a killer's
kiss

Also by William Lashner

Marked Man
Falls the Shadow
Past Due
Fatal Flaw
Bitter Truth (Veritas)
Hostile Witness

William Lashner

A KILLER'S KISS

 WILLIAM MORROW *An Imprint of* HarperCollins*Publishers*

A KILLER'S KISS. Copyright © 2007 by William Lashner. All rights reserved. Printed in the United States of America. No part of this book may be used or reproduced in any manner whatsoever without written permission except in the case of brief quotations embodied in critical articles and reviews. For information address HarperCollins Publishers, 10 East 53rd Street, New York, NY 10022.

Designed by Kate Nichols

ISBN-13: 978-0-06-114346-5
ISBN-10: 0-06-114346-4

For Michael Lashner,

who never ceases to amaze

a killer's
KISS

SUNDAY

They came for me in the nighttime, which is usually the way of it. They knocked so loudly the walls shook. Two men in ties and raincoats. I could see them through the peephole in my door. They weren't wearing fedoras, but they might as well have been.

"It's late," I yelled without opening the wooden door. "And I don't need any magazines."

"We're looking for Victor Carl."

"Who's looking?"

The shorter one leaned toward the door until a walleye filled the peephole. Then he pulled back and reached into his jacket. The badge glinted like a set of freshly sharpened teeth.

"I'm naked," I said.

"Then put something on," said the guy with the badge. "Our stomachs are strong, but not that strong."

In the bedroom I slipped on a pair of jeans and a shirt. I knew who they were before the badge was flashed. I had seen the two of them prowling the corridors of the Criminal Justice Building, where I plied most of my trade these days, defending the riff and the raff. You can always tell the cops in the courthouse, they're the ones laughing and rubbing their hands, talking about where they are going to eat lunch. While they waited in the hallway, I took the time to put on socks and a pair of heavy black shoes with steel tips. When dealing with the police, if you don't protect your toes, they are sure to be stepped on.

I closed the bedroom door behind me before I opened the front door. They strolled in like they were strolling into an art gallery, hands behind their backs, leaning forward as they examined the walls.

"Nice place," said the one who had shown me his badge.

"No it's not," I said.

He stopped and looked hard at me. He was slim and sharp-faced, with clever eyes. "You're right. I was just being polite. But the furniture's not bad. My wife's looking for some new pieces. Is that couch leather?"

"Pleather," I said.

"Well, you certainly can't tell unless you look. You mind if I sit?"

I shrugged.

"I'm Detective Sims," he said as he carefully lowered himself onto the couch and lifted one leg over the other. Sims's suit was freshly pressed, his shoes were shiny and thin-soled. "This is my partner, Hanratty."

"A pleasure," I said.

Hanratty grunted.

"He's big, isn't he?" I said to Sims.

"But a surprisingly nimble dancer for his size," said Sims. "You alone?"

"Not anymore."

"Why is your water running?"

"I was about to shower when you guys knocked."

"We'll wait while you turn it off."

"It's all right. You won't be staying long."

"I don't know," said Sims. "Hanratty might want some tea."

"Do you want some tea, Hanratty?" I said.

Hanratty stood like a block of cement and glowered. He was the size of a linebacker, with thick knuckles and a closely mowed patch of blond hair. The bridge of his nose was crushed like a beer can. I tried to imagine him dancing nimbly and failed. But he sure could glower. I got the feeling if he smiled, his face would shatter.

"Where were you tonight, smart guy?" said Hanratty. Each syllable was like a punch to the kidneys.

"Home," I said. "I don't get out much."

"Spend your nights on your pleather couch, do you?" said Sims. "Eating cheesesteaks, watching that big television set you got there. That's a lonely kind of existence for a man your age."

"Not as lonely as you would think. Every once in a while a couple of cops stop by and chat amiably about my taste in furniture. What division within the department did you boys say you were in?"

"We didn't," said Sims. "You wear any rings, Victor?"

I lifted my hands and showed him. They were free of jewelry.

"How'd you get the cut between your forefinger and thumb on your right hand?"

"I was slicing onions."

"Care if I look at it?" he said.

"That's not necessary. I'm sure it will heal on its own."

"Give him the hand," said Hanratty.

I stared at him for a moment, saw the violence behind his eyes, and then brought my right hand closer to Sims. Sims grabbed it, examined both sides, brought it up to his face as if to kiss it, and then took a sniff.

"That was weird," I said after I jerked it away.

"Yet strangely thrilling," said Sims. "I smelled soap. Always lather up your hands before you shower, do you?"

"Cleanliness is a virtue," I said.

Sims looked around at the disordered mess that was my apartment. "Ever been married, Victor?"

"No."

"Good for you. Trust me when I tell you, it's not all it's cracked up to be. Ever been engaged?"

"Once."

"What happened?"

"It didn't work out."

"Care to spill the details?"

"No."

"Still hurts, is that it?"

"Ancient history."

"Oh, six or seven years is not that long a time. McDeiss says you were pretty broken up about it."

A chill shivered up my spine at the name. I tried to work my jaw but it was frozen. McDeiss was a homicide detective. I put a hand to my jaw and rubbed it back to life. "McDeiss?" I managed to say. "You guys work with McDeiss?"

"You're pretty close with him, from what we hear."

"Not really."

"You've broken bread together, haven't you? Worked a couple of cases together."

"On different sides."

"He's the one who suggested we stop by, ask a few questions, see what you— Wait. Did you hear that, Hanratty? The water just turned off. All by itself."

"The water pressure in the building is erratic," I said.

"Maybe our friend here is not as lonely as he lets on. Why don't you invite your guest out so we can have a little party?"

"Maybe you should mind your own damn business."

"Getting testy, are we, Victor? Got something to hide? Embarrassed by your partner? Or maybe your visitor is somebody's wife."

"Maybe yours," I said.

Sims laughed. His teeth were small and very white. "You want her number? You'd be doing me a favor. Just be sure to take some pictures for the judge. But you'd enjoy yourself, she's a looker. Isn't she a looker, Hanratty?"

"She's a looker all right," said Hanratty.

"She's also a whore," said Sims as he lifted a loose thread from his suit pants. "I think she even slept with Hanratty over there, imagine that."

"No, thank you," I said.

"But she is a looker. Oh, listen to us talk, like men blowing steam around the campfire after a day of fishing. You know how it is with us, when we get together by ourselves, we can't stop complaining about women. Go ahead, Hanratty. Tell Victor who was the woman who broke your heart."

"My mother," said Hanratty.

Sims winced dramatically. "I think we've heard quite enough about that, don't you? So now it's your turn, Victor. Tell us about the girl who left you bare and broken at the altar."

"I was engaged," I said. "Her name was Julia. She ran off and married a urologist. End of story. Not much plot there, I'm afraid."

"What was his name, this evil urologist, or am I being redundant?"

"Denniston. Wren Denniston."

"And how did you feel about Dr. Wren Denniston? Bitter, angry, resentful, with a murderous thirst for vengeance?"

"I got over it."

"Oh, I don't think we ever get over something like that."

"Is this an official inquiry of the Homicide Division?"

"If that's what you want it to be," said Hanratty. "Is that what you want it to be?"

"Why don't you stop holding it in and tell me what this is all about."

It was Sims who broke the news. "Dr. Wren Denniston was found murdered in his Chestnut Hill mansion this evening."

I tried to say something clever, but the words caught in my throat. I caught a whiff of burnt coffee in the air.

"Shot in the head," said Hanratty.

"Imagine that," said Sims. "Can anyone vouch for your whereabouts at around eight tonight?"

"No."

"You sure? We're talking around eight o'clock. No one saw you at the office, at the store, didn't happen to stop into the tap on your way home for a beer?"

"None of the above."

"That's a shame. Makes things a little tougher on you."

"You mind if we look around?" said Hanratty.

"Not at all," I said slowly, "as long as you have a warrant."

Sims smoothed out the pleat on his pants. "So it's going to be like that."

"Yes, it's going to be like that."

"Have you seen Wren Denniston's wife lately?"

"Thank you so much for coming."

"We're talking about Julia Denniston. The girl you were engaged to. The girl who broke your little heart. Have you seen her?"

"But I think it's time for you to go."

"You'd remember her, I'm sure. No flower has sweeter nectar than the old love who broke your heart. Isn't that from an Eagles song? No, maybe not."

"I'm done talking."

"You hear that, Hanratty? He's done talking."

"I heard."

"Which is funny, actually, because I don't think he ever started. What should we do?"

"You know what we should do."

Sims slapped his knee. "Give us a moment, Hanratty, won't you?"

Hanratty glared some more at me, turned his glare on Sims, and then slipped out of the apartment. Sims stood from the couch and came over to where I was standing. He thumbed at the door, lowered his voice to a conspirator's whisper.

"Hanratty wants to bust you right now, jerk you downtown, sweat you in the box. He's that kind of cop. Hands-on, if you know what I mean. But lucky for you I caught lead on this case. You're pals with McDeiss. McDeiss has attracted the eyes of the brass, he'll be head of detectives someday. And word is you're close to Slocum in the D.A.'s office, too. The downtown boys are trying to get him to run against his boss next term. That's a lot of protection for a small-time lawyer who upholsters his couch in pleather. I don't see any reason to ruffle your feathers."

"There's nothing to ruffle my feathers about," I said.

"Good. That's the way we'll play it. Don't worry, I'll find someone to pin this on. I always do."

"What is it you want, Detective?"

"I just want to retire with a pension and a nest egg and spend my days hunting and fishing, that's all." He chucked me on the shoulder. "Remember me at Christmas," he said before following his partner out.

I locked the door after he left and then loped over to the window. I watched the two men leave my building and step over to their car, parked illegally on the far side of my street. They got in and sat. And sat. I was still watching them sitting there when the door to my bedroom opened.

"Who was that?"

I turned. She stood there, trim and tawny, long legs falling out of a towel wrapped tightly around her body. Her head was tilted to the side, and she was rubbing a second towel over her long dark hair as she stared at me. To see her standing in my living room was to see a future devoid of want and strife, all my dreams satisfied, all my hopes fulfilled. She was a worker's paradise in one stunning figure. I stared for a moment, I couldn't help myself.

"It was the cops," I said finally.

"Really? What did they want?"

I looked at her for a moment longer and then turned back to the window. The car was still there, Sims and Hanratty were still there.

"They came," I said without turning around, "to tell me that your husband's been murdered."

Oh, right, like you've never done it.

I don't mean the stonewall-the-cops-while-the-dead-man's-wife-is-lathering-herself-in-your-shower thing. I mean the other thing, the important thing. There is much that is easy in this world: downloading porn, stealing cable, Serbian girls, you know what I mean. But of all that is easy in this world, nothing is easier than falling into bed with an old lover.

"Victor, is that you?"

"It's me all right," I had said into the phone, the soft, level voice on the other end of the line disturbingly familiar. This was before, weeks before.

"Hi," said the voice. "How are you?"

"Fine, I suppose."

"You don't recognize me."

"Not really."

"I should be insulted, but it has been a long time. It's me," she said. "It's Julia."

My heart just then held its breath as it dived into dark, cold waters.

"Hello?" she said. "Are you still there?"

"I'm here."

"It's me."

"Okay."

"Do you have anything to say to me?"

"Let me turn down the television."

I pulled the phone from my ear and sat there for a moment. There is always one that gnaws at the bones. You think of her when the alcohol floats you into a tidal pool of regret. You dream of her still. In the simplest of moments, waiting for an elevator, mailing a letter, the memory of her slices into your heart as naturally as a breath.

"Okay, I'm back," I said.

"Are you still mad?"

"That's a funny question. You get mad when your fiancée flirts with your old pal Jimmy. I think what happened sort of transcends mad, don't you?"

"Is that why you're sending me the letters?"

"What letters?"

"Maybe we should get together and talk about it."

"I'm not sure that's a good idea."

"Then you have to stop."

"But I'm not doing anything."

"How about some coffee, Victor? The letters are a bit deranged, don't you think? And I know deranged, believe me. I'm worried about you."

"I'm not sending any letters."

"Just coffee, Victor. Please."

That was the start, the first step in our version of the old-lovers' tango. You meet again by chance, you meet by design. She's thinking about you, he wants to make amends, she wonders why you're writing her anonymous letters filled with hate. You deny it, although it sounds just then like a pretty good idea. You meet, slyly, surreptitiously, as if your meeting together like this is somehow indecent, as if you already know the way it will end. You ask how he's been, you ask how's her job, how's his mother. You look good, she says.

"So do you," I said. And she did, damn it.

Julia had been a slim, dark girl when she crushed my heart beneath the sole of her boot, and so pretty she'd been hard not to stare at. Glossy black hair, sly eyes, thin wrists, breasts like ripe tangerines, a feline curve to her lips that drew out startlingly indecent thoughts. She had been a walking explanation for the burqa; to see her in the flesh was to want to do all manner of things to her, slowly, over and again. And she had a surprising accessibility that made it all seem deliciously possible. It was that voice, sexy and impassive and sweet, like Honey West's. She was easy to talk to, easy to flirt with, easy to kiss, easy to kid yourself that maybe you understood what was going on inside her pretty skull. But even so, you never lost the sense that she was forever holding something back. It was as if she carried in her heart a truth that could make everything perfect if only she would share it, though you sensed she never would.

At the Starbucks now, elbows atop the bare wooden table, she remained stunningly beautiful, but noticeably older and more prosperously dressed. No more black jeans and loose white oxford shirts, not for her. She had pinned an Hermès scarf around her long, lovely neck, she wore a Burberry skirt, she sported a fragrance, like a Frenchwoman or a grandmother. Still, when she smiled, my heart seized. Did I mention her smile? It was a rare enough sight, true, but so dazzling it hurt. Even the lines around her eyes when she smiled caused me pain. It was as if she had spent all the years after me laughing.

"How have you been, Victor?"

"Fine."

"No, really."

"Fine," I said.

"Okay. I won't press. I know how it is to keep things to your-self. I've been reading about you in the papers."

"Just part of the job," I said.

"Maybe, but you seem to thrive on the notoriety. How's Beth?"

Beth was my erstwhile partner, who had left our legal prac-tice to travel the world. "I suppose she's okay. Last time I saw her, she was heading for a plane to India. She's off to find her-self."

"That sounds exciting."

"It sounds like work."

"You weren't tempted to go along with her?"

"Gad, no. I actually might succeed, and then where would I be?"

"So you're all alone at the firm?"

"At the firm, yes."

"And life's good? Everything's fine? It all turned out great?"

"Sure it did. Doesn't it always?"

"Even Voltaire didn't believe that," she said, eyes glancing first down at her coffee and then back up at me like an invita-tion.

She wanted me to ask. It's what is done at this stage of the reunion, the feigned friendliness and concern. *How are you do-ing? I hope things are going well.* A sort of teeth-grinding po-liteness that hides the truth boiling underneath. But just then, with the lovely face of my betrayal sitting across the table from me, framed by the steam of her latte, I wasn't in the humor to be polite.

"Tell me about the letters," I said.

She reached into her red leather bag—Coach, I couldn't help but notice—pulled out a short stack of envelopes, handed it to me. The envelopes were plain, no return address, Julia's name and address printed in a basic computer font. The postmark was from Center City Philadelphia. I opened one, took out the letter, unfolded it.

"They've been coming for the last couple months," she said. "Every week or so. At first I thought they were nothing and threw them out, but then I got scared enough to keep them."

"Did you show them to the police?"

"I've never shown them to anybody. There is nothing that could be done. And I didn't want to get anyone in trouble."

"You mean you didn't want to get me in trouble."

"I didn't know who was sending them, but it was someone who seemed to know me intimately enough to have a grudge, and you seemed like a logical choice."

She was right about that.

The first one read "SLUT" in big, red, hand-scrawled letters. A designer shoe that fit quite neatly, I thought. I opened the next, and the next. "WHORE. WITCH'S CUNT. FAT SLOB. SLAG-HEAP. BANGSTER. YOU GREEDY BITCH."

I went through them all, noticed the way the *S*'s curved, the *L*'s looped, the way the *E*'s tilted to the right. I placed each carefully in its envelope, handed the stack back to her.

"I never thought you were fat," I said.

"So you didn't send them?"

"No," I said. "I'm sorry to disappoint you, though maybe I should have thought of it."

"You're still upset."

"I'm over it."

"You don't look over it. You look like you just ate an iguana."

"We were engaged," I said. "We were planning our future together. You left me for a urologist. A urologist."

"It wasn't a comment on your masculinity."

"Thank you for that, Julia. The burden of Atlas has been lifted from my shoulders. Why, I might now even be able to get on my hands and knees and scrounge up a bit of my lost self-respect.

Oh, look, under that couch over there, with the dust bunnies and the discarded sugar packets. Yes, it's my self-respect. Glorious day. I now can go on."

"Lower your voice, please. People are looking."

She was pulling back a bit, biting her lip. I fought the urge to bite it with her. I ducked my head, leaned forward like a boxer burrowing forward in a clinch.

"Tell me, Julia, what was it, really, that caused you to betray me like you did? Was it that you couldn't help yourself from running after a doctor? That I actually would understand. I'm Jewish, remember, I'd leave me for a doctor, too. Or was it just the sheer joy of emotionally destroying me? I bet you and the doc had a few laughs over that. Sure you did. I did, too. Look at little Victor, rolled up in a ball in the corner the room. What a hoot. Or maybe the truth of it all is that you simply are a slagheap, whatever the hell that is."

"Is this making you feel better?"

"Yes, actually. Thank you."

"You weren't blameless," she said softly.

"Oh, no, of course not. It was all my fault, wasn't it? I was sleeping with your sister. Oh, but you don't have a sister. Then I must have been sleeping with your best friend. Except I wasn't, was I? I was too busy being faithful. That's a good word. Faithful. You should look it up. It means not screwing around on your fiancé with a urologist."

She put the envelopes back in her bag, stood up from the table. "I think I'm going to leave now."

"Oh, don't go, Julia. We're having so much fun catching up. Why don't you tell me about your wonderful marriage? Why don't we chat about your marvelous life, your Persian rugs in the foyer, your bright expense account at Nordstrom? This was a good idea, wasn't it, getting together like this?"

"Good-bye, Victor."

"That's funny, I've heard that before. When was that? Oh,

yes, at the coffee bar where you worked, with the *fwoosh* of the frother and the scent of scorched espresso, when you told me you were abandoning me for a urologist. A urologist. Well, at least his urine's clear. Clear enough to drink, I'd bet. Hey, that's an idea. Let's the three of us get together sometime and share a pitcher. Won't that be fun?"

These last few sentences were said loudly and to her back as she made her way out of the Starbucks. I looked around. I was being stared at, which felt perfectly appropriate, since I just then felt lower than a carnival geek with chicken blood smeared across his teeth. That was the end of that, I figured, but of course I was wrong.

The explosion of the bitterness that had been bubbling and boiling inside me for years was a perfectly natural part of the whole sleeping-with-the-old-lover thing. Until the bitterness of the ending is drained away, the next phase of the dance can't begin. And it wasn't just my bitterness that had to be bled.

"You pulled away the moment you proposed," said Julia over the phone. She had called, anger seething beneath the placid surface of her voice. Then she called again, repentant. She said she couldn't help herself from calling. And even as I recognized her on my caller ID, I couldn't help but answer. We were each other's wound that we prodded and poked to know we both were still alive. I apologized for my behavior in the Starbucks. She laughed and then blamed herself and then blamed me. For my part, having released my bitterness at an overpriced coffeehouse, I was ready to accept her judgment. And wasn't it just like Julia to nail my pathologies with deadly precision.

"I was scared," I said.

"You could barely look at me."

"I could always look at you."

"It was over as soon as I agreed to marry you. It was like you never expected I would say yes."

"I didn't. You were too pretty, you had the body of a dancer.

I expected you to burn me. Which, of course, you did. But we could have worked through it."

"I wasn't strong enough, Victor. You knew that about me from the first. I needed to be adored."

"And he adored you."

"Madly."

"I always wondered. Where did you meet him?"

"In an elevator. He struck up a conversation, offered to buy me a drink. This was after you started pulling away. I was feeling vulnerable. I let him buy me a manhattan. He had nice hands."

"I don't doubt it."

"And he wore a Rolex."

"There it is, the secret of my undoing. A Rolex."

"It was a very nice watch," she said.

"And you didn't give me a chance after that."

"I did, don't you remember? I told you about him, and you turned away."

"You told me there was someone else. I was supposed to take you out dancing?"

"Yes."

"I wasn't going to fight for you."

"And right there was the problem. I could tell that all you wanted was a way out. So I gave it to you."

"You don't know how much it hurt."

"Yes I do," she said.

Granted, her display of bitterness didn't include the brilliant image of the three of us hoisting a pitcher of piss, but it was plenty tough and plenty accurate, and it hurt like only the truth of things can hurt.

So of course we met for drinks.

We met at a hotel bar, something intimate and classy. At this point the enterprise takes on an air of inevitability. Over drinks we each blamed ourselves for what happened. *It was my fault.*

No my fault. No really, my fault. Okay, your fault. Shared laughter. All part of the dance. And the next part too. *So really, no really, how are you?*

Not so good, either one of us.

Her marriage had died, become a farce. Her husband had shady business dealings and a mistress with blond hair and skinny legs, and she didn't really care. When I met Julia, she had been an art student, pulling espressos at the local coffee shop. Now she didn't know what she would do with the rest of her life. But she needed a change, she said. She was ready to change everything.

And me? My relationships since her had been frank disasters. I was in the same apartment as when she knew me. My legal practice was limping along. When we were engaged I had two partners, both had deserted me, and now I was practicing alone.

"As in love as in law," I said in that fancy hotel bar.

"Things haven't quite worked out the way we had hoped," she said.

"No, not really."

"I'm sorry," she said.

"So am I. But more and more I find that life is nothing but regrets."

"That is so sad."

"It is."

"But I know what you mean."

"And I guess you're just one more on the list."

We parted with a hug and a shrug, a wan good-bye and good luck. As if the purpose of the whole thing was to lance the boils of bitterness that had grown like goiters on our necks so we could both, separately, go forward with our lives. But that wasn't the purpose, was it? And even as I stepped out of that bar, I knew that wasn't it. Because about some regrets in this world there is nothing you can do, but this was not one of them.

She called.

It was late on a Sunday night. I had been lying on my

pleather couch, my shoes off, my head resting on my hands, re-membering the way her lips would part ever so slightly in the middle of sex.

And she called. On my cell phone.

"Victor," she said.

"Where are you?"

"I've been thinking of you."

"Where are you?"

"Victor?"

"Because wherever you are, I'm coming."

"I'm parked outside your building," she said.

And this is the thing about falling into bed with your old lover: it is the best of both worlds. It is new, spanking fresh, spontaneous in the way it only is the first time with someone who has your blood and your soul at fever pitch. But it is also old and familiar, as comfortable as your favorite pair of jeans. The steps, the sounds, the scents, as familiar as hearth and home.

I missed you. I think about you all the time. I'm sorry. Kissing you feels so right. I think I'm ready now, finally, yes. If it wasn't for your husband. Forget about him. It could be perfect. Maybe. We need him out of our lives. He already is, I've already moved on. What got into us? I don't know. I've been in a fever about you for days, for weeks. Are we really going to try again? We can make it work this time, I know we can.

And the words are sincere, absolutely, as sincere as any words can be accompanied as they are with tossed socks and bra hooks coming unloose.

Her shoulder, her neck, the soft underside of her breast, so new and so familiar. The brush of her fingers across my tattoo, the smoothness of her thigh, the taste of her tongue, the delirium that leads to the sweetest step in the sweetest of dances. Because it's not happening just in the present, it's happening in the past and the future, too, and all three are suddenly pure and full of promise. The unzip, the pull down, the kiss of the calf, still taut and lovely, the bite, the laughter, the sigh, teeth clacking, hands gripping, an ecstasy over the horizon so distant and so close it leads to a burning—

And then, smack in the middle, after commitment but before consummation, the knock at the door, a knock so loud the walls shake.

The car was still there, Sims and Hanratty were still there.

"They came," I said to her as I stared out the window, "to tell me that your husband was murdered."

I didn't turn around when I said it. Whatever registered on that lovely face, a reaction of staggering shock or something else, something more frightening, I didn't yet want to see it. It was my legal training kicking in, I suppose. The sad truth about lawyers is that we are fantasists, we make up stories in our heads, stories we can weave for judge and jury, but we don't want to know the reality. And what fantasy could ever be larger than lost love recklessly reclaimed?

"What did you say?"

"Your husband was murdered, Julia."

"Where? How? Victor?"

"At the house," I said. "Shot through the head."

"Victor, stop it."

"Not long before you showed up here," I said.

"Stop it. Just stop it. Please."

There was a quiet for a moment, and then a whispered "Oh, my God," as if she had just put together the meaning of my words, followed by the sound of something falling, collapsing, a long, dangling rope dropping to the ground.

I supposed she would expect me to rush over and help her through it. I supposed she would expect me to act like a human being. But instead I stared out at the cops sitting in the car in front of my apartment building and I thought over a few things. Like how Julia had come back into my life just a few weeks before her husband was murdered. Like how it seemed almost too wrong to be a coincidence. It might all have been a slapstick twist of fate, sure, and every piano that falls out of a fifth-floor window has to land on some sap's head, but if it wasn't pure happenstance, then I was already in serious trouble.

I took another look at the cops in the car, then I pushed myself away from the window and walked over to her.

She was lying quietly on the floor, hands over her face, towels strewn about her naked body. Her jaw was shaking, her breasts were rising with each shallow breath. I stared at her for a moment and wondered what I was seeing. A devastated woman who had just lost her beloved husband? No, surely not that, or why would I be seeing her at all? A cold-blooded killer trying to use me as an alibi or, worse, a fall guy? At first take it added up just like that. But she was so lovely I couldn't stop myself from hoping that she was something in between, and that hope itself was enough to allay for a moment the brutal doubts that had bound tight my emotions.

I bent down, put one arm behind her neck, snaked the other arm beneath her legs, lifted. She was lighter than a woman her size had any right to be. I smelled the shampoo in her hair and felt the silky heat of her skin as I carried her to the couch. I placed her gently on the cushions so she was sitting up. From the bedroom I fetched her a blanket, with which I covered her modestly. From the kitchen I fetched her a beer, which I placed into her hand. She sipped from the bottle once and then ignored it while her dazed eyes darted to and fro. I sat close and petted her still-wet hair.

"Do they know who killed him?"

"No."

"Do they know why?"

"Not yet."

"Was it a robbery?"

"I don't know."

"What do I do now?"

"You need to get dressed," I said.

"Okay."

"The cops are outside. They're looking for you, and they're outside."

"Why are they looking for me?"

"To ask you questions. They want you to help them find out who killed your husband. And they'll also want to know where you were tonight."

"Do they know I'm here?"

"Not for sure, but they suspect."

"They shouldn't know. This was just about us, not about them. I don't want them goose-stepping into our lives."

"It's too late for that. Either they're waiting outside, hoping to catch you leave, or they're waiting for a warrant to be approved by a judge so they can come back and search my apartment. Either way, you need to get dressed."

"I'll go out the back."

"My guess is it's also being watched."

"Where will I go?"

"It doesn't really matter. Once the police spot you, they'll pick you up and take you to the Roundhouse for questioning."

"Police headquarters?"

"That's right."

"They think I did it."

"They'll just want to ask you some questions. And they'll want to know where you were all night."

"Here," she said.

"Before you came here."

She stared out for a moment as something washed through her. Then her eyes went slack and the blanket fell to her waist, exposing her breasts, and she did nothing about it. It was strange to see Julia at such a loss, as if when she heard the news the secret that seemed always to sustain her had slipped away along with the blanket. When she spoke, finally, her eyes still were distant, as if focused on some far shore, and there was a soft, girlish note in her voice.

"Remember when you spoke about regrets," she said. "In the hotel bar. You were thinking of me, which was so sweet it almost made me cry. I was thinking of myself at sixteen, living in Ashland. Ashland, Virginia. 'The Center of the Universe.' That's the town motto."

"I can't imagine you at sixteen."

"I was in the drama club at John Paul Jones High School. *Romeo and Juliet*. I played the lead."

"Forsooth."

"It was a disaster, and yet it was the highlight of my life. Is that sad, Victor, playing Juliet in a silly high-school production being the highlight of your life?"

"Who was Romeo?"

"Nobody. Somebody. A sweet boy. Terrence."

"That name must have made for some unpleasant afternoons on the schoolyard."

"Terry. You should have seen him then, Victor. He was Romeo in his bones."

"I'm getting jealous."

She licked her lips. A worm of emotion stirred in my gut. In all our time together, she had never before rambled on like this about her past, never before let her voice be twisted by remembrance and sentiment. It was as if she were a different woman entirely, open and unguarded, sweetly innocent, the woman I had imagined her to be when first I spied her behind the counter of that coffee joint. I couldn't help myself. I leaned forward and kissed her.

She raised a hand, touched my cheek. "'Thou mayst think my 'havior light,'" she said: "'But trust me, gentleman, I'll prove more true than those that have more cunning to be strange.'"

"Is that Juliet?"

"On the balcony. But it proved to be a lie, and I've been paying for it ever since."

Was I a fool to think it was my misplaced trust and my betrayed hopes that had been plaguing her all these years?

"It's time to go home," she said.

Was I a fool to wonder if my heart was the home for which she yearned?

"I'm here," I said.

"I know, but I want to go home."

Yes, I was that fool. I stood, straightened my spine to a lawyer's posture. "You can't go back to your house," I said. "It's now a crime scene. The coroner would have already picked up the body, but there will be yellow tape across the front door, there will be technicians taking prints and searching for evidence. There will be blood."

At the word *blood*, her eyes focused, as if some red and sodden image had snapped her back to the present and its prickly predicament. She pulled the blanket up to her neck. She noticed the beer in her hand and took a long drink.

"I'll just stay here," she said.

"The cops are going to find you, Julia. It's better for you if you find them first."

"What do I tell them?"

"Either you tell them the whole truth or you tell them nothing. Those are your choices."

"Which should I do?"

"Do you have an attorney?"

"I suppose. Wren did, at least. Clarence, Clarence Swift."

"Then you should call this Clarence Swift and ask his advice."

"But what about you? Why don't you be my lawyer?"

"I can't represent you. I'm a witness to your whereabouts. If I try to represent you, they'll have me disqualified immediately, and it will gum up everything. But as a friend, I would advise you for the time being to tell them nothing before you talk to your lawyer."

"I didn't do anything, Victor."

"It doesn't matter. They can twist things. And I don't trust the guys they assigned to the case."

"Do they think I killed him?"

"The spouse is always a suspect until she's cleared."

"What do you think?"

"It doesn't matter what I think."

"But you just kissed me. Would you kiss me if you thought I was a killer?"

"Go get dressed," I said.

She took another long drink of the beer, nodded a couple of times, and then stood. As she turned away from me and walked into my bedroom, the blanket still clutched to her front, I caught a view of the length of her naked body, from the back of her head to her thin heels.

Lovely neck, I thought. A sweet arch in her spine. Nice legs. To answer her question, even if my worst suspicions had been right, I'd still kiss her. And more. See, I never believed that part about Sam Spade. Sure he would have turned in Brigid O'Shaughnessy, but only after. That's the way we're wired.

When she came out of the bedroom, she was fully dressed, with makeup in place and lipstick bright, her red handbag like a shield at her side. She looked like a woman who had made a decision. I turned to the window again, peered out at the street. The car was still there, Hanratty and Sims were still there.

"They're waiting for you."

"I'm ready," she said, her voice firm.

"I'll take you down, introduce you, stay with you as long as they let me. Do you remember what I said?"

"To say nothing."

"Good. If they press, tell them you want to see your lawyer."

"Okay."

I walked toward her, took hold of her right arm to lead her to the door, but she didn't follow. Instead she pivoted forward into my chest. The top of her head tickled my nose. We stood there for a while. And then she tilted her face up and stood on tiptoe and kissed me. And I let her. She kissed me, and her body eased and sagged into mine, and we fit together, like we fit together before, like we were made one for the other, and I kissed her back. I liked it more than I should have liked it, considering the dead man and the questions that remained. But I didn't like it as much as I did before the knock on my door. It still had the past, present, and future in it, but the idealized sheen was gone, and I could see them now for what they truly were: soiled, paranoid, dead.

"You seem to have recovered from the trauma," I said when I pulled away.

"You want to know the truth, Victor?"

"Not really."

"I'm not broken up that he's dead. The truth is, the last few months I couldn't stand the sight of him."

"Let's try not to tell the cops that. As soon as they can, they're going to separate us. They're going to try to turn us against each other. That's what they do."

"Are you going to turn against me?"

"I'll do what I can for you."

"Even after what I did?"

"It was both our faults, isn't that what we decided? The best way to play it right now is for both of us to say nothing. Can you manage?"

"I'm good at saying nothing. You can trust me."

"We'll trust each other," I said.

"We're in it together."

"Sure," I said, still holding on to her arm as I walked her to the door. "In it together."

I stopped at the entrance to the kitchen, grabbed a dish towel from the counter, and wiped her lipstick off my lips.

"Now let's go meet the cops," I said. "Their names are Sims and Hanratty. Hanratty is the big one. Watch out for Sims."

They put me in a small green room in the Roundhouse. The table was cheap, the chairs hard, the place smelled like sweat and vinegar and dead mice. But you had no excuse not to look snazzy, because the room had a great mirror on one of the walls in which you could straighten your collar and check your teeth.

Julia was in an identical room somewhere in that same ugly building. I assumed they were giving her the business. Sims was whispering sweet nothings into her ear; Hanratty was banging on the table. But no matter how tough it got, I figured she was holding up just fine.

Julia always had a place deep within the recesses of her emotions where she could retreat, a sanctuary from which even those who loved her the most were barred. It exists in all of us, that last place that others never reach, but in Julia it was a cavernous castle, with a fearsome moat and chains on the doors and evil dwarfs as guards. Even Gollum couldn't have slipped inside. If Sims had chased her into her sanctuary, it didn't matter how hard Hanratty banged on the table or knocked on the door, they weren't getting in.

When we came out together from the door of my apartment in the middle of the night, the two cops climbed out of the car as if they had been expecting us all along. Sims was kind and courteous, uttering solicitous words to the grieving widow, holding the rear door open as he offered us both a ride. Hanratty glared at me with a brutal little smile on his granite face. I was getting a pretty good idea of the range of Hanratty's facial expressions. And the drive east, toward the river and the Roundhouse, had been almost jolly. Sims had talked about his planned retirement, how big would be the trout, how clear would be the air.

"You ever fish in Montana, Hanratty?" said Sims.

"I don't fish," said Hanratty.

"Fly-fishing, I'm talking about."

"I don't fish."

"Neither do I," said Sims. "And I've never been to Montana. But I'm going as soon as I get my twenty-five. The land's cheap and the trout are jumpy. I've been reading up. *A River Runs Through It*."

"Runs through what?" said Hanratty.

"Montana," said Sims.

"What river?"

"I don't know. The Mississippi, maybe."

"The Mississippi doesn't run through Montana."

"Where does it run?"

"Iowa."

"Who the hell goes to Iowa to fish flies?"

"Don't ask me, I don't fish."

"Well, let me tell you, Hanratty, you don't retire to fish flies in Iowa. Montana is it."

"What river?"

"Who the hell knows the name of a river in Montana?" said Sims. "Any ideas, Victor?"

"Take up knitting," I said.

It was quite an act—if vaudeville were still alive, they could have taken it on the road—but it wasn't putting me at ease, like they intended. At the Roundhouse they were pleasant as could be, gallantly opening doors, offering up cups of cop coffee, tepid, bitter, and thick.

"Can you wait in here a moment, Victor?" said Sims, gesturing toward the small green room.

I went in and sat down. Sims closed the door, leaving me in there alone. I checked myself in the mirror. No jacket, no tie, haggard and unshaven and sallow. In a green room, under fluorescent lights, even a cherub looks like an ax murderer.

I tried to fathom the depths of the trouble into which I had fallen, and I failed. Things were happening above and below, all around. I could sense their shapes and movement, but the purposes remained mere shadows. Still, I knew the taste of trouble and this was it, oily and electric, with too much salt and a bitter pinch of cumin. Oh, yes, I was neck deep. Sims seemed ready to help me out, for reasons that left me feeling squirrelly, but Hanratty had a hard-on for me, I could tell. Is that a baton in your pocket, Officer, or do you just want to smash my face against the wall?

A knock on the door. It swung open, and a young uniform poked his head inside. "Detective Sims thanks you for your patience and says he'll be with you in just a moment."

"That's what he said an hour ago."

"I'm sure it won't be too long."

"I'm glad you're sure," I said as he closed the door behind him.

I drummed my fingers on the table. I stared at my watch. I tried to think it through.

How to handle the next few hours, the next few days as the cops investigated the murder of Dr. Wren Denniston and found themselves someone to pin it on, was the question plaguing me. And the answer, I knew, hinged on Julia. Was she the love of my life, a savior who had returned to rescue me from an increasingly dismal existence? If so, then I needed to do all I could to protect her. What false story wouldn't we concoct for true love? What crime wouldn't we commit? And hadn't the two of us agreed, in my apartment, to trust one another, not to turn each on the other, and, at least for the moment, to keep our mouths shut?

On the other hand, if Julia had opened our rapprochement for the sole purpose of using me as a lifeline out of a brutal crime she planned to commit, then she was nothing but a manipulative psychopath set on endangering both my physical and emotional well-being. Of course, what else could one expect from an old girlfriend, and about par for the course in my relationships, but something to avoid nonetheless. And the easiest way to avoid it was to sing like a rock star and wash my hands of the whole foul mess.

The problem was, I couldn't figure out who she was, which I suppose was a clue right there. I mean, what kind of relationship was possible if I was unsure of the basic psychological makeup of the object of my affection? She could be just a messed-up girl or a dark-hearted murderess? Either way I was in for trouble.

And I couldn't help but wonder why she had finally come back to me, and why now? I thought about the letters Julia had shown me. "SLUT. WHORE. WITCH'S CUNT. FAT SLOB. SLAGHEAP. BANGSTER. YOU GREEDY BITCH." Something about the letters seemed to be the clue to everything. It was the letters, she said, that had caused her to call. If she had written them herself, she couldn't have found a sweeter opening. And who says she didn't? Write the notes, stuff them in plain enve- lopes, drop them into the mailing slot to set up the old lover to take her fall. Even finding her fingerprints on the letters would tell us nothing. Mine were now on them, too. If she had sent the letters herself, then she had been setting me up from the start. But then again, if someone else had sent the letters, maybe the sender should be the prime suspect.

I tried to think it through, but the night had already been too long, and I was too tired, and I failed.

I checked that the door was unlocked. It was, which made me feel strangely vulnerable. I slipped out of the room, swiveled my head like a leopard escaping from his cage, and then explored just enough to find a bathroom.

It hurt when I peed. My testicles felt heavy and bruised. At least I wouldn't have to lie about that. When I stepped outside the bathroom, with the intent to traipse up and down the hall looking for Julia, the same young uniform was waiting in the hallway to kindly lead me back to the green room. I thought I heard a click after the door closed. I tried the knob again. This time it was locked.

I sat and sighed. I twiddled my thumbs. I leaned back, kicked my legs out, watched my beard grow in the mirror. My head lolled on the top rail of the chair, and I fell asleep.

It was at that very moment, of course, that the door burst open and Sims and Hanratty marched into the room.

Hanratty closed the door and leaned on it, barring any attempt to flee. Sims sat down across from me and smiled like a kindly uncle, you know, the kindly uncle who feels your muscles through your sweatshirt to tell you how strong you are and asks you down to the basement to take some pictures.

"Sorry to keep you waiting, Victor," said Sims.

"Oh, I bet you are," I said, wiping my eyes with the heels of my palms. "Where's Julia?"

"She's being taken care of. She's with her lawyer right now, as a matter of fact, a nice gentleman named Clarence Swift. He's been quite helpful, I must say, more helpful than his client. But we're close to getting this thing wrapped up without her cooperation, except for a few minor details which we hoped you could help us with."

"I doubt I could help you with anything."

"Don't be so sure, Victor. We think your help can be enormous."

"Like the fat lady at the circus," said Hanratty.

"Are we talking about your mother again, Hanratty?" I said.

"Let's start with tonight, shall we?" said Sims. "When did you meet up with Mrs. Denniston, and where?"

I closed my eyes, tried to figure out what I should do, failed, and decided instead to punt. "You haven't read me my rights."

"You're not a suspect, Victor. We don't need to read you your rights, which you, anyway, know better than we do. But we would very much appreciate your full assistance."

"And I would appreciate a full body massage."

"And a happy ending, too, I assume."

"Are you volunteering?"

He shook his head wearily. "You're not going to help."

I glanced at the mirror. "Not tonight I won't."

"Maybe Hanratty here can persuade you," said Sims. "My wife once asked him over to help rearrange our furniture. He made a mess of it, of course, smashed china, battered walls. Like a bull in the bridal section of Macy's. I wouldn't want that to happen to your face, not that it couldn't use some rearranging."

I rubbed my jaw.

"Make it easy on yourself, Victor."

"I don't think so," I said. "One of those rights you failed to read to me is the right to remain silent. I don't exercise much, but I'm exercising that."

"We could subpoena you and drop you in front of a grand jury."

"And I could plead the Fifth unless you give me immunity." I turned to the mirror and grinned. "Are you ready to give me immunity, right here and right now?"

"What did I tell you?" said Hanratty.

"Victor, Victor, Victor," said Sims, each recitation of my name accompanied by a shake of the head. "Why are you making this so hard? You're only going to hurt yourself. There is no use trying to protect her."

"I'm not trying to protect anyone," I said, "but myself."

"Siding with her is not the way to do it. This is what we've got so far, and you can figure out for yourself what it adds up to. Dr. Denniston was shot once, straight on. There was no apparent forced entry, no apparent robbery, no evidence of a struggle. The live-in housekeeper, a woman named Gwen McGrath—who makes a fabulous pecan pie, or so we've been told by Mr. Swift—said there was a loud argument between the Dennistons while she was still at the house. Not, she informed us, an unusual occurrence. In the middle of the argument, Mrs. Denniston told Gwen she could go on out for the evening. Gwen, who has a standing date for Sunday dinner with a man named Norman, locked up behind herself and set the alarm, leaving only the doctor and the wife in the house. When she came back a few hours later, about nine o'clock, she found the alarm activated and the house empty, except for Dr. Denniston dead in the library."

"With the candlestick?" I said.

Sims smiled vaguely at the comment. I tried not to show how shaken I was.

"A single bullet in the forehead," said Sims. "No weapon has yet been found, but Mr. Swift kindly informed us that Dr. Denniston did have a revolver, a quite shiny one, he told us. He kept the gun in the safe."

"Is it still there?"

"We don't know, we haven't been able to open it yet, though a representative from the safe company will be at the house tomorrow. According to Mr. Swift, the combination was apparently known only by Dr. Denniston and his wife."

"It's nice that Mr. Swift has been so helpful."

"Isn't it, though?" said Sims. "And he is very interested in you, our Mr. Swift. Wanted to know your relationship with Mrs. Denniston. Wanted to see everything we had with your name on it."

"Curious fellow."

"That's an understatement. So what we need to know from you are the answers to three small questions. As soon as you help us with our questions, we can arrange for you to be taken home. How does that sound?"

"I sure could use a shower."

"You don't have to tell us," said Hanratty.

"And if you cooperate now, we'll keep you out of it for as long as we can. We won't call you before the grand jury, we won't disclose your name to the papers."

"And that helps me how?"

"Do you really want all the papers harping on your relationship to the dead man's wife?"

"As long as they spell my name right," I said.

"Victor, Victor, Victor. Can we begin?"

I thought about it for a long moment. Sims smiled easily and waited. Hanratty looked like he was struggling to keep from banging on the table with my head.

The whole factual recitation by Detective Sims was solely designed to convince me they had the goods on Julia Denniston, and I must say it had worked quite well. If everything he was telling me were true, who else could have committed the murder? And if she had committed the murder, then all my lowest paranoid suspicions were also true. I had made her a promise, and I owed her something, I figured, our past required it, but what did I owe her, really, other than the truth? And it's not like she didn't already have a lawyer on her side.

"She called me about ten from outside my apartment," I said finally. "I invited her in. She was there when you guys showed up."

"Showering," said Hanratty.

"She asked if she could. I said it was okay."

"I bet you did," said Sims. "Do you mind if we run forensics tests on your apartment?"

"Knock yourselves out. Just be sure your guys screw the drain cover back into the shower floor."

"How long had you been seeing her?"

"After she ran off with the now-dead doctor, we lost contact until a couple of weeks ago. She had been getting some strange letters. She called to ask if they were from me. I said they weren't. But the renewed contact allowed us to work out some unresolved issues."

"What kind of issues?"

"Personal issues, Detective."

"Were you screwing her, Victor?"

"It all comes down to that, doesn't it?"

"It usually does."

"The details are none of your damn business."

"But they are, you see. With a husband dead and the wife in your apartment shortly after the murder, it is definitely our business. Were you screwing her?"

"No."

"Really? That's strange, especially with her soaping up in your shower like that."

"I'm more disappointed than you are."

"What happened?"

"I was unbuttoning her pants and unhooking her bra the very moment you boys knocked."

"Oh, that's good," said Sims. "That's ripe."

" 'Ripe' is not quite the word I'd use."

"And you'll sign an affidavit as to all this?"

"Type it up."

"Okay," said Sims. "That wasn't so hard, now, was it? I'll leave you in the good graces of my partner while I rustle up a CSI team and have the affidavit prepared."

As soon as Sims left the room to talk to the assistant district attorney standing behind the mirror, Hanratty walked to the table and leaned over me. I could feel his hulking presence, smell the bad cop coffee on his breath. He placed his hand on the back of my head and pressed gently.

"I think Sims is missing half the story here."

"Maybe," I said without turning around, "but I'm not the half he's missing."

"I think you been slipping it to her for a good long time. I think, drunk on love, you both decided the easiest way to keep the fireworks going was to kill the husband. I think you and she hatched the whole damn thing."

"Don't think so much, Detective, you might strain something."

"Anything you want to tell me right now? Anything you want to get off your chest?"

"I have nothing else to say."

"Oh, you've got plenty to say, baby. And you're going to spill it, all of it, before this is over. I'm not going to rest until I get the whole truth from you."

"Then you're going to be very tired," I said.

A few minutes later, when Sims came back into the room, I was wiping off a thin line of blood from my brow. My head had accidentally rammed into the tabletop, imagine that. I guess Detective Hanratty didn't like the crack about his mother.

"Had an accident?" said Sims as he placed the affidavit before me.

I read it carefully, made a few minor changes, signed it. And with that, I believed I had signed my way out of the whole damn thing. Julia now was on her own.

"Very good," said Sims. "By the way, you ever hear of a guy named Cave?"

"Cave?"

"That's it. Miles Cave?"

"No."

"You sure, Victor?"

"I'm sure."

"Okay, fine. Wait here just a moment, and then we'll take you back to your apartment and conduct the search. And, Victor, take my advice, why don't you. From here on in, stay the hell away from old girlfriends. Nothing but trouble. It's like my grandmother always said."

"What's that, Detective?"

"Old flames burn deadly."

MONDAY

I was half blind and bleary with weariness when I arrived at the courthouse the next morning. There wasn't much on my docket, a young man's future was all. His name was Derek Moats, and Derek was in trouble.

"Where you been, bo?" he said when he spotted me outside the Criminal Justice Building. "You told me to get here a half hour ago, and here you are, stumbling up with your tie all awry."

"I knew I'd show, Derek," I said as I adjusted my knot. "It was you I was worried about."

"I was here from when you said, and I'm the one looking sweet, not like I just stepped out the crapper. Late night with the ladies, bo?"

"Let's call it a late night and leave it at that." I gave him a quick inspection. "Nice hair."

"Combed it out just for the judge. And I wore what you told me to."

"You look fine. Are you ready?"

"I was born ready."

"You were born, we know that for sure, the rest we'll figure on the run. Remember what I said, how to play it?"

"Course I do."

"Good. Now go on in there and sit where I told you. I have someone I have to meet first."

Commonwealth v. Derek Moats. It wasn't much of a case, one of a long series of short trials arising from a simple roundup at a crowded drug corner in North Philly. After a number of undercover buys, the uniforms had swarmed in from all sides, forming a ring and herding a group of suspects into the center. The undercover cops then identified the young men who had been doing the selling. It was an effective way to clean out a corner, but a scattershot form of justice. Derek was caught in the hoop and pointed out by one of the undercovers, but he claimed he wasn't doing the selling.

"So what were you doing there?" I had asked him.

"Hanging," was his answer.

"Hanging?"

"There's girls on that corner you would not believe," he had said, "and every one of them just waiting for a little bit of Derek."

The little-bit-of-Derek argument wasn't much of a closing, but it was about all I had, unless I could discredit the identification. Because of the ID, I had opted for a bench trial. Juries are always taken in by clear identifications—he's the one, yes, him—but judges know that the simple identification is often the most unreliable part of a criminal case. That was the knowledge I was banking on.

Half an hour later, I was sitting at the counsel table, leaning back with a quiet little smirk on my face as A.D.A. Johnstone, a fierce young prosecutor, came to the crucial part of her direct examination.

"What time was it," she asked, "when you made the purchase?"

"About two o'clock in the morning," said Detective Pritzker, a burly man with a long, shaggy beard, looking quite awkward in his suit and tie. He obviously would have been more at home in the motorcycle leathers he was wearing the night of the arrest.

"Was it dark?"

"The sun wasn't out, if that's what you're asking, ma'am. But at that location there are plenty of streetlamps, and with all the headlights from the traffic, it was more than bright enough for me to see who I was dealing with."

"And so you had a clear view of the man who sold you the heroin in People's Exhibit One."

"Objection," I said. "There is no testimony yet as to the actual contents within that glassine envelope."

"Are you contesting the contents, Mr. Carl?" said the judge.

"I'm contesting everything, Your Honor."

"I'll sustain the objection for the time being," said the judge. "Let's get on with it."

"And so, Officer Pritzker," said A.D.A. Johnstone with annoyance now in her voice, "you had a clear view of the man who sold you the alleged heroin in People's Exhibit One."

"Yes, I did," he said.

"And do you see him in the courtroom today?"

"Yes, I do," said Officer Pritzker, staring now straight at me as if he were preparing to steal my lunch money.

"Can you point him out, please?"

He reached out his arm and pointed his finger at the man sitting next to me at the counsel table, the man in the usual defendant's seat, and then he swiveled his arm until his finger was aimed at a different man in a suit and tie sitting in the last row of the courtroom.

"He's right there," said Pritzker. "Sitting in the back row, in the gray. That's him."

A murmur went though the courtroom. I swiveled in my seat, seemingly stunned at the revelation.

"Officer Pritzker," said A.D.A. Johnstone, "are you sure?"

"The lawyer is trying to trick me, is all," said the witness. "I heard that's the way he works. He's got a reputation. But I'm a step ahead. The guy I bought from is him in the back."

The judge leaned forward on the bench and hissed down at me. "Mr. Carl, are you playing games in my courtroom?"

"Would I do something like that, Judge?"

"Unfortunately, yes, you would. But not without consequences. Who is the man sitting next to you at counsel table?"

I looked at the young man next to me, hands clasped before him, eyes staring down. "Your Honor," I said, "the young man sitting next to me at counsel table is the defendant, my client, Derek Moats."

Officer Pritzker, on the stand, snarled at me and then said to the A.D.A. in a harsh whisper loud enough for the whole courtroom to hear, "He's lying."

"Your Honor," said the A.D.A., "this is highly irregular."

"Yes it is," said the judge. "Mr. Carl, if I may ask, who is the man in the suit whom the officer identified?"

"I believe the man in the suit," I said, "is an intern with the public defender's office."

"What is he doing in my courtroom?"

"I invited him, Judge. He's trying to learn about the criminal justice system, I told him this could be an instructive case."

"You invited him, did you? And it's just a coincidence, I'm sure, that the intern you invited into the courtroom and your client both look quite alike."

"They do? I hadn't noticed."

"They were talking outside the courtroom," said Officer

Pritzker. "The lawyer had his arm around his shoulders, giving him orders. I saw it."

"I was advising a young man who is seeking a career in the law," I said.

"I bet that's what you were doing," said the judge. "And doing it right smack in the view of the witness. Okay, this is what we're going to do. Ms. Johnstone, I want you to take custody of both these men right now and figure out who is who. Match fingerprints if you have to. How long will that take?"

"Give us an hour, Your Honor."

"Fine." He checked his watch. "Come back in an hour. If the man in the suit is the defendant, Mr. Carl, there will be hell to pay, both in the sentencing of your client and for you personally after I hold you in contempt and make my report to the bar association."

"That sounds a little harsh, Judge."

"Be glad it's not the old days, Mr. Carl, where I would have pulled your ticket and had you flogged. But if it truly was, as Mr. Carl claims"—he paused, looked down at the docket on the bench before him—"Derek Moats, the defendant, sitting next to Mr. Carl this whole time, then, Ms. Johnstone, your witness blew the identification, your case is dead, and I expect it to be dismissed forthwith. Do you understand?"

"We could still make the argument that—"

"I don't want to hear arguments. It will be dismissed, is that clear?"

"Yes, Judge."

"Any questions?"

"No, Judge."

"And, Mr. Carl, don't you dare leave this courtroom until Ms. Johnstone makes her report."

"What about lunch?"

"Eat the desk, I don't care, but you stay right here."

"Yes, Your Honor."

"Okay then," he said with a bang of his hammer, "we're in recess. I need to take a pill."

I signaled to Derek not to say a word to anyone and watched as A.D.A. Johnstone and two police officers escorted the two young men from the courtroom. Then I sat down and leaned back to wait.

Just at that moment, a massive weight fell onto my shoulder and almost sent me reeling backward to the floor. I angrily jerked around and spied a huge man, with broad shoulders, an expanding stomach, and a face like a boxer who had bobbed when he should have weaved. Detective McDeiss of the Homicide Division. And he was shaking his big old head at me.

"That was cute," he said.

"You think so?"

"Which is which?"

"I am an officer of the court, Detective."

"You're also incapable of telling the truth."

"Not this time."

"So he identified the wrong one?"

"Yes, he did."

"Then I assume that you are quite proud of yourself for tricking a servant of the people."

"Quite. But I didn't have to trick him, he tricked himself. You heard what he said. I have a reputation. But my client wasn't selling anyway. He was in the wrong place at the wrong time."

"Just like you," he said as he dropped something onto the table.

I looked down, felt my nerves fizzle.

It was the *Daily News*, the chronicle of high crimes and low misdemeanors of the residents of our fair town. And spread across the front page was the picture of a fine stone house and the headline MANSION OF DEATH.

I hadn't had time to check the papers that morning, so I paged through it quickly, stopping at the article. It gave a few details of the Denniston murder and mentioned that the doctor's wife was still in police custody. A statement about the investigation was made by Detective Augustus Sims, who simply confirmed that the wife of the deceased was being held for questioning. And the paper also quoted Julia Denniston's attorney, Clarence Swift, as forcibly denying that Julia had anything to do with the tragedy and urging the public to come forward with any information about the crime. "In my modest opinion," he was quoted as saying, "as the investigation continues, the evidence will completely exonerate Mrs. Denniston." My name was conspicuously absent. I must say I was a bit surprised to find that Sims had honored his word and kept me out of it. Maybe he was more trustworthy than I supposed?

Nah.

I closed the tabloid, tapped the cover. "Nice house."

"Did you have anything to do with it?" said McDeiss.

"No."

"You sure?"

"Stop it. Of course I didn't."

"That's what I thought. Guns aren't your style."

"Still, you sent Sims and Hanratty over to my place in the middle of the night."

"I remembered your connection to the dead man's wife. I brought it up to the captain, tried to use it to get assigned the case."

"Really? To protect me?"

"To ensure justice and promote domestic tranquillity."

"You wanted to nail me personally, huh?"

"Like a toothache. But the captain didn't let me anywhere near the case and gave it to Sims."

"Just my luck. What can you tell me about him? Nice guy?"

"Watch yourself."

"Why?"

"Just be careful."

"I'm more concerned about Hanratty."

"Hanratty's okay."

"He thinks I'm somehow involved."

"Of course he does. Any cop worth his salt would. But he'll find out what really happened one way or the other. That's all he cares about. With Sims you never know. He plays to his own agenda. Sims is more politician than cop."

"And we all know how well politics mixes with truth."

"Hey, did you really not have sex with her?"

"Word gets around, I guess."

"We all got a laugh out of it. And it's too bad, since she's quite nice-looking for a killer."

"You sure she killed him?"

"Sims seems to be sure. You still have feelings for her?"

"We have a past," I said.

"I understand. But the reason I came over is to give you some friendly advice. Sims is a bulldog. He'll sniff here, sniff there, take his time in figuring out who he wants to charge with the murder, but once he's got his teeth into your leg, he's impossible to shake off. And funny thing about his cases, when they start getting shaky, evidence starts popping up as if from nowhere."

"You don't say."

"So here is my advice. Don't let your unresolved feelings from the past betray you into doing something stupid. Stay the hell away from this case, Victor, at least until Sims decides who to charge. Right now he's focusing on the wife. But if he starts focusing on you, then, boy, you might think you know what trouble is, but you'll find out you were underestimating it all along."

Generally I am disinclined to follow the advice of those in authority. I think it comes from the difficult relationship I have with my father. Either that or I am simply a dope. When I am told, repeatedly, to stay the hell out of a thorny situation, I find myself somehow compelled to get involved.

But not here, not now.

Both Sims and McDeiss had advised me to stay away from the Wren Denniston murder case, and I was fully disposed to follow their advice. It wasn't because they had badges—I don't heed no stinking badges—it was because something inside me was screaming the exact same thing. The suspicion that had gripped me as soon as two hard homicide dicks trooped into my apartment and gave me the third degree had only grown thicker as I learned the details of the crime. Reclaimed love had turned to outright paranoia in the flash of a gunshot.

So I would not be visiting, not be investigating, not be aiding in her defense. Despite our promises one to the other to maintain silence, I had already told the police everything I knew. And now, going forward, I would not be a valued support in Julia Denniston's time of utter need as Sims worked like a bulldog to build a case against her. She had betrayed me in the past; I was going to abandon her in the present. It seemed a fair enough trade to me. But she had a right to know.

I could visit her in the prison, tell her the way I was feeling, advise her that she was on her own, but that would require an actual modicum of bravery and class. So I decided instead to write her a letter.

Dear Julia,

Or should it have been "Dearest Julia"? Or "My Dearest, Dearest Julia"? Or "You Murderous Skank"? It was hard to get a grip on the proper address for a former fiancée who was soon to be indicted for murder. Where is Emily Post when you need her?

I want you to know how important these last few weeks have been to me.

I liked the tone of that, a sharp, clinical detachment, like we were working out the details of a business transaction rather than performing our little tango.

In a way we were able to recapture something that was lost so long ago, when you betrayed me and married that urologist asshole whom you have most recently murdered.

So much for detachment. And was it oxymoronic to call a urologist an asshole? I crossed out everything after "so long ago."

I know that this is a most difficult time, and I very much would like to be by your side as you pass through it.

Did that sound a little bitter, as if I would enjoy the spectacle of her disintegration?

But the exigencies of the situation make that impossible. As a material witness, I have been repeatedly ordered by the authorities to stay away from you and your defense. I believe it is imperative for both our benefits that I do so.

That was actually pretty good, precise and filled with legal nomenclature while still making my cowardice appallingly apparent. I considered it sort of a noble gesture on my part, my spinelessness undoubtedly making the whole abandonment thing less painful for her. Sometimes I'm so noble I can't stand myself.

I'm sure you are in excellent legal hands and that your attorney will do everything possible to ensure a just result.

This was actually a lie. I was pretty sure that Clarence Swift, whom I had never yet met, was in over his head, but there was nothing I was willing to do about that. And the "just result" thing was a double-edged sword, wasn't it? If you are innocent, I hope you get off, and if you are guilty, may you rot in jail.

Look me up if you beat the rap, and maybe we can resume precisely where we left off.

The sentiment was true, absolutely, I could still feel her warm flesh, but I'd have to rewrite that a bit, don't you think?

Sincerely,

As opposed to "Sardonically," or "Cynically," or "With All Due Self-Preservation."

Victor

At least that part I got right. The rest needed some work.

I opened my desk drawer, pulled out another sheet of paper so as to give it a second go. When I pushed the drawer closed, it caught on something.

Not a surprise, really. While that drawer is not normally an exemplar of neatness, it was now an unholy mess. The contents had been rifled, as had the contents of my bureau and clothes closet, my kitchen, my linen closet and bathroom. They had taken the sheets off the bed, the towels off the rack, had swabbed the shower, had taken apart the drain of my bathroom sink and pulled out all the gunk in the elbow. It wasn't hard to figure out what they had been looking for: They had been looking for blood, Wren Denniston's blood.

And with all that rifling, they had obviously pushed something in the way of my drawer slide. I reached in, felt nothing that would stop the drawer from closing, tried shutting it again, and failed. I could either work on the letter or solve this mystery once and for all, and working on the letter was proving more difficult than I expected. So I slid the drawer all the way out of the desk and reached inside, and that's when I felt it. Something, yes. Something smooth and soft.

I grabbed hold and pulled it out.

A little purse, zippered shut. Red. Leather. Coach. About the size of a small hand, Julia's hand, zippered shut to hide everything inside.

When I realized what I had found, I dropped it onto the desktop as if it were burning my fingers. It sat there, red, on my desk, like a warning fire.

Dear Julia, you sly little minx,

She learns her husband has been murdered. She collapses to the floor in anguish. After a few moments of dazed reminiscence, she goes into the bedroom to prepare for her rendezvous with the police, and what does she do? She dresses, and packs, and stuffs her red Coach purse behind a desk drawer, stuffs it in so cleverly that a team of Crime Scene Search technicians executing a search warrant don't find it. That told me all I really needed to know about the guilt of Julia Denniston.

I should give it to the cops, without delay, turn it over like a good and honest citizen, an officer of the court. Yes, I should. Except that Julia wanted desperately to keep it from their prying eyes. It was one thing to answer questions truthfully and then wash my hands of her, it was quite another to voluntarily turn over evidence to those trying to imprison her for the rest of her life. I am a defense attorney as much by instinct as by choice.

I picked up the purse, felt its weight, a few ounces maybe. I rubbed my thumb across the leather and felt something underneath, something hard and cylindrical, like a fancy pen. But what pen was worth hiding from the police? Montblanc? It would be nothing to unzip the purse, peek inside. It would be nothing to uncover the secret she was trying to maintain.

I drew my hand away, shook my head. I should give it to her lawyer, Clarence Swift. She wanted to keep it from the cops, and by giving it to Swift I would be facilitating that choice. Then it would be up to Swift to decide what to do with it. He could examine it closely, learn its secret, decide what to turn over, what to keep hidden. With him it would have protections of the attorney-client privilege that it could never have with me. Except that if Julia wanted Swift to have it, he would already have come knocking. She had hidden it from him, too.

I reached my hand once again toward it, gently rubbed the tips of my fingers over its supple red finish. It was worn and soft, like flesh. Like Julia's flesh in those few rare moments before the cops came knocking, warm and yielding, hungry, ecstatic.

Stop, I told myself. Toss it, burn it, chop it with an ax and drown it in the Schuylkill River. If I did it right, no one would be the wiser. Whatever was inside, whatever evidence, whatever clues to the murder of Julia's husband or the state of Julia's soul, would disappear right along with the supple leather.

Yet even as I plotted on how to rid myself of its dangers, I could feel it drawing me toward it. I leaned close and smelled its scent, an aphrodisiacal combination of leather and expensive French perfume. For a moment I lost myself in the erotic promise of the bouquet. Hints of fine oil, champagne, the French Riviera, balsamic and vanilla, musk and passion. And as I breathed it in, as deep as my lungs would allow, I knew, quite simply, that I wouldn't give it to the cops, or give it to Clarence Swift, or render it unto ash. I had thought our old-lovers' tango had reached its sordid conclusion, but of course, as usual I was dead wrong.

Whether I liked it or not, I was in the middle of Wren Denniston's murder. My neck was on the line, and the more I knew, the more I found out, the safer I would be. I wasn't the type to let evidence disappear, to let secrets lie fallow, to let the soul of an old lover remain hidden from my view when there were clues right in front of me. No, I wasn't the type. But it wasn't only that.

Did I still have feelings for her? had asked McDeiss. Of course I did. Old love doesn't disappear; it is too potent an elixir for that. Instead it burrows deep into bone, like a parasite, waiting until just the right moment to reassert itself and sabotage your life. It arises like an ache in the middle of the night. It crawls up your throat with the taste of bile when you kiss someone new. It grips your soul and shakes you senseless.

It turns you stupid.

I picked up the small Coach purse, gently grasped the red leather pull of the zipper, yanked it open, and in that one sudden movement I was suddenly all in.

The knocker on the big green door was a bronze coiled snake, with its forked tongue sticking out. I lifted it and dropped it twice.

Knock, knock.

While I was waiting for the "Who's there?" I looked around at the poorly lit front lawn, at the large dark BMW parked in the circular driveway, at the brick and white-pillared arbor off to the side. The stone house was big all right, not quite a mansion, like the papers were calling it, though the "of death" part was surely accurate. In the gloom of night, it had a forbidding mien, like a cantankerous old man in a wheelchair, legs covered by a tartan blanket, with money in his wallet and evil in his heart.

Knock, knock, knock.

The door opened a crack. "I heard you the first time," came a voice, creaky and slightly Southern. "What you want in here?"

"I'm looking for Wren Denniston," I said.

"Don't be a fool," came the voice. The door opened a little wider, and I could see her there, tall and thin with short gray hair and raw hands, a trim white-and-blue dress. "I spent all day dealing with reporters banging on the door and crawling through them bushes. I've heard more lies than a priest in confessional the last three days. I don't need to hear yours, too."

"I don't understand," I said. "I'm just looking for Wren. He told me to stop on by when I got to town. This is his house, isn't it?"

"I never said it wasn't."

"Then I'm at the right place. Is he in? Can you just tell him that I'm here?"

"What you say your name was?"

"Taylor, Anthony Taylor. Wren will know me as Tony."

She cocked her head, narrowed an eye. "How do you know the doctor?"

"We were at Princeton together. In the same eating club."

"You look younger than him."

"He was a couple classes ahead of me, and I live clean. If he's not in, just tell Julia that Tony is here. She'll know me."

"Julia, huh?"

"His wife."

"You really don't know."

"Know what?" I said.

"Where are you from?"

"Columbus," I said. "Just got in this afternoon."

She stepped out, wagged her head left and right, and then pulled me through the doorway before shutting the door behind us both. "Maybe you should have a seat," she said. "In the living room, Mr. Taylor. I have some terrible news."

Her name was Gwen, and she was a lovely, dignified old woman who had worked for Wren Denniston for years, starting when he was a boy, and she'd worked for his parents in this very same house. Her eyes welled as she broke the brutal news of his murder to one of Wren's old college pals. I patted her hand, and gave what comfort I could, and I felt like a cad the whole time I was doing it, but I've done worse in my life. And I had good reason to be there.

When you need to find the truth about a murder, there is no better place to start than the killing ground. Except I didn't need the cops to know I was snooping around, or Julia to know either, for that matter. So I wasn't Victor Carl this night. Instead I reached into the sad history of our city's baseball past, pulled out one of the few names that still shone, and became Tony Taylor, Princeton grad. I sort of liked the sound of that: Princeton grad. Maybe I should have actually studied for my SATs.

"I came back and found him myself," said Gwen as she poured me some tea out of a fine china pot. I was sitting on a green couch in a cavernous blue living room stuffed full with French-style chairs and couches. She was sitting across from me, holding the pot with a steady hand. "All that blood and him lying there, pale and dead with that black mark on his forehead and the back of his head gone. It was horrible, Mr. Taylor, just horrible. Would you like more pie?"

"Yes, thank you. I have to say, Gwen, this is the best pecan pie I've ever had."

"My cousin sends me the pecans from back home, fat and fresh off the tree." She cut a slice from the thick brown pie sitting next to the teapot on the coffee table. "Fresh pecans make all the difference. When I saw the doctor lying there, I just screamed and screamed, which was silly, since there was no one to hear it. But I couldn't help myself."

"Of course you couldn't."

"More freshly whipped cream?"

"Yes, please. The pie is too rich without it."

"That's the way I make it," she said. "That's the way my mother made it, and she taught me how. Right away I called the police. They came quick, but even so it was too horrible being in the house. I waited outside for them to come."

"I understand completely. Where was Julia?"

"She was gone. They were arguing when I left. I had dinner plans. Norman buys me dinner every Sunday night. So I left them to their argument. It's not like it was a startling event, the two of them going at it."

"What were they arguing about?"

"Something personal to them. But, to be truthful, they didn't need an excuse."

"Who was usually right?"

"Now you're going to get me in trouble. More tea?"

"I'm fine, thank you."

"The doctor was . . . well, you know, being old friends, like you are."

"He was prickly, even in college," I guessed.

"That he was. He wrestled all through prep school and college, as I'm sure you know. He told me once that wrestling was the truest expression of his inner nature. All that twisting and violence, the domination by the man on top. And I don't think he changed much over the years."

"What about Julia?"

"The missus is a little more complicated. But she is a kind soul, a sweet woman who I took to right away. We have a special bond. It might not seem it, but she needs taking care of, and in her own way she lets me do just that. The poor missus didn't understand what she was getting into when she married the doctor."

"What was she getting into, Gwen?"

Gwen lifted up her teacup, took a sip. "It was a marriage, Mr. Taylor. And, if I can confide—"

"Of course you can."

"Some loves die hard and some never die at all."

"Are you talking about Julia's love for Dr. Denniston?"

"No, dear, I'm not."

I turned my head to hide the emotions that must have flitted across my face. Was ours the old love that had never died in Julia? Of course it was, and it was indescribably sweet to hear how she had described it to someone else. And if I were to be true to myself, I had to admit that our love held the very same place in my heart. So maybe my foolish hopes from the night before had not been so foolish after all. Suddenly, in the midst of the current darkness, there seemed to be something bright over the horizon, if I could only steer us past the shoals. I looked around at the richness of the furnishings, the sturdy bones of the manse, the housekeeper who seemed to come along with the deed. Julia, my darling Julia.

"Where's Julia now?" I said with complete disingenuousness.

"She's still being held by the police. But we expect her back home tomorrow."

"We?"

"I and her lawyer. Clarence Swift." She sniffed a bit, as if at a peculiar smell. "Do you want to see where it happened?"

"I don't know. Do I?"

"He was your friend. You should see it, as a memorial, don't you think? Maybe leave a token like they do at those street-corner shrines whenever a child gets shot in the city."

"Could I finish up my pie first?"

"Of course, dear. Do you have enough whipped cream with that?"

After putting down my fork and smacking my lips—I hadn't been lying, about the pecan pie at least—I followed Gwen out of the living room into the wide central hall. Toward the rear of the house, there was a pair of closed double doors on the other side of the hallway and a piece of yellow tape wrapped around the door handles.

"The police told me not to go into this room," she said.

"Then maybe we should stay out."

"No, thank you," she said, unwrapping the tape. "I've lived in this house for more than thirty years. I won't have anyone telling me where I can and can't go. This way."

She pushed open the doors, turned on the lights, led me into a spacious den with wood-paneled walls and beamed ceilings. It smelled a little damp, and a little rusty, and a little ill, like a sickness had come over the place. A large mahogany desk was set by the windows, a round green-felt poker table stood in the corner, and a huge flat-screen television hung over the marble fireplace. Surrounding the fireplace was a wall of bookshelves, covered with trophies on which little wrestlers were posed like bullies with back conditions, ready to strike. The walls and furniture were so highly polished the whole room gleamed. It would have been a room fit for *Architectural Digest* if it weren't for the patches of dark powder over the walls and windows or the sprawled squat figure outlined on the bloodstained carpet.

"That's where I found the doctor," said Gwen. "Just like that. I wanted to clean up the blood, but they wouldn't let me. I'm not going to wait much longer."

"Where was he shot from?"

"Over there," said Gwen, pointing to the end of the bookshelf in the rear corner of the room.

One of the wooden panels beneath the books in that corner was slightly off kilter. I stepped over to it, gently pulled. The false panel swung open to reveal a gray metal safe.

"They got that open this morning," said Gwen. "Brought a man in from Ohio to do it. There were some papers, some baseball cards, stuff. But no money, when there was always money. Everyone's wondering where the money got off to. And then, of course, the gun."

"What gun?"

"He kept a gun in the safe, but that was gone, too."

"Was that the gun that killed him?"

"That's what they think."

"And they really think that Julia killed him?"

"They do."

"What do you think, Gwen? Did she?"

"Course she didn't. Why on earth do you think I let you in here and stuffed you full of pecan pie?"

"Excuse me?"

"I made that one for Norman. With the last of the pecans, too, so he'll be eating apple until I get a new batch. But when I saw you at the door, I knew right away the last pecan pie was going to you."

"I'm missing something here."

"I remember seeing Tony Taylor play at Shibe Park," said Gwen. "Lithe and handsome, skin like polished ebony. He was dreamy. You, sir, are no Tony Taylor. But I knew who you were as soon as I opened the door, Mr. Carl. The missus had tracked your adventures in the paper over the years. We used to laugh at the stories. And then she mentioned you more recently. In fact, you were being discussed in the argument last night before Dr. Denniston was killed."

I looked at the figure outline on the carpet. "Really? That's not good."

"Not for you, and I guess not for the doctor neither, the way it turned out. I figured you were here to help Mrs. Denniston, and so I decided to help you. You don't think I thought you were an old friend from Princeton, did you?"

"Yes, actually."

"My mama didn't raise no fool, Mr. Carl."

"Mine obviously did."

"Princeton." She shook her head. "But the missus called when they first took her to the police station and said that you were going to help her, and so I decided to help you."

"With the pie."

"There's not much a dose of Karo and molasses can't help. So, Mr. Carl, is there anything else you want to know?"

I looked around the room, thought about it for a moment. "I heard the alarm was activated when you came back last night."

"That's right."

"Who knew the code?"

"The doctor and the missus. Me, of course. A few others. That Mr. Swift. A couple handymen that worked on the house. It wasn't a well-kept secret."

"Clarence Swift had the code?"

"Mr. Swift was almost family to the doctor. It was like he lived his life through the doctor and the missus. Mr. Swift was here almost as much as I was."

"How about a guy named Miles Cave?"

"I never met him, but I think he was an old school friend of the doctor's," she said. "I told the police about him. Recently I had heard his name being discussed by the doctor over the phone. Something about money, I could tell. A lot of the doctor's calls at the end were about money. The calls involving that Cave fellow seemed to be more heated than most. I'm no detective, Mr. Carl, but I told the police and I'm telling you: I believe this Miles Cave has more to do with what happened than the missus. You want to find out what happened, you ought to start by finding him."

I looked at the safe, at the figure sprawled on the blood-stained carpet, at the big-screen television. I tried to figure out the scene the instant before the violence, the shooter there, the dead man standing there, the safe open.

"Is this just the way the room was when you found it?"

"Yes, sir. The police haven't let me touch much of anything."

"No struggle, then, no bashed pottery or books thrown?"

"No, sir."

"What did the police take with them?"

"They cut some stuff off the carpet, they dusted the whole place."

"Tell me about Julia. How has she been doing lately?"

"I don't know, Mr. Carl. She seemed distracted the last few

weeks. It's always tough to get a grip on the missus. She keeps a lot to herself."

"How about her health?"

"The same as ever, I guess."

"Is she on any medications?"

"How would I know?"

"Oh, Gwen, my guess is there isn't much you don't know. I suppose you've cleaned up her medicine cabinet now and then."

"There are some pills prescribed by the doctor. Women's stuff, I think. And some Valium. For muscle pain."

"I bet. Does she drink much?"

"Not as much as the doctor, but she has a glass or two now and then."

"Anything more serious?"

"What are you getting at, Mr. Carl?"

"I don't know," I said. "Is that her car in front?"

"That's right. She called from jail and told me where she left it. I had Norman drive me over to pick it up."

"Anything interesting inside?"

"No, sir. And the police went through it as soon as I brought it back."

"I figured. Can you do me a favor? Can you call me when she returns home?"

"Sure I can. Anything else?"

"Only whether or not I can take the rest of that pie home."

"I'll box it up for you."

"Why, thank you, Gwen."

"You going to save her?"

"Maybe," I said. "If she deserves to be saved."

"We all deserve that, Mr. Carl."

9

TUESDAY

He was waiting for me in my outer office when I came to work the next morning, a slight, dome-headed man with outsize shoes and a striped bow tie. He leaned forward in his chair, his small mouth pursed with worry, his long, pale hands wringing one the other. He might have been my age, or he might have been fifty, it was hard to tell with his wispy red hair and wide forehead. When he saw me, he lifted his chin.

"Victor Carl, is it?" he said.

"That's right," I said.

He rocked to his feet, still bowed forward at the waist, as if in a perpetual cringe. His hands continued to rub each other strangely. It was an insectile gesture, calculating and submissive at the same time, like a male praying mantis wringing his hands before sex.

"Mr. Carl, hello. Yes. It is an honor to meet you, indeed. An honor." His voice was whiny and dispirited, and the way he enunciated "honor," he might as well have been telling me what a burden it was to be in my presence. "I apologize for dropping in unannounced like this. You can be assured that I wouldn't bother a personage of your high status and accomplishment if it weren't so vital. But could you possibly, perhaps, spare a moment in your busy day for me? If it is in any way inconvenient, we could do it at another time, certainly. Everything at your convenience, of course."

I stared at him and then at my secretary, Ellie, who had an amused expression on her face. She subtly pushed forward a card on her desk.

I looked at the card, swiveled my head to look at the man and then back at the card. SWIFT & SON, it read. REAL ESTATE MANAGEMENT. TITLE INSURANCE. MORTGAGE BROKERAGE. LIFE AND DISABILITY INSURANCE. And then, in the corner, in tiny print: CLARENCE SWIFT, ATTORNEY-AT-LAW.

"Mr. Swift?"

"Clarence, please," he said, interrupting me. "Call me Clarence. There is no reason for you to be so formal with the likes of me."

"Fine, Clarence. You were Wren Denniston's lawyer?"

"More than that, sir. We were friends, the best of friends. We spoke constantly, hatched plots together. His father did business with my father, and that was a bond that kept us together. I still can't believe he's gone. Not an hour goes by where I don't start to pick up the phone and only then remember."

He pulled a giant handkerchief from his inside jacket pocket, wiped the shine off his wide forehead, blew his pointed nose.

"I'm sorry for your loss," I said.

"Yes, thank you," he said as he flicked the handkerchief back into his jacket. "It's been a most traumatic couple of days. I am at sea, Mr. Carl, marooned on a floating piece of flotsam. Not even jetsam, sir, but flotsam."

"Very understandable. Why don't you step into my office?"

"Oh, thank you, sir, thank you. That is quite extraordinary of you to make the time to see me on such short notice."

"Think nothing of it," I said as I gestured to the hallway.

When he was situated in a client chair across from my desk, I stepped out of the office for a moment and returned to Ellie.

"Any calls?" I said.

"A few," she said, handing me my messages.

"I need to talk to Derek Moats, the defendant I represented yesterday. Can you try to find him for me?"

"I have his cell-phone number. Do you want me to set up an appointment for him here?"

"No," I said quickly. "Not here. Just find out where he'll be tonight. Tell him I have a job for him, if he's willing."

"Fine."

I glanced down the hallway. "What do you think of our Mr. Swift?"

"Peculiar, isn't he?"

"Yes. How would you feel if your life was in his hands?"

"Concerned."

"I suppose you should hold all my calls."

When I returned to my office, Clarence Swift was just closing the briefcase on his lap and locking it shut.

"Looking for something?" I said.

"Just consulting my scheduler to see what is next. A man of business must always keep himself busy, my father used to say."

I sat behind my desk and stared for a moment at the strange-looking man before me. His chin was pointy, his pursed mouth was just the right size for his thumb. And his philtrum was extraordinarily deep. You know what a philtrum is, it's that groove that runs from your nose to your mouth, that thing we never think about, but it was hard not to think about it with Clarence Swift. It was so deep he could have stored his loose change in there.

"I so appreciate your seeing me unawares like this, Mr. Carl," he said. "I've heard much about you, in both the papers and from Wren. Poor old Wren was quite the raconteur, always quick with the telling jab and the illuminating tale. He'll be so missed. And you'll be gratified to learn, I am sure, that you were often a favorite subject."

"Oh, I bet I was."

"It is from my bond with Wren that rises my commitment toward Julia," said Swift. "You must believe that I would do whatever is humanly possible for her. She is a fabulous woman."

"Yes, she is."

"Truly extraordinary."

"I agree."

"Wondrous in oh-so-many ways."

I eyed him for a long moment. "Are you married, Clarence?"

"Engaged."

"Good for you."

"My fiancée, Margaret."

He pulled out his wallet, opened it, dug deep until he pulled out a bent and spindled photograph of a large woman holding a gray cat. The woman was stout and hardy, with big-knuckled hands and floppy ears. Ouch.

"We often had dinner together with the Dennistons," said Clarence, looking at the photograph with a depressed gaze before sticking it back into his wallet. "We were all so close."

"So tell me, how is Julia holding up?"

"Hanging on as best she can, under the circumstances," he said. "I think she has a slight cold."

"A cold, huh?"

"Yes. It's understandable, the tragedy weakening her defenses."

"I'm sure that's it."

"It has rocked us all. But this is no time to be paralyzed by grief. We must put away our own personal anguish and sally forth. And so here I am, thrust into the role of defender, determined to do my best for poor Julia. Though, of course, I don't expect my meager experience in such matters can compare with the achievements of your brilliant career."

"It hasn't been that brilliant," I said.

"You're being modest, but I would expect no less. It is a certified truth that the greater the man, the greater the humility. And you, Mr. Carl, are living proof."

"I'm not that humble either."

"Still, Mr. Carl. Still."

"Call me Victor," I said.

"That would be a privilege." He bowed his head in gratitude, as if I were a lord granting some great favor to a serf. "One of the reasons I have come today, Victor, is that I am trying to understand all that Mrs. Denniston was doing on the night of the murder. A timeline, so to speak. That is what they always do in the television shows, is it not? And so I am quite interested in what she was doing at your apartment when the police finally found her. The police detective has already given me your statement. The handsome one—"

"Sims."

"Right, Detective Sims. I much prefer him to the other one, the big Irish one, who comes off as quite a brute. But Detective Sims seems much more reasonable."

"Oh, he's a great guy, he is."

"He's actually been very helpful."

"I bet he has."

"So, Victor, do you have anything to add to what you told the police?"

"No, the statement is still operative."

"Still operative. That's a funny phrasing. Quite atypical, don't you think? May I ask you straight out what is the exact nature of your relationship with Julia?"

"No."

He sat back awkwardly, stared at me over his pointy nose. "It would help my preparations tremendously."

"I don't see how. And in any event it's personal."

"Personal? Oh, my."

"If you want an answer, Clarence, simply ask your client."

"Yes, well, she hasn't been, how do I say this"—he leaned forward, lowered his voice to a whisper—"as cooperative as I would have hoped."

I tilted my head a bit. "She's not talking? Even to you?"

"No. Do you have any idea why?"

I did. We had made a deal, a deal she had kept but that I had violated at the first convenient moment.

"No," I said. "No idea. But she is being smart not to talk."

"I don't think it is smart at all. I have advised her, of course, that she should cooperate completely with the authorities. That is simply what one does after a great tragedy. But she has sadly not taken my advice. Which is too bad. I'm afraid if she doesn't talk to the police soon, they are going to become suspicious."

"That boat sailed long ago."

"But it is not too late to turn the tide. I was as surprised as anyone when Julia called from police headquarters, but since that moment I have been working like a demon. And you'll be gratified to know, I'm sure, that I have poor Julia's case well in hand."

He pulled out his handkerchief, blew his nose while staring at me, stuffed the handkerchief back in his jacket.

"Well in hand," he repeated.

"That's interesting," I said, "because it appears from the papers that they are building an airtight case against her."

"A flimsy case of circumstantial evidence only, Victor. A tissue of lies that I can, that I must, pull apart. And preparations are being made."

"What kind of preparations?"

"As her attorney, you must understand, I am not at liberty to say."

"The cops mentioned a guy named Cave. Miles Cave. Have you ever heard of him?"

Clarence sucked his teeth as he stared at me a moment. "No. Never. But I will get to the bottom of everything, Victor, trust that at least. And, like I said, Julia's case is well in hand."

Well in hand indeed, I thought. It didn't take but a glimpse to size up Clarence Swift. He was eager, earnest, humble, and harmless, all fatal traits in a defense lawyer. And in court, no matter whom the D.A. put against him, he'd be terminally overmatched. If Julia had to depend on him in a murder trial, she'd be lost.

"What kind of law do you normally practice, Clarence?" I said.

"Mostly wills and such, taxes and real estate."

"Have you ever defended a murder charge before?"

"Not precisely."

"Ever tried a criminal case?"

"The son of one of our clients was arrested for driving under the influence."

"How'd that turn out?"

"Well, he had failed his Breathalyzer, Victor, and there was not much anyone could have done."

"I suppose not."

"I know this won't be easy, being Julia's bulwark against the ravages of false accusation. But trust me when I tell you, I have her case well in hand." Clarence raised a long, bony finger in the air. "She'll be free and clear before you know it."

"I wish I had your confidence."

"Which brings me to the other reason I have come today."

"Go ahead."

"I understand you paid an uninvited visit to the house last night."

"That's right."

"It must have been a disappointment to learn that Julia was still being held by the authorities."

"I got over it."

"I am working out a deal with the district attorney to have my client released. She could be out quite soon."

"That's great news."

"Yes. 'Tis. But that might cause other problems in the investigation. So this is what I request, with all due respect, from you, Victor. It would be best for everyone, I believe, if you could manage to stay far away from Julia. No more visits to the house, no more rendezvous at your apartment or surreptitious meetings in hotel bars."

"Hotel bars?"

"There is no need to stoke the suspicions of the police about a relationship between the two of you, no matter how misguided. No need to set tongues to wagging. As Julia's attorney, I am asking that you don't see her or communicate with her in any manner until this matter is resolved."

I thought about that for a moment. "You don't have the right to ask that."

"Maybe not, but think of it as a favor to me."

"I don't owe you a favor."

"Then think of it as an urgent request from her attorney. One that, if you refuse, might result in serious consequences."

"Consequences?"

Clarence lifted his briefcase from his lap, stood. "Thank you so much for seeing me on such short notice. It was quite generous of you."

"Consequences?"

He walked to the door, stopped at the entranceway, and swiveled his head. "I will keep you informed of the progress of the case and any further information I might be needing. I'm sure the two of us will work famously together. Famously."

"What kind of consequences?"

"Good day to you, sir," said Clarence Swift. "A most earnest good day."

I sat in my car and stared out the window at the front of the Denniston house.

It looked altogether less disturbing in the late-afternoon sun. A lovely home in a lovely neighborhood where a loving family could pursue its lovely future. Which of course I knew to be a lie. This wasn't a home that protected with its warm embrace, it was a heap of stone and wood in which the twisted destinies of flawed people played out to their bitter ends. Usually that meant divorce and desolation, other times it meant a slow descent into decrepitude and madness, and sometimes it meant murder.

Yet I couldn't help myself from driving over, parking on the street, waiting as if in stakeout for some blessed arrival. Gwen had called with the ring of excitement in her voice. Mr. Swift was waiting at the police station with his car. He had worked out something with the authorities. The missus was coming home.

Shortly after I showed up, a boxy black Volvo pulled into

the circular drive and parked behind the BMW. Clarence Swift bounced out of the driver's seat of the Volvo, jumped around the car, bent at the waist as he obsequiously opened the passenger door. He remained in a bow as Julia left the car and headed toward the house as casually as if she had just come back from a routine day of shopping and lunch. Clarence Swift slammed shut the door and slipped into position beside her, his mouth at her ear, talking and whispering and importuning as they walked inside the house. The big green door closed behind them both.

I had the urge to run over, yank open the door, grab hold of Julia, and swing her around in the air, which was peculiar, because Julia was not a grab-hold-of-and-swing-around-in-the-air kind of girl. I could just imagine her puzzled expression, wondering what on earth I was doing. But I also had the paranoid urge to get the hell out of there, to run away and stay away and not allow myself to be drawn any further into the murderous mess she had made of her life. I was poised between two equal urges that left me paralyzed.

So I sat and thought about our shared past, our blighted present, our possible futures. One involved a lovely life in that very house, drinking champagne bought with Julia's dead husband's money, making love on Julia's dead husband's bed. The other involved me sitting in prison, growing old with my roommate Bubba while Julia shopped for scarves at Nordstrom. I thought about what I had found in the purse snuck behind my desk drawer and wondered which future that made more likely.

Clarence had said she had a cold. A cold indeed.

About half an hour after they had arrived, Clarence left the house and closed the door behind him. Before entering his car, he lifted his chin as if he had sensed something. I crouched down lower in my seat and kept staring. With his head swiveling back and forth like a dog's head sniffing the air for a stray squirrel, it was as if a mask had slipped from his features. No more was he the humble and overmatched attorney. In this unguarded instant, I saw something else, the truth behind his fawning manner, and this is what I saw: Dylan Klebold in the flesh.

You remember Klebold, the quiet boy who went to school one day and started blasting away with a sawed-off shotgun and a TEC-DC9 semiautomatic. Before his big day at Columbine, Klebold wrote in his day planner, "The lonely man strikes with absolute rage." And now here was Clarence Swift, scanning the landscape with a cold anger, as if everything his gaze alighted upon were about to be obliterated.

And then Clarence Swift was in the Volvo, and then he was pulling out of the circular drive. I ducked lower as his car passed mine and stayed down until I was certain he was gone. Not the bravest of acts, I admit, but something about that meeting in my office had told me to be cautious of the peculiar Mr. Swift. And it wasn't just the threat of unpleasant consequences if I tried to see Julia that was causing my caution, though the flash of Klebold in his features added a little jolt to his warning. Swift had known about my meeting with Julia in a hotel bar. How had he known that if Julia wasn't talking? And why did it bother him so much? Between the time he stepped out that door and the time he drove away, in my eyes he had morphed from an overmatched attorney to something far more frightening.

When I was sure he was gone, I popped up and stared again at the big green door. Was I going to go in and see her? Was I going to start it all anew, despite the fear that had blossomed along with the desire? As I dithered, someone else beat me to it.

A Jaguar, gray and predatory, passed my car, slipped into the circular driveway, stopped at the door. The rear passenger door opened, and a man climbed out, a broad bus of a man with a huge belly and a bushy black beard. He wore sandals and white pants and a loud print shirt, as if he had just stepped off the streets of Bangkok. He looked around, much the way Clarence had looked around, and then walked quickly, almost skippingly, to the door, lifted the serpent knocker, and let it drop loudly once, twice.

Gwen opened the door, gave him an astonished stare, and let him in. I checked my watch. When the door opened to let him out, I checked it again.

Seventeen minutes. Not much of a visit.

The way he was dressed, it wasn't a business call, he wasn't a plumber or the air-conditioner guy, he wasn't a banker, he wasn't anything I could figure. And for sure he wasn't Julia's normal type, pretty much the opposite, actually. Maybe he was a proctologist.

He climbed back into the rear of his Jaguar. It started to rumbling, pulled out of the driveway, and drove quickly away from the house. I started my car and followed.

I don't know how quickly my tail was marked, but after turning left and right and right again, I followed him down a rather narrow street, where he disappeared. The street was blocked by a parked truck. I stopped the car, peered through the windshield, and then checked the rearview mirror, where I spied the gray Jaguar parked right behind me and two men striding toward my car, one on either side. The first was a thin, dark man with hooded eyes and a black leather jacket. The second was Julia's visitor.

When he reached my window, he dropped his thick hands on the edge of the door and peered down at me with a strange, dull gaze, as if I were nothing more interesting than a fly buzzing harmlessly by his ear.

"Who are you?" he said. His voice was a gravelly, accented growl that seemed to have originated somewhere in a bad Cold War movie. Russia? Uzbekistan?

"I'm nobody," I said. I glanced through the passenger-side window. The thin, dark man was reaching into his jacket, scratching his side. At least I hoped he was scratching his side.

"Why you following me?" said the man with the beard.

I turned my head back to him. "I liked your car?"

"You have good taste for a nobody, but I think you're lying. What is your name, nobody?"

"Victor Carl."

He continued staring at me for a moment with the same dull, uninterested eyes, before his mouth, beneath the black beard, opened and closed, as if he had just swallowed the annoying fly, and his eyes snapped into focus.

"I know you," he said.

"I don't think so."

"Yes, yes, I do. Victor Carl. You were the one she threw to garbage heap when she ran off with Wren. It was you."

"Who?"

"Oh, don't be silly man. Victor Carl, yes, yes. So let me guess. You were sitting in car outside her house, thinking romantic thoughts, when you saw me visiting and grew insanely jealous. For how could she prefer a skinny runt like you when she had chance with real man like me? So you decided to find out who I was. Isn't that right?"

"That would be a little weird, wouldn't it? Me sitting outside her house, just watching."

"Yes, it would. Demented, actually. Are you demented, Victor?"

"Well, when you put it that way . . ."

"So, my friend. Let me introduce myself. Gregor Trocek, at your service. And my companion is Sandro. Go back to car, Sandro. Don't worry. Nothing to fear from man like Victor, who can let someone like Wren Denniston steal his woman."

Sandro stared at me for a moment, still scratching at something beneath his jacket, then nodded and bared his teeth like a hyena before heading back to the car.

"So tell me," said Gregor Trocek. "What can I do for you, Victor?"

"I was just wondering who the hell you were?"

"A friend of the beautiful Mrs. Denniston. Through her husband. The doctor and I were business associates."

"So you were merely giving your condolences to the grieving widow?"

"That, too." He tilted his large head and narrowed his eyes. "But we should talk, yes. For you would not believe what wonderful coincidence this is. Even as you were following me, quite badly, I might add—you need work on your technique, Sandro could teach you—but even as you were following me, I, too, was looking for you. Are you hungry, Victor Carl?"

I quickly glanced at my watch.

"Never trust man who checks clock to see if he is hungry," said Trocek. "Pleasure follows no timetable. What does gut tell you?"

I looked up at him for a moment. There was a merry sort of knowingness in his gaze. I wondered what it was he knew.

"That I'm ready to eat," I said.

"Good boy. Follow me, I know a place."

And from the size of him, I was sure he did.

We ended up in a busy Spanish joint in Old City called
Amada, just the two of us at a high butcher-block table next to a
bar with hams hanging from the ceiling and wooden casks in the
wall. The décor was spare, the crowd was hip, the sign outside
read TAPAS Y VINOS. Trocek was familiar enough with the spe-
cialties of the place to order for us both without a menu, provid-
ing us each a tall beer and a wide selection of appetizers on little
plates. I pawed at the octopus and marinated white anchovies
while piles of cod croquettes and crab-stuffed peppers disappeared within the maw hidden in Trocek's beard.

"I love Iberia," said Trocek with a lecherous growl. "The food,
the sun, Portuguese girls. I have a home in southern Portugal, in
the Algarve."

"That sounds nice."

"Nice? Nice is for schoolboys with pimples on their chests."

"Have you ever been to Nice?"

He looked at me for a moment, pulled at his beard for a bit, and then stuffed a folded piece of Serrano ham into his mouth.

"Even thugs in Iberia, like Sandro, have special quality. A cruelty that comes from too much sun and not enough honest work. He is from Cádiz, the unemployment capital of Europe. He had much time to learn his current trade."

"He seems quite sweet, all warm and fuzzy. You mentioned that you visited Julia for business. What kind of business?"

He ignored my question, stabbed a slice of chorizo with his fork, and pointed it in my direction. "That must have hurt, when Wren snatched Julia from right within your embrace."

I lifted my beer, looked for a moment at the tiny bubbles rising in it before taking a sip. "Yeah, well, life sucks."

"He used to love telling that story," continued Gregor. "His how-we-met story. He'd have his arm around her neck when he told it, and in the middle of it he'd give her a little squeeze. 'I rescued her from some shyster,' he'd say. That was word he used, and he always laughed when he said it. Shyster."

"Jew shyster?"

"No."

"I'm surprised."

"It was implied."

"And what was Julia's reaction?"

"Oh, you know Julia, she doesn't react much. But he would laugh and laugh."

"I'm so sorry that he's dead."

"Me, too," he said as he speared a ring of calamari with his fork. "He was quite a valuable friend. Long ago we were partners in a business venture to sell used medical equipment to the poorer countries of Eastern Europe. We were performing great public service." He stuck the calamari in his mouth and chewed. "Sadly, we were shut down by pack of petty bureaucrats—there were libelous reports of diseases being spread by our product—but we remained friends. And later he was helpful in treating certain conditions that arose from my unique lifestyle."

"It's always handy to have a urologist on call."

"Indeed it is. He will be missed. In fact, we should drink toast to him right now."

I lifted my beer. "To Dr. Wren Denniston, that son of a bitch."

"Yes," he said, lifting his own beer in response. "To that glorious son of a bitch."

He downed his beer in a quick series of swallows, slammed the glass on the table, wiped his mouth with the back of his hand, snapped his fingers for another round.

"In fact, Victor," he said. "You might find this peculiar, but we talked about you last time we spoke."

"Me?"

"Yes, you." Trocek swirled a tentacle of squid in black ink and deposited it in his mouth. A squirt of the ink stayed on his thick lower lip, dripping into his beard. "He asked me to kill you."

"What?"

"Kill you."

"Come again?"

"Should I shout it?"

"No, that's fine." I felt my nerves fly loose, like a flock of startled swallows, and then settle again. I looked quickly around the restaurant, leaned forward, lowered my voice. "Me?"

"You."

"Gad."

"Yes."

"Why?"

"It seemed Wren somehow discovered that his dear Julia was seeing someone behind his back. Meetings at coffee shop and hotel bar. Tell me, Victor, does anyplace ooze wanton and anonymous sex more than hotel bar? And then he discovered that the someone his wife was seeing in hotel bar was you."

"We're just friends."

"Which was why you were parked on her street this very afternoon, staring at her house with longing eyes."

"How did Wren find out? Did he tell you?"

"I think he had spy on her."

"And what did you tell him?"

"It was hard to turn offer down. First, the money was good. And second, Sandro so likes the work. I have very little scruples, it's major part of my charm, but killing you seemed overreaction. As friend, I strongly advised him to forget about it."

"Thank you."

"You're welcome. But Wren was just talking anyway. He was always great talker. Not great doer, actually. Aside from the wrestling and stealing his wife from you, he was pretty much failure. Not much of doctor, not so successful in business. And even in wrestling, a monster from Iowa broke his back and ended career, so that did not work out either. Leaving Julia as his only real achievement. And then you come along, trying to snatch her back. You can see from where was born his upset. I told him to get grip. It was just wife, not like it was mistress cheating on him. Now, that would be serious. That is worth sending Sandro. Were you sleeping with his mistress, too?"

"I wasn't sleeping with anyone."

"Now you are not being serious with me. But still I found it curious that day after he told me he wanted you murdered, he ended up dead."

"Curious?"

Trocek jabbed at a shrimp, dipped it into the butter sauce until it was covered with bits of garlic, delicately placed it between his teeth, and chewed slowly. "It's like ambrosia, isn't it?"

"The shrimp?"

"No, not shrimp, though that, too, is quite good. I was in love once. I was young, she was younger. I've never recovered. I spend my life now trying to recapture feeling. It's never quite same, though, is it? Ultimately a quest doomed to failure. It can never be same because we are no longer same. But the moments of anticipation, the fleeting sensations as you slowly peel off her clothes and think that maybe, this time, it will stir you equally. Well, that delicious moment of anticipation is what I live for now. It is worth everything."

"I think you have the wrong idea."

"I would kill for it."

"I didn't."

"But would you, Victor? That's the question."

"Why is that the question?"

"How far would you go to recapture love?"

"Is this rhetorical?"

"I'm looking for Miles Cave," he said. "Do you know him?"

"No," I said.

"We were in business together, Wren and Miles and me. Wren was go-between, so I never met this Miles. A friend from school, Wren said. But now, with Wren gone, I need to find him. That's why I visit Julia. She said she didn't know him either, which is quite strange. Wren told me Miles Cave was friend he could trust. I would expect he would have introduced such friend to his wife."

"Maybe not."

"Maybe yes. Are you defending her out of gallantry, Victor, or is it something else?"

"What is it you're getting at?"

He gestured to one of the plates. "Garbanzos con espinacas?"

"I've suddenly lost my appetite."

"Pity, no matter what befalls me, I never lose my appetite. What do you think of Detective Sims?"

"I don't."

"Personally, I wouldn't trust him. His shoes are a bit too French, don't you think? But I am quite taken with Detective Hanratty. He's all jaw. You don't see jaw like that outside of old American movies or the sporting field."

"You met them?"

"No, please. I make practice of avoiding police. But I also make practice of knowing who I am dealing with, and in this case I seem to be dealing with this Sims and this Hanratty. What do you think they would say if I showed up and told them of my last conversation with Wren?"

I rubbed my thumb down the side of my beer, leaving a trail in the condensation.

"And what would they say," continued Trocek, "if I told them that right after my conversation with Wren I called Julia and relayed to her what Wren had requested of me?"

"But that would be a lie."

"Would it?"

"She would have told me."

"That would be the obvious conclusion, yes, whether it happened or not. And, of course, other conclusions would be drawn. Maybe she told. Maybe you both panicked. Maybe you decided it was kill or be killed. Don't look so worried. You could plead self-defense. From what I know of American law, it would fail, but you could plead it. You would not be standing there with just your peter in your hand."

"She never told me, and I didn't kill him."

"Details. Now, I know you've lost your appetite, Victor, but you simply must try the foie gras and orange marmalade. It is as bright as a bite of a young girl's tongue."

"They won't believe you."

He shrugged, spread the concoction on a strip of toast, swallowed, and swooned. "They won't have to," he said as he slathered another piece of toast. "They can trace the phone records. A call from Wren to my hotel room and then a call from the hotel room to Julia's cell right after."

"What do you want, Mr. Trocek?"

"I want to find Miles Cave. He has something of mine."

"Maybe you should use the Internet."

"I found a Miles Cave on the Internet, yes, in upstate New York. Sandro paid him visit. Nice man, but, unfortunately, not the one. Sandro was careful with the fingers, preserved them in

ice, at least the one he didn't keep, so maybe they've been reat-
tached, who knows with the wonders of modern medicine? I
hope so. You see, Victor, at heart I am a humanitarian. But the
pity is that I am one of those poor deluded souls who is led by
his peter, and my peter is all business. So still I am seeking my
partner."

"I don't know who the hell he is or where the hell he is."

"Then maybe start looking. And maybe give Julia little nudge
to jar her memory."

I sat back, lifted up the beer. It was a bit early, but I still
drained it and looked immediately for the pretty young waitress
so I could order another. I had never dreamed of a fat guy with a
black beard sticking tapas in his craw, but even so, this son of a
bitch was my worst nightmare come alive. Was he lying? Maybe,
except what he told me explained why Gwen had heard Wren
and Julia Denniston fighting about me the night of Wren's murder. And even if it was a lie, it wouldn't much matter. If Trocek
spilled, Hanratty's hard-on for me would grow only harder. And
it would be just as bad for Julia as it was for me. It wouldn't
make much difference then who pulled the trigger, motive was
motive and conspiracy was conspiracy and both of us would go
splat.

"Dessert?" said Gregor Trocek. "They have very nice fried
milk with orange and butterscotch."

"No, thank you. I'm ready to throw up as it is."

"Trust me, Victor, it's to die for."

"Tell me about it."

I sat and drank another beer and watched him shovel the
brown concoction into the hole in his beard and tried to think it
through. No matter how you sliced the fried milk, I was in a vise.

"What do I do after I find this Miles Cave?" I said.

Trocek reached into his shirt pocket, took out a card, slipped
it across the table. It had no name, just a phone number.

"Don't do anything rash," said Trocek. "Just give me call and tell me where he is. Sandro will take it from there. And with call, my conversations with Wren and Julia on the eve of his murder will disappear."

"I'll see what I can do."

"Don't see, do. And do quickly."

"I didn't kill your old friend Wren."

"That's sweet," he said, "but really, I don't care."

Okay, so this is what I had. There was a dead doctor. There was a cop who thought I had murdered him. There was a squirmy lawyer with the facial expressions of a teenage mass murderer who was threatening me with unpleasant consequences. There was a Russian gangster with a Spanish henchman and a taste for young Portuguese girls who had been asked to kill me. There was an old school chum of the dead man's named Miles Cave who had gone missing and yet seemed to be at the center of everything. And there was a girl who was either the key to my future or a cold-blooded killer trying mightily to make me her fall guy.

When did love get so hard?

It was enough to send me driving deep into the dark, drug-addled heart of North Philly to find some answers. Before I fell any further into the mire, I needed to learn the truth about Julia Denniston, and I figured it took one dark, drug-addled heart to know one.

I was in a single-file line of cars moving slowly down North Fifth Street as if at a Taco Bell drive-through. There was an SUV from New Jersey in front of me, a Trans Am with what looked like a couple of suburban kids behind me. The street was well lighted, music was playing, crowds were swarming around the intersection. It was like a party, festive and bright, with a cash bar.

"What can I do you?" said a kid who sidled up to my window. He had to rise on tiptoe to get a view.

"Isn't this a school night?" I said.

"I got a special deal for you, mister. How about a lady to go with your goods?"

"Does your mom know you're out here tonight?"

"It's my moms I'm talking about."

"That is so sweet. You just won my Son of the Year award."

"Come on, let's go. I got a business to run."

"It looks to me like you're the one being run. How often do you get picked up by the cops?"

"I don't. They sweep in here, I just tear. I'm so fast all they see is a blur."

"What about the bullets? You outrun those, too?"

"If I have to, sure."

"I must say, you are enough to bring tears to a man's eyes."

"You here to buy or to cry?"

"Neither, really. You know Derek Moats?"

"Skinny guy, never stops talking, combed-out Afro."

"That's the one."

"Don't know him."

"Here's a ten," I said, slipping him a bill. "Derek told me he'd be around tonight. Go find him and tell him Victor Carl will park a block down and wait for him. Then why don't you go on home and get some sleep so you'll be fresh and ready for school tomorrow."

He looked down at the bill, back up to me. "It's going to take more than a dime to save me."

"You want to be saved?"

"Hell, no."

"Just tell Derek," I said as I took my foot off the brake pedal and slowly drove away. If you put a dog in a room and shock him, he'll leap around and bark like crazy. If you shock him again and then again, shock him without rhyme or reason and without giving him any way to stop the shocks, he'll eventually stop all the leaping and barking and just lie down on the floor and take it. It's called learned helplessness, and sometimes this city makes me feel like a dog on the floor with an electrode up his butt.

"Hey, bo," said Derek a few minutes later when he leaned into the passenger window of my parked car.

"I thought you weren't in the business."

"I told you I don't sell. I'm just hanging with my boys."

"They pick you up again along with your boys, my tricks won't work a second time."

"Did you come here to lecture me, or did I hear something about a job?"

"Get in," I said.

With Derek inside the car, I drove a bit, away from the drug corner, toward an area more residential. I parked and turned on the overhead light.

"What's up?"

"I want to show you something, but you have to keep it quiet."

"Something good?"

"No," I said. "Something not good at all."

I reached down beneath my seat and pulled out a small red zippered purse and handed it to Derek.

He looked at it, front and back. "Coach," he said. "Nice. Bet it fits in right fine with your man purse."

"It's not mine, Derek. Open it up."

He took hold of the zipper pull, opened the purse, and emptied its contents on the little tray between our seats. A wad of cash, a lighter, a silver spoon, a hypodermic needle with the point capped in plastic, cotton balls, packets of alcohol swabs. And small plasticine envelopes the size of a postage stamp, all of them empty, the picture of a cat printed in black ink on the side of each. Derek stared at the little pile, rubbed the stubble on his chin, dramatically grimaced, like he was diagnosing a swollen appendix.

"You know, just having this stuff is illegal," he said.

"I know."

"Looks like some high-class society fly is hopped on H." He leaned over the tray, sniffed the air. "Yep, that's what it is."

"I'm curious about the little packets."

"They're all empty."

"They weren't when I found the purse. I emptied them into the toilet."

"Now, that was simply a crying waste."

"Do you recognize the stamp?"

"Black Cat," he said. "It's the mark of a Jamaican group working out of Hunting Park. They have all kinds of names for their stuff, depending on where it's sold. Face to Face, Viagra, Turbo, Versace, Viper, Blue Label."

"Where's Black Cat sold?" I said.

"Don't know. It changes corner to corner."

"I want to find where it's being sold and by whom."

"Where did you say you found all this stuff?"

"I didn't."

"And why you want this information for?"

"It's personal," I said. "Can you just help me out here?"

"How much?"

"Ten bucks an hour."

"What's your middle name, McDonald? Come on, bo. Fork it over."

"What about the money you still owe me for your defense?"

"What's that? I paid you a retainer."

"That didn't even cover trial prep. You still owe me for the trial itself."

"Apples and oranges. You want my help or what?"

"Twenty an hour, then, but that's it."

"Okay, though this might take a while."

"I figure."

"There's a guy I know who might know what you want to know. You want to meet him?"

"Sure," I said.

"Tonight soon enough?"

"Perfect."

"You got cash?"

"I got cash."

"Good, let's go get ourselves a drink. You like Red Stripe?"

"The beer?"

"Yah, mon, the beer," he said, lilting his voice into an island accent. "Have your cash ready, bo. We'll be eating goat and drinking Red Stripe tonight."

"Goat?"

"Tastes like dog, but with a kick."

"Sounds yummy," I said.

It was just a shed, set up on an abandoned lot hard by the railroad tracks, surrounded by a pile of abandoned cars, with electricity hijacked from the bus depot next door. A squatter of a place, the kind that sprouts wild and free of rent and regulation, until the Bureau of Licenses and Inspections gets wind of it and shuts it down, only to see it spring up in some other locale. And the word gets out again, and the clientele arrives, and the place shudders back to life.

"I know Barnabas," said Derek to the tall, thin man in dreads sitting by the door. The boards nailed haphazardly around the door were shaking to the heavy bass of a reggae beat.

"You may know Barnabas, me bredren," said the man at the door in a slow voice, "but does Barnabas know you?"

"We're cousins."

"For real?"

"Our grandmothers are related."

"How about the dundus with the suit?"

"He's with me."

"A badge?"

"Now, why you want to go insulting me like that?" said Derek.

"So who you be, mon?"

"Just a guy looking for a time," I said.

Derek stared at me for a moment, like I had suddenly turned into a circus clown. "Don't be Joe."

"Who's Joe?" I said.

"Apparently you." He turned back to the man at the door. "Is Barnabas around? Why don't you call him outside and explain to him why you're making his cousin stand here and wait like a dog?"

"All right, keep your cool. No offense meant. Just be doing my job is all."

"You letting us in?"

"Go on ahead."

As we were stepping through the sagging doorway, the tall man shot out an arm to stop my progress. "You better not be badge."

"Do I look like a cop?"

He stared for a moment and then laughed. "No, mon, for real you don't. Go on in and enjoy yourself."

The inside was far bigger than it appeared from the street, not wide but long. Rusted industrial fixtures hung from the rafters, dropping bright cones of light through the smoky haze. A makeshift bar ran along one side of the room, a small stage was set against the middle of the other, tables and chairs and a few ratty booths were scattered around the edges of a dance floor. The place smelled like spilled beer and sweet tobacco and the sizzling fat of barbecue. A loud band was playing on the stage, most of the tables were taken, the dance floor was already crowded.

"Ooh, lookie that," said Derek, leaning toward my ear and

shouting over the pounding music. He pointed to the dance floor with his chin. "That's a caboose and a half. I'd like to hitch up my locomotive to them booty cheeks."

"Can we just find who we're looking for?" I shouted back.

"In due time, bo. But first we have to scope out the opportunities."

"Well, we're being scoped ourselves right now, I can tell you that." And we were. Heads turned when we walked into the bar, and they remained turned as they registered my presence.

"You shouldn't have worn that suit," shouted Derek.

"I don't think it's the suit."

He gave me a quick up-and-down. "You are a little pasty, I must say."

"Are you really Barnabas's cousin?"

"I'm a friend of a friend of a cousin, but that's close enough to count around here. There's an empty booth over there."

As we edged our way through the dancers, a man bashed his shoulder into mine and turned without apologizing. Derek stopped for a moment to dance with a woman in tight jeans who was sashaying by herself to the music. I pulled him away by the sleeve, and together we slipped into a booth with ripped leatherette seats and a scarred wooden table.

"Why did you yank at me for?" he said. "She was into me."

"What's the plan?" I said.

"Loosen up, bo. Really, now. A place like this, you got to groove to the island rhythms. Undo your tie, unbutton your collar, lay back, blow a little weed, relax."

"I don't want to groove, and I don't blow weed. All I want is to find some answers."

"Okay, cool. I admire a man knows what he wants. The guy I need to talk to is at the bar. You see him? Dude in the overalls with the black porkpie and tats up and down his arms?"

"Dark glasses?"

"That's the one."

"Big, isn't he?"

"He's got guns, I'll say that for him. And his arms aren't tiny neither. His name's Antoine. He's sort of a free agent, flits from group to group, is allied with no one so is accepted by everyone. Takes odd jobs even as he works for his own agenda."

"What agenda is that?"

"Hard to say. He's like a community rabble-rouser."

"I bet."

"Let me go on up, fetch us some beers, maybe invite him to join us for a drink. He'll know who's selling the stuff. But you can't rush these things, bo. You got to wait until the time is ripe. Until then there are a couple of sweet things at the bar that are waiting for a little Derek. You see the one with the hair, giving me the eye?"

"Is that what she's doing?"

"Want me to bring one back for you?"

"Just a beer and your friend, please."

"While we're here, Victor, we might as well enjoy ourselves."

I didn't think that was going to happen.

Derek stood, bobbed his body to the music. "Be back in a flash."

I sat in the booth, eyed the whole of the shack as Derek made his way to the bar, felt my paranoia grow. This was not my usual crowd. I didn't really have a usual crowd, more loner than joiner am I, but whatever that crowd might be, the denizens of an outlaw reggae shack in the wilds of North Philly certainly didn't qualify. I sat with my hands clasped on the tabletop, my knuckles whitening, and waited for Derek. Despite his promise, he didn't seem on the verge of returning. He stood at the bar, hitting on a pair of tightly packed women, leaving me in limbo.

I saw more and more faces turn in my direction. Wondering what the hell I was doing here, no doubt. I was wondering the same thing. A small group seemed to be staring my way. I glanced away and then glanced back. They started moving toward me. I looked for Derek, he was focused on a very stretched tank top. The group got closer. Things were starting to get tense.

Then I saw an apparition move across the dance floor, broad-shouldered, thick-necked, with a countenance of angry irritation. He had grizzled gray hair, and wore a white smock smeared with blood, and as he walked slowly toward me, the group that had been heading in my direction halted their progress and stepped aside as if the old man were death itself.

Or maybe I was projecting.

He came right up to my table, placed his fists, knuckles down, on the wooden surface, leaned forward, stared at me with pitiless eyes.

"Who the devil are you?"

"Victor?" I said, my voice a questioning squeak.

"Where you hear about this place?"

"From Derek. He's Barnabas's cousin."

"I don't have no cousin Derek. What the blazes you want here, man?"

"Goat?"

He tilted his head, narrowed his eyes, stared at me for a long moment.

"Jerked or curried?" he said finally.

"Is the curry hot?"

"Hot enough for the likes of you."

"Done," I said. "And a Red Stripe, please."

He stared a moment more, pursing his lips, and then he turned around and made his slow way back toward the dance floor. When he reached the group that had been eyeing me, he stopped, stared at them for a moment without saying anything, shook his head, and moved on. The group took a hard look back before retreating to the bar.

A few minutes later, Derek slipped into the seat across from me and plopped three Red Stripes on the table. The guy with the massive arms and the porkpie hat sat down next to me and slid over until I was pressed against the wall. He turned and stared, his eyes hidden completely by his dark glasses.

"You see that girl at the bar with those thighs and the rack?" said Derek. "Man, she was all over my ass. Shaking her thing like I wasn't getting a good enough view as it was with the way her top was like three sizes too small. She might have been a size four in grade school, but that was before she started eating a whole haunch of cow for lunch. Oh, man, going to have to give her a free sample tonight, no doubt about it."

"Can we get to it?" I said.

"Sure, man. No problem. I'm just saying did you see that rack?"

"Derek."

"Calm yourself down. We're just having a friendly here. Bo, this is my pal Antoine. Antoine, this here is my lawyer, Victor Carl."

"Pleased to meet you," I said.

Antoine grunted.

"Antoine here is the one with all the answers," said Derek. "Funny thing, though, bo, he didn't like them questions you was asking. So he's got a question of his own."

Antoine turned his head and stared at me a bit more.

"Antoine wants to know," said Derek, "why you so interested in who's selling that Black Cat. And since, bo, you never done told me, I didn't have an answer for him."

I glanced at Antoine. He seemed like he would just as soon crush my skull with those arms of his than hear any of my legal tap dancing. In times like these, I've found, when your body, if not your soul, is in mortal danger and there seems to be no way out, sometimes all that is left is for you to tell a story. And it better be a good one. And if you to want to tell a good story, among a pack of males, there's one perfect opening line.

"There was this girl," I said.

There was this girl.

I first spied her when she brought me an espresso in a coffee bar in Old City. She had bronze skin, dark hair, a lovely, suggestive mouth. I was taken breathless at first sight. When you saw her, you envisioned a certain kind of life, a private life ennobled by a singular obsession with a singular woman. Secret passions, teeming emotions, long walks by the river, sex on the rooftop, foreign films, visits to Paris, bad poems, summers at the lake, shared memories, her head on your shoulder as the years twirled around the stillness of your love. You looked at her and you saw it all, uncoiling, and when she turned away to clear another table, it vanished, quick as that, and you felt strangely bereft.

That was Julia.

Of course I was smitten, from the very first. With her looks and her body, she was many steps out of my league, except there was something about her, some sweet passivity, maybe, that made anything seem possible. She had no humor of her own, but she laughed at my jokes. She didn't talk much about her life, but she seemed interested in mine. I didn't expect that she would go out with me, but I couldn't not ask. I figured there was no way she would sleep with me, but I couldn't not try. It was inconceivable that she would actually marry me, but I couldn't not propose. And at each step of the process, she acceded to my ever-more-desperate requests, as if she were being swept off on a voyage not of her choosing but one she couldn't bring herself to halt.

And so we were engaged.

"You a dog," said Derek.

"Yeah," I said, nodding.

"And the sex?"

"What about it?"

"Was it rocking?"

"Derek, don't be a jerk."

"But he's smiling, isn't he? Look at that boy smile, Antoine. Bo, you a down-and-dirty dog."

"Maybe. But this is what I discovered: In love, as in boxing, it is always dangerous to move up in class."

"So what happened?"

"What had to happen," I said. "She left me and broke my heart. Up and married a urologist instead."

Antoine laughed.

"A urologist," said Derek. "That is cold."

"Tell me about it."

"Still hurts?"

"Like someone ripped out my spleen."

Just then the old guy with the bloody smock, Barnabas, showed up at our table with a tray. He slammed down a bottle of Red Stripe in front of me, spun a bowl with a light brown stew over rice onto the table, dropped a napkin and fork beside it.

"Goat," said the old man.

"Freshly killed?" said Derek.

"Listen close, you can still hear the bleat," said the old man.

"What are those?" I said, pointing my fork at some white chunks. "Potato?"

"Cho-cho," said the old man, staring at me, waiting for me to taste the concoction. "And them yellow things is Scotch bonnets. That's the heat."

I speared a small piece of meat with my fork, stuck it in my mouth, gave it a careful taste.

"My gosh, that's good," I said. "That's just terrific."

Barnabas beamed.

" 'My gosh, that's good,' " said Derek in a radio announcer's voice. "Could you be more white?"

"But it is," I said, and I wasn't just blowing smoke, though the curry was hot enough. The stew was surprisingly delicious, the meat tender and tasty, the cho-cho and onions sweet. I pushed the yellow Scotch bonnets to the side, but my tongue still burned. I grabbed the Red Stripe, took a deep pull. The beer tasted like it was made purely to wash down curried goat.

Derek leaned toward the stew. "It does smell good. Get me some of that, old man."

"Anything for my cousin," said Barnabas.

Derek winced. "Sorry about that. Hey, Antoine, you want some goat?"

"Nah, mon," said Antoine, in a thick Jamaican accent. "Just another bokkle Red Stripe, maybe."

"Goat, the other red meat," I said. "Who would have figured?"

"Another curry, then, and some more beers when you got the chance," said Derek. "All this listening about old love, it builds up a thirst."

"Old love?" said Barnabas.

"Victor here was telling us about the girl that broke his heart," said Derek. "You still pine for her, bo?"

"Every day," I said.

The old man looked at me for a moment and then eased himself into the seat beside Derek.

"There is always one," said Barnabas.

"Don't we know it," said Derek with a sad shake of his head.

"I been married, it's been now more than thirty-five years," said Barnabas. "My wife, she's a saint. We got children together, grandchildren, a great-grandson just got born. Named after me. My years with my wife have been the happiest of my life. But there is this one girl."

"You tell it, Pops," said Derek.

"Melinda. It's been thirty-seven years since I seen her. Have no idea what the years they done to her. But if Melinda shows up tomorrow and says 'Let's go,' well, you'd need send out the dogs to find me, brother, because I'll be gone."

"I believe it," said Derek.

"Gone."

"Your wife know?" I said.

"She's got her own," he said, "but he's fat and lazy and can't get out the house no more. He not coming north, that's for sure. But Melinda, one never knows."

He pushed himself out of the seat, sighed an old-man sigh, full of bone weariness and long-accepted regret.

"I can still smell her skin," said Barnabas. "Smooth and sweet-scented, like polished rosewood."

"So who is yours, Derek?" I said after the old man had ambled off. "Who is the old love that still haunts?"

"Who, me?" said Derek. "Nah, not me. I'm cool."

"You lie," said Antoine.

"Don't do me like that, Antoine."

"Derek still in love," said Antoine. "For always and ever."

"Shut up, man. All right. No biggie. There was one. Tamiqua."

"What happened?" I said.

"We were together. From grade school, even. And then I started playing, and she acted like it was some crime, and that was it. She upped with some other slob and moved to New York."

"Still hurt?"

"I'm over it."

Antoine laughed. "Hell he is. Tamiqua, she only wanted for Derek a make something better for himself. All Derek wants a do is hang. So now he hangs alone."

"Not alone."

"Not with Tamiqua."

"What about you, big guy?"

Antoine pointed those dark glasses at Derek. "Sam," he said.

"Samantha," said Derek, nodding his head.

Antoine tilted his head and stared until Derek involuntarily pulled back.

"Whoa," said Derek.

There was a moment of awkward quiet.

"What does all this duppy love have a do with Black Cat?" said Antoine.

"It's my Julia," I said. "The guy she left me for was murdered on Sunday night, and she's the main suspect. I'm looking into it and I discovered this." I pushed away my now-empty plate, took out my wallet, let a few empty plasticine squares float to the table. "She had these on her the night her husband was shot. They were full, along with the whole needle-in-the-arm kit. I just want to know when she got them and why."

"The why's pretty obvious, isn't it?" said Derek. "She's a hop-head, your old love."

"Maybe, but she doesn't seem like it. And that night I didn't see any marks on her skin."

"Got a good look, did you? All the hidden places?"

"Good enough."

"You are a dog," said Derek. "The night she kills her husband you're hooking up with her. Bo, I got to say, I'm almost impressed."

"The murder happened at a pretty specific time. She told me she was out of the house at the time, wandering around. But maybe she was wandering over to buy herself a couple of fixes when her husband was being shot in the head. I thought it was worth a try. Her life may be on the line."

"She broke your heart, she smacking up, she maybe killed that man," said Antoine. "Why you still a care?"

"Old love," I said.

Antoine stared at me for a moment with his dark glasses and then said, "When was this killing?"

"Sunday. About eight o'clock at night."

"You got picture?"

I took a photograph out of my jacket pocket. Antoine and Derek leaned over to get a look.

"Bo," said Derek, nodding his head.

"Pretty like money," said Antoine. "And if I get what you need, what promises you make me?"

"Promises about what?"

"About them police, about them lawyers, about keeping Johnny Crow off our backs."

"The people who get hold of this will only be concerned about the guilt or innocence of the woman. Whatever else is involved, any trouble, I'll handle it myself."

Antoine turned to Derek. "You trust him?"

"He's my lawyer. He got me out of a scrape with a certifiably slick move. Whatever comes up, he can handle it."

Antoine thought about it for a moment before stuffing the photograph into the center pocket of his overalls. "You don't want a be disappointing me, Victor Carl," he said. "Wait here. I be back."

As soon as Antoine left the booth, Derek leaned forward. "Can you believe that? Big old Antoine going all Brokeback on us. Damn, you never can tell where that shit will start breaking out."

"Shut up, Derek."

"Hey, I'm cool with the down low. I'm man enough it don't

threaten me. But Antoine? Damn. I'll have to watch my step around that big boy, turn off the charm."

It wasn't long before Antoine was back at the table. He stood before us, his massive hand on the neck of a young, smooth-faced kid with nervous eyes.

"This likkle bwoy be Jamison," said Antoine, tightening his grip on the kid's neck. "And Jamison, he has something he need a tell you."

It was after midnight, and a better man might have been able to stay the hell away, but I am not a better man.

After hearing what Jamison had to say in the Jamaican juke joint, I was shaking. I know what it feels like to have your worst fears confirmed, but to have them discounted utterly was a whole new sensation. Was my luck changing after decades of relentless calamity? It seemed so very much as if it was. And it was that lethal sense of euphoric possibility that sent me scurrying right over to that mansion of death in Chestnut Hill.

I parked in the circular drive, bounded out of the car, dropped the knocker again and again onto the green door. I paced around in a circle as I waited, jammed my hands in my pockets, pulled them out again, knocked once more.

It was Gwen who answered. Her feet in slippers, her robe clutched with a strong hand about her waist.

"You know what time it is?" she said.

"I know, I know. But I need to see Julia. Can you wake her?"

Gwen glanced behind her, into the house, then peered for a moment over my shoulder before yanking me inside.

"She's been awake," she said. "She hasn't slept yet, just sitting in that room, drinking and staring at nothing."

"What room?"

"That room. The one. The same one the police went through again this morning before the missus came home."

"They were here this morning?"

"Oh, we had a busy day. First the police, then Mr. Swift and the missus, then an old friend of the doctor's, that Mr. Trocek. He just stayed a bit. A few others paid respects. It was only you who didn't come."

"Things were hectic, I couldn't get away," I lied, "but I'm here now, and I need to see her."

"Come on," she said. "I'll take you."

Gwen led me through the foyer, to the entranceway that led to Wren Denniston's trophy room. The double doors were closed, but the yellow police tape was lying flaccid on the floor.

"You find anything yet?" said Gwen.

"Maybe," I said.

"About Mr. Cave?"

"No."

"You need to find that Miles Cave. You'll tell me when you do?"

"Sure I will. But what I found is even better."

"Is it going to help her?"

"I hope."

"She's in there," said Gwen. "When the last guest left, she took a bath and then came right down to that room and sat."

"Okay," I said.

"I tried to make her go back upstairs. To get some sleep at least. It's not healthy sitting there all night. In that room. With the blood still on the carpet. I'm cleaning it tomorrow, I am, Mr. Carl. I don't care what they say."

"You do that."

"Go on in, then, if that's what you're going to do," she said.

I thought Gwen would announce my presence, but she just stepped back to clear my path. I gave her a final glance and then put my hand on the doorknob. It felt strangely hot, but that must have been my own excitement, because I was excited, so excited I ignored the warning expressed on Gwen's features as I turned the knob, pushed open the door, and stepped inside.

"Julia," I said. "Julia."

The room was dense with shadow, only a few shafts of light stabbing through the gloom. The outline of the body of the dead doctor was a mere suggestion on the carpet. Dull gleams bounced off the welter of wrestling trophies. I smelled the smoke before I spotted her, sitting deep in the corner, on a leather easy chair, the tip of a cigarette glowing. As best as I could tell, she was wearing a man's shirt, unbuttoned, and nothing else. One bare leg was tucked beneath her, her arms were crossed. A slash of light fell across her eye and cheek.

I had wanted to rush in and sweep her up in a great hug, but a woman sitting like that, in the dark, as defensive as that, even nearly naked, is impossible to sweep anywhere. I stopped suddenly when I saw her, but it wasn't only her posture that halted my charge. The sight of her, thin and nearly naked, in the darkness, sad and threatened, bare legs, bare throat, an air of hostility floating about her as thick as the cigarette smoke, all of it filled me with a desire that was paralyzing. It was as if the whole of my bizarre phobias and fixations were assembled into a perfect instrument for my enthrallment. The very air crackled with my wanting. If she had blown on me, right then, the mere touch of her breath would have toppled me backward onto the floor.

The glow of her cigarette rose to her face and brightened before she slowly pulled it out of her mouth and let loose a long exhale. I staggered back.

"I've been waiting for you," she said finally.

"I . . . I . . ." Gather yourself, boy. "I had been told to stay away."

"By whom?"

"The cops. Because I'm a material witness. And also by your lawyer."

"Clarence told you to stay away? Now I understand. He can be very intimidating. Did he brandish his bow tie at you?"

"I didn't want to cause you any more trouble. But now I need to see you. I have great news." I looked around. "What are you doing in this room?"

"Savoring the memories."

"Is that his shirt?"

"It's cozy."

"Julia."

"And it still smells like him. The cigars I hated and the cologne that made me want to vomit."

"You shouldn't be in here. Wearing that. There's still blood on the carpet. And what are you doing smoking? You don't smoke."

"I picked it up in prison."

"You were there two nights."

"Two nights more than you," she said.

She put the cigarette to her lips and inhaled again before tapping her ashes into an empty crystal liquor glass on the table beside her. Beside the empty liquor glass was an empty bottle.

"You didn't kill your husband, Julia."

"No?"

"I know it for sure now."

"You didn't before?"

"How could I?"

"Because I told you I didn't."

"You told me you'd marry me, too."

She took a moment to fiddle with the cigarette, take another inhale. "So that's where we are, Victor, in an endless loop."

"No," I said. "Not anymore. That's over, all of it is over. I'm going to help you now."

"I don't need your help. I have Clarence."

"Clarence is out of his league. Clarence is going to help you into a jail term if you let him. But I'm not just talking about the murder investigation, Julia. I found the purse you left in my desk, I followed the clues within it. I know what you were doing at the time of your husband's murder. You were buying drugs from a dealer named Jamison. And I can prove it."

"Don't."

"I can get you cleared."

"Keep your nose out of my business."

"I won't. You're an addict. You're buying heroin regularly from a street dealer in North Philadelphia. You have a problem, and you need help."

"I do have a problem, Victor, but it's not what you think."

"Clarence said you had a cold in jail. I bet it's gone. I bet as soon as you got out of jail and had a moment alone, you had your little fix and cured it right up."

"If you're so clever, sweetheart, then why are you always wrong?"

I went to her, knelt in front of her as if she were a child, placed my hand on her bare leg. Even as I knew her to be half drunk and loaded with hop, I couldn't stop thinking how beautiful she was. I could smell the soap on her, make out the swell of her breast beneath the shirt. The skin on her leg felt warm and smooth. I patted it gently, then let my hand fall so my palm was flat on her flesh. My head swam as if it were I who had emptied the bottle, not she.

"Julia," I said, trying to regain control of my senses.

I looked up at her. She stared down coolly.

"Now that I know you didn't kill your husband, we still might have a future together. If you get help, go into treatment, deal with the drug thing, we'll be free to start again and this time do it right. Without any encumbrances."

"That's all life is, encumbrances."

"We can be free of them."

"You never knew me, did you, Victor?"

"I loved you."

"It's not the same thing."

"But you have to admit the truth if we have any chance."

I grabbed her right arm, pushed up the sleeve, turned her wrist so the underside of her arm glowed dully from a dim shaft of light. She didn't do anything to stop me. The skin was flawless. I grabbed her left arm and tried to do the same but felt a sharp, jabbing pain on the back of my hand.

I snatched my hand away, and sparks flew from the cigarette she had jammed into my flesh.

I jerked myself to standing, backed off, lifted my burned skin to my lips. She sat there calmly, staring at me with dead eyes.

"What the hell was that?" I said.

"Clarence showed me your statement," she said. "It read like a Harlequin romance. 'I unbuttoned her shirt. I unhooked her bra.' If the law doesn't work out, you can write bodice rippers."

"I just told them the truth."

"That's funny. I thought we agreed not to tell them anything."

"With all the evidence they had, the only thing that could help you was the truth."

"It was never about the truth, Victor. It was about keeping what was ours to ourselves. About keeping what was growing again between us private, because that was the only way it had a chance to survive. And we agreed. And the first bit of pressure, you blurted out everything."

"I was just trying to help you."

"You were just trying to save yourself."

"Maybe I was. But now I'm going to save you."

"You have no idea what you are doing."

"Where are you shooting it?"

"I'm not."

"Are you smoking it, snorting it? How are you using it?"

"You're refusing to believe me again."

"But you had the kit in your purse. You were buying drugs

from Jamison. And you hid it in my desk to keep it from the police."

"Maybe all that wasn't for me, Victor."

I looked at her, stepped back, and thought about it for a moment. Then I turned my head until I was staring at the vaguely outlined body on the carpet.

"Your husband?" I said.

"I won't talk about it, Victor."

"You have to."

"No I don't. Leave it alone."

"I can't."

"Promise me you'll leave it alone," she said.

"Julia."

"Promise me," she said coolly as she tossed her cigarette into the empty glass, "or go away."

"Why?"

"Because I'm asking. Shouldn't that be enough?"

She unfurled the leg that was curled beneath her body and stood from the chair. Her shirt flared open, exposing the whole of her breasts, the hollow of her belly, the narrow black straps of a lacy lingerie bottom. She stepped toward me until we were an arm's length apart. Even though we weren't touching, I could feel her, like a heat all across the front of my body, a magnetic heat pulling me forward.

"You said you loved me," she said.

"Yes," I said, trying to catch my breath.

"If it was ever true, then that should be enough."

"Okay," I said.

"So no more questions about the drugs and who they were for. No more questions about where I was when my husband was killed."

"No more questions."

She stepped forward and put her hands on either side of my neck. "And we'll trust each other again."

"Yes."

"Good," she said, and then she pulled my head toward her and kissed me.

And this is what she tasted of. She tasted of alcohol, sweet and swollen. She tasted of tobacco, dark and loamy. She tasted of yearning and desperation and a fatal sadness. And oh, yes, she tasted of deceit.

"So what do we do now?" she said after she stopped kissing me, and grabbed my wrists and pulled my hands out from beneath her dead husband's shirt.

"Breathe?" I said.

"About the police."

"Oh," I said. "Them." I bit my lip to try to bring the feeling back. "We can do nothing and see what happens."

"Or," she said.

"Or we can find out who the hell really killed your husband."

"What if I don't care who it really was?"

"The police care."

"Do they? Or do they just want to find someone to pin it on?"

I thought of Sims and his political smile. "I don't know."

"Why don't we find out?" she said.

"You want us to find someone to blame."

"If you think it will help."

"An innocent dupe."

"Maybe not so innocent. But someone to draw attention away from us. At least for the time being."

"A fall guy."

"Yes."

"That's what I thought you were making of me."

"Oh, Victor," she said as she grabbed my tie. She pulled me close, kissed me quick, then let me go and turned away. "Don't be silly."

"So who do you have in mind?"

"I don't know. I'm just thinking."

That's what I did for a bit. Remember I said her kiss tasted of deceit. That's what I was thinking of. She was keeping something from me, something crucial, I could tell. But just then I didn't want to dig for it. So I searched where the light was better.

"Tell me about Gregor Trocek," I said.

She spun around. "How do you know about Gregor?"

"I had an early dinner with him just tonight."

"With Gregor?"

"We shared tapas and beer. And he told me a peculiar story. That your husband tried to hire him to kill me."

"Gregor and his stories."

"But I believed him. And I'm afraid the cops will, too."

"What if it's true? Is that bad?"

"For both of us. The cops will know that your husband found out we were seeing each other again."

"But it was almost innocent."

"Almost," I said. "That's a hole big enough to drive a prison van through. It gives us both a motive."

"So what do we do?"

"Gregor said he's looking for Miles Cave. The police asked me about the very same name. Do you know this Cave person?"

"No," she said.

"Ever hear of him before?"

"An old friend who had something to do with Wren's business."

"What was he, a patient?"

"No, not a patient. Wren had retired from medicine."

"A little young for the old-age home, wasn't he?"

"The retirement was not wholly by choice. Wren was sued. By a bitter transsexual whose sex-change operation went bad."

"There was a lawsuit?"

"It didn't go well. After the loss, the hospital suspended his privileges. So Wren, who had been losing interest in penises anyway, found a new profession in money management."

"What did he know of money management?"

"Not enough, I suppose. The company, called Inner Circle

Investments, was having trouble. And one of the names I heard Wren mention in his business conversations was Miles Cave."

"Was he a partner?" I said.

"I don't know."

"An investor?"

"I never met him."

"And you told that to Gregor?"

"He was a bit skeptical, but he didn't know Miles Cave either."

"So," I said, rounding out the vowel as I thought it through, "no one knows who this Miles Cave is."

"I suppose."

"A mystery man who might be the key to everything."

Julia looked at me for a moment, her face a cipher as she worked it out, and then she smiled. "So he might be the one," she said.

"He might."

She stepped up to me and grabbed my belt. "How do we find out?"

"We do the most obvious thing."

She leaned forward, rose on tiptoe, kissed me again. I reached inside the shirt, grabbed her waist, pulled her close, kissed her back. Even as the figure sprawled on the floor stared gape-mouthed at us both, I kissed her back.

You want to know what deceit tastes like? It's sweet. Like honey. Charged with electricity. Laced with amnesia. It is why adultery will never go out of fashion, why sincerity fails, why sex with strangers is more fun than ever it ought to be. It is the very taste of old love reclaimed, which might be the sweetest deceit of all. The taste of her made me stupid, and the more I tasted it, the stupider I wanted to become.

She pulled away slightly, moved her chin to the side, her lips to my neck. "What do you mean, 'the most obvious thing'?"

"You want to find the dirt in this world, there's only one route to take."

"What's that?"

"Follow the money."

I bent her back like a bow and snapped at her ear.

"Maybe it's time," I said, "for the grieving widow to claim her marital assets."

WEDNESDAY

I had a moment of clarity the next morning, when I spied Julia Denniston walking up Locust Street to meet me in front of the offices of Inner Circle Investments.

She was well dressed, in widow black, of course, her figure thin, her legs long and well shaped. Her stride was her usual careless glide, but now with the edge of some intriguing sense of purpose. Her head, covered by a black, wide-brimmed straw hat, swiveled easily on her proud neck, her inky black hair was silky and well coiffed, the flow of her arms was loose. She was a lovely woman, absolutely, as lovely as hundreds who walk back and forth on Locust Street each day. But she wasn't as young as the woman who first caught my eye in that coffee bar, and there was now a brittle disappointment that showed in her tense eyes. Objectively, she was nothing to get all shivery about, nothing to get stupid over. You put her in a lineup and you'd pass her by and pick that one, the other one, with the green eyes and the breasts of a Big Ten cheerleader.

What the hell was I doing?

Then she spotted me and smiled, and I remembered. I remembered the fever I had felt the night before, the fusion of desire and remembrance. She wasn't just another appealing woman on the street, she was my heartbreak and my history and my hope.

She came up to me, put her hand on my forearm. "Hi," she said with a lover's intonation, which meant she had a long memory, because we still hadn't as of yet consummated our reunion. The night before, she had pushed me away even as her earlobe was pinched between my teeth. It was late. Gwen was still awake. It was too soon after her husband's death. It was like he was still in the room. "All the better," I had said, with the tact of a brontosaurus in heat, but still she had pushed me away and still I had let her.

"You ready?" I said now, as we stood outside the building.

"I suppose." She glanced up at my hair, squinted a bit, looked back into my eyes. "So you think this Miles Cave gambit will work?"

"We'll see."

"It would be good, Victor. For us, I mean."

"For us?"

"It would give us a chance."

"A chance to stay out of jail, maybe."

"More," she said. "If we can send the police off chasing after this Miles Cave, that might give us the time we need to undo all the regrets. He could be our last best chance."

"Just so long as he can take the fall."

"Yes," she said, her chin rising at the flat tone of my voice. "Just so long." She looked at me, reached a hand to my cheek, and then let her eyes drift up again. "What's wrong with your hair?"

"You don't like it?"

"It's like an oil well vomited on your head."

"I bought some gel. When we meet this Mr. Nettles in your husband's office, I want to look just right. Today, in order to find out what I can about our boy Miles Cave, I'm playing the part of your slick, amoral lawyer, out to grab for you everything he can, including the wallpaper and the desks."

"Don't you think you overdid it a bit?"

"Absolutely. A little gel looks like you're trying. A lot of gel looks like you're trying way too hard. And way too much gel makes you look like a demented grave robber, which, for today's purposes, I think, is perfect."

Inner Circle Investments was housed in an old brownstone with a series of metal plaques bolted into the stone by the door. There were lawyers' offices, there was a psychiatrist, and there was Inner Circle, taking up the whole of the third floor. An almost perfect combination, I figured. First you give your money to a broker, then you get your head examined, then you sue.

"Mrs. Denniston, hello," said Ernest T. Nettles as he bounded out in shirtsleeves and suspenders to greet us in the deserted outer office. "We are all so sorry for your loss. I've only recently come aboard and so didn't know your husband very well, but I've heard much about him."

"Thank you," said Julia softly, as if fighting back tears. Nice job on her part, I thought.

"Mr. Carl, it's a pleasure to meet you, too," said Nettles. "I'm sorry the secretary isn't here, she would have wanted to greet you both personally. She is at the courthouse, doing some filing or other. Come, come into my office, both of you. Let's talk."

We followed him through the doorway and into a desolate hall lined with empty offices, until we reached his, a nice corner job with dark wood furniture and oil paintings of sheep. Nettles was a cheerful man, short and stocky, with round glasses and shaggy gray hair. He gestured us to sit on a couch, he sat perched on an easy chair beside us.

"Do you know yet when the funeral will be, Mrs. Denniston?" said Nettles.

"As soon as the police release the body," said Julia.

"Please let us know. We've had many calls from those who wish to pay their respects."

"Thank you."

"Have you ever been up to the offices before, Mrs. Denniston?"

"No. Wren very much liked to keep his personal and business lives separate."

"A fine policy," said Nettles. "An excellent policy."

"In fact," she said, "he never mentioned you to me."

"As I said, I've only just come aboard. I've been hoping to have a chat with you in the last couple of days, but I've held back because of the tragic circumstances. But now here you are. And with your lawyer, no less." He clapped his hands together and rubbed, glanced at me, and then let his gaze wander up to my gelled hair. "So what can I do for you both?"

"As you are aware, Mr. Nettles," I said, "the death of Mrs. Denniston's husband has been a cruel shock. But that doesn't mean the necessities of life halt."

"Of course they don't," said Nettles.

"And as her attorney I've advised Mrs. Denniston that she has the responsibility to look after her late husband's assets."

"Of course she does."

"And that is why we are here, Mr. Nettles. We need an accounting of Dr. Denniston's financial stake in this company. And, if I may be blunt—"

"You may."

"A sense of how his widow might turn it into ready cash."

"Of course. That's what anyone would want."

"So when can we start?"

"Mrs. Denniston, Mr. Carl, please be aware that our records are completely open and you are more than welcome to send your accountants in to scour our books."

"Thank you," I said.

"As you can see, we have much more space than we need at present. We can set aside a few offices for your team to make itself at home while it examines every scrap of paper. With our files and databases, it shouldn't take more than a few weeks to get a solid grip on the exact details. But maybe I can save you the expense."

"That would be most kind," said Julia.

"If you want a ballpark figure of the exact value of your husband's share of Inner Circle, Mrs. Denniston, I could give that to you right now."

"Are we talking liquid assets?" I said.

"Yes, I suppose."

I leaned forward, smoothed the hair at my temple with the base of my palm, wiped my palm on the other palm and then back again, and then wiped both palms on my pant legs. Is it just me, or is the revelation of the exact numbers when dealing with great gouts of cash quite exhilarating? The number scrawled on a paper, the number given in a hushed tone, the first number in a lucrative negotiation.

"Go ahead, Mr. Nettles," I said. "Make our day."

"The value of Dr. Denniston's share of Inner Circle Investments is"—he cleared his throat—"I'm afraid, nothing."

My jaw dropped. I lifted a hand and pushed it back up. "Nothing?"

"Zilch. Zero. Nada. Actually, less than nada. Dada, you might say. I expect when the final numbers are run, and the lawsuits shake out, Dr. Denniston will owe Inner Circle quite a large amount."

"How much?" said Julia matter-of-factly.

"I don't want to give an exact figure now, but it is substantial,

Mrs. Denniston. A full accounting will be presented to you shortly. I'm sorry to say that there will probably be litigation."

"I don't understand," I said. "How could that be?"

"Well, you see," said Nettles, "from what I understand, there was an embezzlement by a minor clerk at a small bank in Taipei."

"Excuse me," I said. "Mrs. Denniston is broke because of some corrupt clerk in Taiwan?"

"Yes, actually. When the theft was discovered, the bank collapsed. Which bankrupted a medium-size manufacturer in Jakarta. Which cut the supply line to a large manufacturer in Shanghai. Who failed then to satisfy its order to Wal-Mart. Which subsequently canceled its contract with the Shanghai manufacturer. When the news got out, the stock of the Shanghai manufacturer fell precipitously on the Hong Kong exchange. All of which provided barely a ripple in U.S. markets. Except for one hedge fund, which, while searching for undervalued foreign companies, had been quite long on the Shanghai manufacturer's shares. A little too long, perhaps."

"I'm not sure I'm getting the connection."

"Are you aware of what Inner Circle Investments was, Mrs. Denniston?"

"No, not really. Wren didn't talk about business with me at all."

"Inner Circle was an investment vehicle in which funds were invested in a single entity, a specific hedge fund run out of Connecticut. One of the principals of the fund was Joseph Borden."

"Wren's oldest friend."

"Exactly. The fund was primarily financed by institutional investors, but Mr. Borden granted Dr. Denniston the sole license to bring individual investors into the fund. Dr. Denniston invested pretty much all his own money and solicited funds from most of his friends and associates and their friends and associates. It was a cozy arrangement, actually. For the hedge fund, it meant a steady stream of cash; for Wren and his investors, the returns were outstanding. Everyone was happy until—"

"An embezzlement in Taipei," I said.

"Yes, exactly. It's funny how these things work, like the fluttering wings of a butterfly causing a tornado half a world away. The hedge fund didn't survive the fall."

"I bet the investors in Inner Circle were not very happy," I said.

"The letters we have on file are heartbreaking."

"You mind if I get a look?"

"No, of course not. If you have the time, Mr. Carl, I'll make them available to you right after our meeting. And you should know, Mrs. Denniston, your husband fought valiantly to keep Inner Circle alive, paying out investors as best he could."

"How could he pay them?" I asked.

"As I understand it, he mortgaged everything he had to keep Inner Circle going. And then, of course, people were still lining up to invest. The past performance of Inner Circle was excellent, and the demand remained high."

"Didn't they know the hedge fund had collapsed?"

"It appears, and this is being looked at now by the authorities"—Nettles leaned forward, lowered his voice—"the prospectus wasn't updated."

"But wouldn't that be illegal?" said Julia.

"I'm afraid, yes," said Nettles, with a touch too much glee. "Can you spell Ponzi?"

I tried to take all this in as Nettles smiled calmly at us and I felt the gel melt on my head and drip down in thick, oily rivulets. I didn't mind that Wren Denniston, the man who stole my fiancée so many years ago, was a crook. I rather liked that. No, what was flooring me was the "nothing" word.

Nothing. Zero. Zilch. Nada. Dada. Mama. Crap.

I had thought that Julia would be loaded with her husband's cash—it was an assumption underlying everything that had kept me up at night—but now that was disclosed to be another of my false dreams. Everything was mortgaged, everything was lost. Step back and be on your way, no money here. I looked at Julia, and she seemed to transmogrify right before my eyes into someone else, someone older and dowdier.

Sometimes I disgust even myself.

But I wasn't the only one thrown for a loop here. Julia's face was strangely serene, yet when I looked into her eyes I could tell that something was throwing her, badly. How could I be surprised at that? An empty bank account is enough to throw a horse. She was distressed, and I was distressed, and I bet all the Inner Circle investors were distressed, too. But our friend Ernest T. Nettles, he wasn't showing a bit of anguish himself.

"What is your role in the company, exactly?" I said to Nettles. "Are you a partner? An accountant? What?"

"Oh, yes, I'm sorry," said Nettles. "I thought you knew. I've just recently been brought on by the U.S. Trustee, who has been empowered by the bankruptcy judge to run what's left of the company. I thought you knew that Inner Circle was in bankruptcy."

"No," said Julia.

"Your husband didn't tell you?"

"No," said Julia.

"He was tight-lipped, wasn't he? Chapter Seven."

"What's that?" said Julia.

"Liquidation," said Nettles. "My job is to collect what we can and then liquidate all the holdings for the benefit of the creditors, who, unfortunately, are many. I don't think anyone is going to get anything out of this. But there is something."

"Something?" I said.

"One chance to give a little back to all those who lost so much. Do you know what a preference is in bankruptcy law, Mr. Carl?"

"I've never done much bankruptcy."

"A preference is a payment made on the eve of bankruptcy to a specific creditor. It's not fair for the officers of the failing company to favor one creditor over the others, and so the Bankruptcy Code provides that the trustee can get that money back to be distributed fairly to all. Which is precisely why I was so gratified to hear that you were coming this morning, Mrs. Denniston."

"Why is that?" she said.

"While it is not totally clear—there is a discrepancy between the company's books and the bank records—there does appear to have been one significant preference payment made which we are trying to get a handle on."

"How significant?" I said.

"One point seven million dollars," said Nettles. "The full amount invested by one of the investors."

"Yowza," I said.

"And we want to get it back," said Nettles.

"I bet you do."

"But there is one slight problem," said Nettles. "We can't seem to find this investor. The U.S. Trustee has asked the FBI for its assistance, and yet we still have not had any success. Now, since most of the investors were friends or associates of your late husband, I was hoping you could help us get in touch with him."

"Who is it?" said Julia. "What is his name?"

He didn't really have to answer, did he?

I was alone in one of the empty offices at Inner Circle Investments, sitting at an empty desk, surrounded by empty walls,
with a single thick file in front of me. The phone was discon-
nected, the hallways were deserted, the hush of failure settled
over everything like a dank, foul blanket. There is nothing sad-
der than a business in its death throes, except maybe a business
that is already dead. And have no doubt, Inner Circle Investments was dead.

Julia had left to absorb the fact that she was penniless, and
Ernest T. Nettles, after escorting me here and giving me the file,
had returned to his own office to continue his liquidation of the
company and the search for the missing preference payment. He
was a jaunty fellow, Ernest Nettles, yet I wouldn't want to be on
his wrong side. I could just imagine him in a skiff, with an eye
patch and a wooden leg, scanning the horizon for his prey.

"Thar Cave blows."

Yes, of course, the one point seven mil had been paid to the mysterious Miles Cave. Who else was so much in demand? I wondered who would find Miles Cave first, Ernest Nettles or Gregor Trocek. I'd have bet on Nettles, and for Miles's sake I hoped I was right, because Gregor wouldn't follow the niceties required by the Constitution. *When Sandro sticks hot poker in your eye,* Gregor would say in his harsh Eastern European accent, *you have right to scream and scream and scream.*

It wasn't so hard to figure out what had happened. Gregor was probably chin-deep in some nefarious enterprise, maybe involving those young Portuguese girls he went on about so rhapsodically. The problem with nefarious enterprises is that the cash they generate is dirty. So how, then, to keep your assets growing? Find an old friend in the investment business, have him bring in another old friend as a straw man, invest the money in the straw man's name as a way to launder the cash. All quite simple, until the straw man withdraws the investment and then withdraws from the face of the earth.

But it wouldn't be only Ernest Nettles and Gregor Trocek on Miles's tail, if I had anything to do with it. Soon I would have to find a way to put Sims and Hanratty on the Miles chase, too, because who was a better suspect for Wren Denniston's murder? If Wren were still alive, he could have pointed the authorities in the right direction, and, once caught, Miles would have had no choice but to give the money back, either to Nettles at the point of a lawsuit or to Trocek at the point of a gun. One point seven mil was a healthy motive for murder.

But there were other suspects now, too, weren't there? A whole mess of impoverished investors, looking for a pound of flesh in exchange for their now-worthless investments. Which was why I opened the file Nettles had given me and delved into the sad trail of destruction that seemed to follow inevitably in Wren Denniston's wake.

The letters in the file were originals, typed on bond or hand-scrawled, and heartbreaking all. They were shouts of pain from the friends Wren had induced to invest in his firm, the letters requesting, demanding, begging. *Where is my money? Give me back my money. My daughter is sick. My wife is dying. I have children to put through college. You're an old friend. My oldest friend. Don't do this to me. I'm going to a lawyer. I'm going to the police. Please, Wren, I'm pleading with you, get me back my money.* The emotions were still so wet and raw it was as if moist, red blood were staining each page.

They were all fools, as far as I was concerned, so rich they couldn't find anything better to do with their money than give it away to a pug like Wren Denniston for him to lose. Yet I couldn't help but feel sorry for them all the same. Who better than I knew the bitter taste of spectacular failure? But I wasn't in that office to exercise my empathy. One by one I read the letters, one by one I wrote down the names and addresses, one by one I created for myself a batch of suspects that would make any cop think twice before dumping a collar on a clever lawyer or give any jury pause before the altar of reasonable doubt.

But wait, what was this? Another letter, stuck in the middle of the pack.

Dr. Wren Denniston
Principal Partner
Inner Circle Investments
Philadelphia, PA 19103
Re: Account #67855

Dear Wren,

As our recent conversations have not gone well, and you have lately been refusing to take my calls, I am having this letter hand-delivered in hopes that I can avoid taking action that you would find distasteful.

We want our money, all of it, and we want it now. We

don't want to hear about shortages or preferences or problems with some stinking bank in Taipei. And don't talk to me about lawyers. We don't want to hear about lawyers. We want our money, all of it, and we want it now.

This is not simply business. You owed me, and I trusted that you would live up to your obligation, and now I feel betrayed. You have screwed me again, and this time I will not sit back and allow you to keep what is mine. Return the money, all of it, or there will be no recourse other than violence.

You will receive no more calls, no more letters, there will be no more attempts at polite conversation. Have the funds wired to my account immediately, or I promise, you will pay the price.

Sincerely,

Miles Cave

There he was, in the flesh, the mysterious Miles Cave. I almost yelped when I saw the letter, it was like discovering evidence of a long-lost brother. So Miles had made his threat and gotten the one point seven mil out while the company teetered on the brink of bankruptcy and the other investors went hungry. It looked like he was demanding it for himself and for Gregor, but once it was wired, he decided to keep it all. Why the hell not? I'd probably do the same. And by now, with money in hand, he was no doubt long gone. He had his own lawyers, he was surely advised about what a preference was, he knew that if he was ever found, by the government or by Trocek, the money would have to be returned, so he found another way. Grab the money, kill Wren Denniston, spend the rest of his life on some beach in Brazil, doing the samba with tawny girls in blue bikinis.

Son of a bitch, I had to admire the guy.

And here, now, in my hand was just the tool I needed to send

Sims and Hanratty to join the chase for Miles Cave. Let them all rush off in search of the great white whale, while Julia and I floated into the sunset on our boat, a smaller, tawdrier boat than I had hoped, absolutely, but a boat nonetheless. I was imagining the scene, the ocean breezes, the gentle waves, Julia's lips pressed upon my neck, when something stopped me.

There was an address at the bottom of the letter. It was a bit smudged, which was why I hadn't noticed right off, but there it was. And from what I could tell, it was a familiar address.

It was my address.

The son of a bitch had been living in my building.

Wait a second. There was something about the signature. The small *i* in Miles. The first two letters in Cave. What the hell?

I took a piece of paper and signed my name and compared the two. Close enough to get my nerves a-snapping. It didn't make any sense, unless . . .

At that very moment, I sensed someone close. Instinctively I dropped the letter to my lap at the same time I looked up. There was a woman in the doorway. She wore a print dress that looked like wallpaper on her sturdy body. She seemed somehow familiar, though I couldn't quite place her.

"Mr. Carl," she said, her voice both high and dismissive. "My name's Margaret. I'm the secretary here. Mr. Nettles asked me to see if you needed any assistance."

"I'm fine, thank you," I said.

"Do you need something to drink?"

"No, really, I'm fine," I said. I looked at her for a moment. Short hair, thick nose, the jaw of a wrestler, knuckles. "Do I know you?"

"Do you dance? Ballroom dancing, I mean. There are monthly events that our club sponsors. You might have seen me competing."

"No, definitely not. I have the grace of an aardvark—after it's been hit by a car. The only thing worse than my dancing is my singing."

"Then I won't bring out the guitar." She looked down at the file open on my desk. "Do you need any copies?"

"Yes, actually." I closed the file and pushed it forward. "The whole file, please. One copy of each letter would be perfect," I said.

"Of course, Mr. Carl." She stepped forward, took the file off my desk, clutched it to her chest.

"Margaret," I said, "has anyone else looked at this file in the past few days?"

"Not that I know of."

"Were the police here?"

"Two detectives, one big and one not so big. They came to talk to Mr. Nettles, and they examined the financial records. The big one left pretty quickly, but the little one stayed quite a while and made plenty of copies."

"But he didn't see this file?"

"No."

"Okay, thank you."

"I'll be right back, and I'll put the copies in a folder for you."

When she left, I lifted the paper that was still on my lap. My address. A signature that had much in common with mine. I read it again and picked out what I hadn't noticed before. *You have screwed me again, and this time I will not sit back and allow you to keep what is mine. Return the money, all of it, or there will be no recourse other than violence.* The letter was a neon arrow pointing right at my heart.

I took a quick glance at the empty doorway and then folded the letter in half, in quarters, in eighths, and stuck it in my pocket. Destruction of evidence, sure. Obstruction of justice, absolutely. But I was in trouble. Some son of a bitch was setting me up.

And by the date of the letter, that son of a bitch had been setting me up from when Wren Denniston was still very much alive.

I went straight back to my apartment after leaving the Inner Circle offices, with a file of desperate letters, all copies, in my briefcase and a single original folded up in my jacket pocket. I wanted to wash the gel out of my hair, sure, but what I really wanted was to figure out what to do with that one original I had swiped. Examine it, hide it, immolate it, I wasn't quite sure, but I was quite sure I wanted to figure it out on my own, without anyone looking over my shoulder.

Which was why the sight of Detective McDeiss leaning against the side of a car parked right in front of my apartment building was so distressing. He was on his phone, staring at me as I approached.

"What's that on your head?" said McDeiss when he clicked his phone shut.

"Gel," I said.

He stared at my hair for a long moment.

"It's stylish," I said. "Quite hip."

"It's quite something. You look like a mortician I know named Prentice."

"Handsome guy?"

"Not really. You want to take a ride?"

"No."

"Excuse me. My sentence was phrased indelicately. It is a statement of fact and not a question. You want to take a ride."

"So that's it, huh? Where to?"

"The Roundhouse. Sims was waiting for you at your office. Hanratty was waiting for you at the Denniston place in Chestnut Hill, in case you happened to show up there again. I had nothing going on, so I volunteered to wait a bit at your home. I just got hold of them on the cell, so now they'll be waiting for you at headquarters."

"Why didn't they just call me?"

"They want to talk, and Sims had the sneaking suspicion that you wouldn't show up on your own. Let's go."

"Can I go upstairs first and wash this crap out of my hair?"

"No."

"It will only take a minute, but it's starting to feel a little—"

"Icky?"

"Exactly."

He pushed himself off the car, opened the rear door for me. "Get in."

"Unless you have a warrant, Detective, I'm going upstairs to wash my hair. The Constitution gives me a right to clean hair."

"You're already a gelhead, don't be a dickhead, too. Get in the damn car."

I got in the damn car. McDeiss was right, I was being a dickhead. I had my reasons to squawk, first to get that gel out of my hair and second to ditch the incriminating fake letter before I showed up at police headquarters, but to start asking about warrants and bitching about the Constitution with McDeiss was all wrong. He was a Philadelphia homicide detective, he had a caseload to choke a goat, when he said he had nothing going on, he was lying. He had volunteered to wait at my apartment on the odd chance that he could get to me before Sims did. He was trying to help, he had something to say, and I was being churlish by giving him lip before he said it.

"Do you have any idea what the hell you're doing, Carl?" he said as we drove toward the Roundhouse. He was in the driver's seat, I sat in the back. I felt weirdly like an old Southern Jewish lady.

"Not really," I said.

"It certainly shows," he said, glancing at me through the rearview mirror. "Because you are screwing yourself big-time. I thought I advised you to stay the hell out of this until Sims finally charged the wife."

"You did."

"So that's why you're rushing all around town with a blackjack in your pants and a bottle of gel on your head?"

"Er . . ."

"Just so you know, questions are being asked about you. And not just by Hanratty."

"I didn't do anything."

"Spare me the tears. It doesn't matter what you say or if I believe you or not. Right now what matters is what Sims believes, and what he can convince the D.A. of. You're making things too easy for him. And he's not pulling this crap out of thin air."

"What does he have?"

"That's not my place, Victor. It's his case, he discloses what he needs to disclose on his own time. But I'm telling you not to be a fool. The focus of the investigation is shifting. The wife's lawyer has been whispering in Sims's ear."

"Clarence Swift is an eel."

"Maybe, but that only means Sims has found a fellow member of the species. And he's been listening."

"He's right to be listening. She didn't do it."

"Now, see, there you go again. How do you know? How do you know anything, you fool? How do you know you're not being set up by a spider with dark hair and nice legs?"

"Because I found her alibi."

McDeiss shot me a look through the rearview mirror. "Is this an alibi she manufactured and pushed you to find?"

"No," I said. "I found it on my own, and she made me promise not to tell anyone."

"I don't understand."

"Neither do I. But it's tricky, because the main alibi witness himself was committing a crime at the time, and so he won't want to testify either."

"What the hell are you talking about?"

"Do me a favor and grab a look at the coroner's report on the dead man. I'm wondering specifically about the toxicology findings. And on the wife, too, if you can manage it."

McDeiss drove on in quiet for a moment. "Drugs?"

"Just take a look."

"You talk to this witness personally?"

"Yah, mon," I said, with an island lilt.

"Where? Jamaica?"

"Closest thing we got."

He glanced again at me through the mirror. "You understand, Victor, that if she has an alibi, that makes you the more attractive suspect."

"With this gel in my hair, I don't think so."

"You should have just walked away when I told you."

"It's not so easy."

"Why not?"

I didn't answer, because in truth I didn't have an answer.

"What is it, Victor?" said McDeiss. "You think you love her?"

"I don't know."

"Shouldn't that tell you enough right there, son?"

"Maybe we both changed. Maybe it will work out this time."

"And in your experience we all get better as we age?"

"No."

"But still you're willing to gamble your life because you think if only everything will go away—the dead husband, the cops, the suspicions, the fear—if everything can disappear, maybe that old love will blossom anew and save your stinking life, is that it?"

"Yeah. Why not?"

"Past performance."

"She's not a horse."

"You gave her your love, and she stepped on your face when she left to marry someone else. Then this someone else, he gave her his love and his name, and he ended up with a bullet in his head. There's something wrong with her. There's a hole in her heart. It's what ruined the thing you had in the past, and it's only gotten deeper. She's not going to save your life, she's going to tear it apart for good, if you let her."

"So what should I do?"

"Give Sims everything you have, give him the alibi if you insist on trying to save her life, and then stay the hell away from her."

"It won't be that easy."

"Why not, Victor?"

"Isn't love worth risking everything for?"

McDeiss was quiet for a long moment, and then said, "You're an ignorant son of bitch."

The same green room with the large mirror, the same smell of sweat and vinegar and dead mice, the same clot of suppurating fear at the base of my throat. So why did the room suddenly seem smaller than before?

"We just wanted to chat a bit, Victor," said Sims, sitting across from me at the table, his hands clasped before him as unthreatening as a preacher's. He wore a gray suit, a dark purple shirt, an unctuous smile. "I'm sure you don't mind."

"Don't be so sure," I said.

"Did you hear the hostility in his voice, Hanratty?"

"I heard," said Hanratty. His back was against the door, his jaw was pummeling a stick of gum.

"I thought we were friends," said Sims. "I thought we had an understanding."

"Is that why you sent McDeiss to my apartment to scoop me up like one of the usual suspects, because we had an understanding?"

"There are a few things we need to clear up," said Sims. "Nothing major, just timeline matters. The night of Mr. Denniston's murder, you were home."

"That's right."

"Doing what?"

"Nothing."

"Be more specific, please," said Sims. "Were you watching TV, ironing your shirts, jacking off to Internet porn, reading the Good Book, what, exactly?"

"Nothing."

"How many times did you go out after you got home from work?"

"I didn't."

"You sure? We received a report that you went out."

"What kind of report?"

"And after you came back," said Sims, "Mrs. Denniston called, isn't that right?"

"I never went out."

"Did she call you on your cell or your landline?"

"I don't remember, but I figure you have the records already, so you can tell me."

"Cell. And when you got the call on your cell phone, where were you?"

"Home."

"Doing what?"

"Nothing."

"Don't be cute."

"I'm not the one wearing the puce shirt."

"You don't like my shirt?"

"It's quite puce. And who the hell told you I went out that night anyway?"

"It came as an anonymous tip."

"And how does that work in court, exactly?"

"Not so well in court, but it's boffo before the grand jury.

Now, before that night, had she ever been up to your apartment?"

"No."

"Did the two of you have any furtive assignations at the Denniston mansion?"

"No."

"You sure?"

"I never saw the place."

"Did you hear that, Hanratty?"

"I heard," said Hanratty, still pounding like a heavyweight on the gum. The way he was staring at me, it was almost like he was staring through me. Involuntarily my hand reached up and touched the pocket where sat the letter that was meant to frame me but good.

"I think he's holding something back from us," said Sims.

"He's been holding back all along."

"But I don't think he means to. It's just that he's a lawyer, he can't help himself."

"Hey, guys," I said. "I'm here, remember?"

"We found your fingerprint in the Denniston mansion," said Sims, staring now right into my eyes. "On the panel leading to the safe where the gun was kept. The gun that was taken on the night of the murder. The gun that we suspect killed the doctor."

"Now, how did your fingerprint get there if you never saw the place?" said Hanratty.

"I never saw the place until Dr. Denniston was murdered," I said, as calmly as I could manage. "I assume you picked that up on your second go-round, the morning before you released Mrs. Denniston. The night after the killing, I visited the house and talked to Gwen. She took me into the room, showed me the safe. I must have touched the panel then. You can ask her, although I assume you already have. I assume it because if you hadn't, I would be under arrest. Am I under arrest?"

"He wants to know if he's under arrest," said Sims.

"Let me work on him a bit," said Hanratty. "I'll squeeze

something out of him. It might not be the truth, but it sure will be fun."

"Let's give him one more chance before we resort to fireworks," said Sims. "You know, Victor, we're only trying to help you here, but you're making it so difficult. We've got the fingerprint. We've got pictures of you and the dead man's wife together even while the husband was still lying cold in the morgue. And we know that the dead man knew about the two of you."

"How do you know that? Another anonymous source?"

"From the beginning I suspected the wife, and I still do. And what has convinced me even more than the evidence arrayed against her is her unwillingness to cooperate. Despite her lawyer's advice."

"Her lawyer is a fool."

"Yes, isn't it wonderful? But she's not taking his advice, she's not answering any of our questions. So maybe we were hoping that you could convince her to open her mouth. We have some very specific questions that need answers. Based on her current situation, the answers could only help her case. Without her cooperation I'm afraid that she is heading straight toward an indictment."

"But you're on the wrong trail," I said. "She wasn't at the house at the time of the killing."

"You're sure of it."

"Yes."

"He's sure of it, Hanratty."

Hanratty just stared and chewed.

"She has an alibi," I said. "And I found it."

"You found her alibi," said Sims with an unconcerned voice. "Really, now?" He looked up at Hanratty, raised an eyebrow. "Tell me all about it."

"A kid named Jamison," I said. "I found him at an unlicensed Jamaican juke joint last night. He was with her at the time of the murder."

"And what, may I ask, were the doctor's wife and this Jamison doing that night together?"

"You'll have to ask her."

"But she's not cooperating."

"Well, there you go. Maybe you'll find out at trial."

"He's a cutie-pie, isn't he?" said Hanratty.

"And where is this juke joint you mentioned?" said Sims.

"I can't tell you."

"Let me rearrange his face," said Hanratty.

"If you choose not to tell us the details," said Sims, "and she chooses not to cooperate, then maybe we'll choose not to believe you."

"Suit yourself, but you might want to turn your attention to other suspects, since there's a gaping hole in your case against Mrs. Denniston."

"It's not a hole. Even if the alibi pans out. You can still be guilty of murder if you don't pull the trigger. We'd just have to add conspiracy to the murder charge."

"And who would be the co-conspirator?"

"Tell him, Hanratty."

"You," said Hanratty.

"Surprise surprise," I said. "Hanratty thinks I'm guilty. The thing you're both missing is the why. Why would we want to kill her husband? I admit that she was an old girlfriend. I admit that we were trying to figure out if we wanted to try again. That might be a bit unseemly, but it's not a crime, at least not in this state. Divorce is legal, last time I checked. So there's no motive."

"What about the prenup?" said Hanratty.

I tilted my head, felt sweat pop up like popcorn on the back of my neck. "Prenup?"

"Don't even bother, Victor," said Sims. "A sharp guy like you, if there's a prenup, you know about it. The way it worked, if she left him, she got not a penny."

"But there was nothing to get. It turns out the doctor was broke. Nothing to him, and you know it, too."

"But maybe you didn't."

"If I was sharp enough to know about the prenup, I would have been sharp enough to get a grasp on the guy's net worth before shooting him in the head for his wife, don't you think?"

"Hanratty doesn't think you're that sharp. Hanratty wants to bust you right now."

"And Hanratty thinks his haircut is quite becoming. But you know better than to charge anyone until you check out the suspects with the best motive of all."

"Oh, yeah?" said Hanratty. "And who are they?"

I raised a finger like I was about to perform a trick. Julia and I had planned to set up Miles Cave as the prime suspect for the murder, but that was before I realized someone was setting me up to play the Cave part. The letter in my pocket would stay there until I got home, when I would destroy it, I decided. But even with Miles Cave out of the picture, when it came to those with motives against Wren Denniston, there was no shortage of options. I lifted my briefcase onto the table, opened it, pulled out a file with the words COMPLAINT LETTERS written in Margaret's script on the cover, spun it across the table toward Sims.

"These are the letters from the investors who lost money with Inner Circle Investments, irate investors who all seemed to blame Wren Denniston for the loss. Some of the letters are pretty strongly worded. One said, and I quote, 'You bastard, you deserve to die.' You might want to look at that one twice."

As Sims reached for the file, I pulled it back. "Mine."

"We'll make copies and then give them back," said Sims.

"Just be sure you do. I might need them if you fellows keep trying to lay a frame around me and Julia."

"You don't trust me, Victor, do you?" said Sims.

"Not an inch."

"But a centimeter maybe? At least that. Tell me you trust me a centimeter at least. Because, believe it or not, I want to help you. Listen to me, Victor. I admit I might be wrong about Mrs. Denniston. And I admit I might be wrong about you. As a matter of fact, there is nothing I want more than to prove it. Help me prove it."

"How?"

"Talk to Mrs. Denniston. Tell her to answer our questions. Tell her to cooperate for both your sakes."

"And if not?"

"What do you think, Hanratty? How would our boy Victor look in orange?"

"Peachy," said Hanratty.

When I got home from the Roundhouse, I set a little bonfire in the bathroom sink. Then I took a long shower to wash off the sweat from the interrogation and the gunk from my hair and the oily sheen left on my skin from proximity to Sims. Showered and shaved, powdered and puffed, I put a towel around my waist and called Julia.

"How are you?" I said.

"Bewildered."

"I understand. Today was a shock, I'm sure. Do you want me to come over?"

"No."

"But I need to see you. Right away."

"I don't think we should see each other," she said. "Not now and not for a while."

"Why not?" I tried to hide the whine in my voice but failed abysmally. I was showered and shaved, powdered and puffed, and ready for action. "There is something important I need to talk to you about."

"So talk."

"I don't want to do it on the phone."

"I'm surprised. It's easier taping a phone call than wearing a wire."

"Julia?"

There was a strange pause, and then she said, "Where were you this afternoon, after you left my husband's office? Why didn't you call me right away?"

"I was detained."

"Lawyers are always so busy."

"No, really detained. By the police. They picked me up at my apartment. They had questions."

"And you had answers, I'm sure."

"They didn't want my answers, they wanted your answers. What are they asking you? What are you refusing to give them?"

"They keep asking about Wren's business affairs. But I don't know anything about Wren's business affairs. I never cared enough to learn. I guess that makes one of us."

"Julia?"

"You should have seen your face, Victor, when that Nettles character told you my husband didn't have any money. It was like one of your pathetic little dreams was crawling underfoot and he had stepped on it and squashed it flat."

"I was simply surprised. Weren't you?"

"Not about that. I could tell that things had gone wrong with Wren's business. By the end his mood had turned so sour it could only have been caused by financial disaster. What surprised me was you. You were so shocked I almost felt sorry for you, even though it wasn't your money. And then I learned you were at the police, blabbing away, and I figured you found a way to deal with your disappointment."

"Who told you I was at the police?"

Another pause. "Did you do what you promised? Did you tell them about Miles Cave? Did you start them on the chase?"

"No," I said. "I couldn't. Something happened."

"Yes, something has happened. I hoped we could trust each other. From the start that's what I hoped. And you promised me that we could."

"We can, still."

"I don't think so. Not anymore."

"All I want to do is help you."

"No you don't, Victor. You can't forgive me, so you're going to pay me back."

"That's not true."

"Even if you don't recognize it yet, that's what you're doing."

"Julia, listen. Things are getting hairy."

"Shave."

"Someone's trying to set me up."

"I feel the same way."

"Why didn't you tell me about the prenup?"

"Would that have tempered your interest?"

"It would have been nice to know about a prenuptial agreement between my old fiancée and her murdered husband when I'm being questioned about the murder. Julia, we need to stick together if we're going to get through this. I know you didn't kill your husband, and you know I didn't kill your husband."

"Do I?"

"Stop it. Just stop it. This is going from bad to worse. Someone is playing us both, one against the other."

"Oh, Victor. All the scheming and plotting, the whispered warnings and secret messages."

"What whispered warnings?"

"When did love get so hard?"

"I had that very same thought."

"It's not supposed to be like this. Why can't it just work out and everyone be happy until they die?"

"It can. We still have a chance to make it work."

"No, I don't think so anymore. I thought we did, truly, but I can see now any chance we had was murdered along with Wren."

Another pause, and the soft whisperings of a voice not Julia's.

"Is somebody there?" I said.

"Take care of yourself, Victor."

"Who's there? Julia? I'm coming over."

"Don't. We need to stay apart. They're watching us both."

"Are you okay?"

"No, no I'm not, Victor."

"Let me come over."

"Gwen will take care of me, she always does."

"Is she there now, Julia? Is it Gwen who's with you?"

"I'm sorry, Victor. For everything I've done. And everything I'm going to do. I'm sorry."

"Julia?" I said. "Julia."

But I was talking to the ether, because she was gone, leaving me with the peculiar sensation that I had just been involved in a three-way skirmish between a horny toad, a chameleon, and a snake.

And the horny toad had lost.

THURSDAY

Something woke me up that very night. I couldn't tell if it was
a dream or a noise doing the waking, but I was already awake
when I heard the refrigerator door open. You know the sound, the
pull of the handle, the *thwump* of the door unsealing, the rattle of
bottles, as prosaic a domestic sound as exists in this world.

Except I live alone.

I rolled out of bed and landed on my feet as quietly as I could
manage. Light was slipping through the crack at the bottom of
the bedroom door. I looked around for something to grab. My
clock radio read 4:06 before I yanked the cord out of the wall
and raised overhead the heavy rectangle with its sharp edges.

The hiss of a beer bottle being opened. A swallow. Some sort
of soft conversation and then the television being turned on.
There were at least two of them, and they weren't trying not to
be heard, which was troubling. Did they even know I was here?

I crept to the bedroom door, slowly turned the knob, gently pushed the door ajar, silently peeked through the crack, the clock radio held high and ready.

I guess I wasn't as silent as I thought.

"Hey, bo," said Derek Moats, sitting in my easy chair, feet propped on the coffee table, remote in one hand, beer in the other. He stared right at me with a not-so-bright smile. "You want to join us?"

I pushed the door fully open, the clock radio still hoisted, and took a step forward.

"What the hell are—" was all I got out before I saw the other man, standing by my dining table, tall and broad, with tattoos and dark glasses and a porkpie hat. It was the big guy from the Jamaican juke joint. And he wasn't looking too pleased.

"You remember Antoine, hey, bo?" said Derek.

"Yes, of course." And strangely, even though they had broken into my apartment, as I stood before the two of them in my boxers and T-shirt, I suddenly felt humiliatingly underdressed. "What's going on?" I said, lowering the clock radio so it covered my crotch.

"Antoine just wanted to go for a ride," said Derek. "Catch you up to date on the news."

"News?"

"I guess you haven't heard."

"No," I said. "I haven't heard. But couldn't we discuss this at a reasonable hour, and maybe at my office?"

"Antoine thought you'd want to hear it right away and see it in person."

"That was kind of you, Antoine."

"And without no delay."

I looked at Derek, who was no longer smiling, and then at Antoine, who was just then scratching a thick bicep.

"You mind if I get something on?" I said.

"It'd do us all a favor if you did," said Derek. "But don't take too long, and don't make any calls, all right? Antoine is feeling a little antsy right about now. Ain't you, Antoine?"

Antoine didn't respond.

"I'll be back in a minute," I said. "Make yourself at home."

"We already done that," said Derek, raising the beer. "You got that HBO?"

"Sure," I said.

"Groovy. I think they got them strippers on this time of night."

Back in my bedroom, I put down the clock radio, slipped on a shirt, a pair of jeans, the heavy black shoes with the steel toes. This was getting to be an unpleasant habit. I glanced at the phone beside the bed and debated using it, but then who would I call? The police? And say what? That a client and his pal, who had helped me find an alibi for an accused murderer, had broken into my apartment and now I wanted them arrested? No, I wouldn't call. I'd play it cool. I could play it cool, sure. But first I had to check out the bathroom, because, frankly, having these two guys in my apartment in the middle of the night scared the piss out of me.

"All right, gentlemen," I said, with as much confidence as I could muster as I walked to the refrigerator. I opened the refrigerator door, leaned in, took out a beer of my own. "Let's hear it."

"Turn off the set, mon," said Antoine. "We going now."

"Ah, Antoine, dude, look at the size of her mammaries. You could feed small countries with them beauties."

"Turn it off," said Antoine. Derek did as he was told. "You made me promises," Antoine said to me.

"Did I?" I unscrewed the bottle top, took a swig, coughed embarrassingly when too much went down my throat. That's the way it is when you're racked with fear, even the most instinctive acts are no longer instinctual.

"You made promises."

"Okay, yes. I did."

"You said you keep them police out of it."

"I said I would do that if I could. And I only told the bare bones of what I learned."

"Old saying," said Antoine. "If fish nevva open him mouth, him wouldn't get ketch."

"What the hell does that mean? What happened?"

"Let's be going now, Derek," said Antoine.

"I'm not sure if I really want to go for a—"

"Why this bwoy keep jabbering?" said Antoine. "Derek, why this bwoy, he still jabbering?"

"I don't know, man. He's an idiot, I guess. You mind if I turn the telly back on, see if that girl with the rack is still dancing?"

"Let's be going," said Antoine.

"Damn shame to miss all of that," said Derek as he stood up from the chair and dropped the remote. "What about the beer? There's some left in the fridge. Shame to waste it on Victor, isn't it?"

"Take it," said Antoine.

"I had enough of this urban blight," said Derek, as he drove my car north, through the dark city streets. Antoine was sitting next to Derek in the front seat. I was alone with my anxiety in the back.

"I was thinking about moving out to the burbs," said Derek, in a monologue without end. "I could kick up my heels, watch the big screen. Or maybe find some desperate housewife desperate for a bone. That's what I hear about them burbs, full of women just looking for someone who knows how to treat them right while the husbands are toiling for the green."

"And you're just the one they're looking for," I said as I stared out the window, trying to figure where we were headed.

"Why not? Maybe a place in Jersey. That would cinch it, don't you think? Jersey housewives, as ripe as them Jersey tomatoes. Just not as red. And without the stems."

"Where are we going?"

"You be seeing soon enough," said Antoine.

Derek turned left and then right again, past dark streets with collapsing houses and junked-up yards. And then we hit the railroad tracks, and I felt a sense of dread, which deepened when I smelled the smoke.

"One of them big houses," said Derek. "You know them things they building on every last open lot, all turrets and windows and the fancy driveways. Like what T.O. was doing them sit-ups in front of. That was in New Jersey, wasn't it?"

"I think so."

"That's what I want. What does that set you back, Victor?"

"About a million," I said.

"Really, for that crap? Got to work on my balling, I suppose."

The smell of smoke grew stronger. We followed the tracks down toward a passel of bright, blinking reds and blues and a ring of arc lights.

We drove slowly past the lights. Fire trucks and police cars, all in front of some abandoned lot, surrounded by a pile of abandoned cars, the arc lights illuminating a smoldering pile of cinder, covered by twisted bits of corrugated metal. The stench of burning turned my stomach.

A group of uniformed cops and firemen was surrounding a man, who peered past the crew of officials and right into the car as we passed.

Barnabas.

My stomach turned again until it twisted into a knot.

"They came tonight," said Derek. "The police. A swarm of them, like bees, and burned it to the ground."

"The police burned it down?"

"That's the way it played."

"Barnabas was running an illegal juke joint," I said. "The police were trying to close it down. I'm sorry to see this—Barnabas's goat is terrific—but what does that have to do with me?"

"It not about the club," said Antoine. "They wasn't there about the club."

"Then what were they after?"

"Jamison," said Antoine.

"They were asking everyone about him," said Derek. "Who he was. Who he worked for. Where he could be found. They didn't look so friendly, bo. They didn't look like they was going to pin some medal on his chest."

"Did they find him?" I said.

"Nah, mon," said Antoine. "And when it come clear that they not, that no one be giving that bwoy up, they cleared the place, and that's when the fire it started."

"Is everyone okay?" I said.

"Everyone got out," said Derek. "But Barnabas lost the club. And he couldn't stop asking about the man in the suit who came in just one day before the police."

"I get the idea," I said, and I did. "It doesn't make any sense. Where's Jamison now?"

"Gone," said Antoine. "And whatever it was he told you that night, that's gone, too. You going to forget it happened."

"Jamison is the alibi for a woman who is facing life in prison," I said.

"He not catching on so quick," said Antoine to Derek. "Didn't you tell me he was clever, bwoy?"

"I must have been overestimating him," said Derek.

"That don't seem so hard," said Antoine.

Antoine turned around in the front seat and stared right at me with those dark glasses of his. "Now, here's the story as it concerns you, Mr. Victor Carl. The folks that Jamison was selling for, they are not happy that Jamison is on the run. He was a good bwoy for them. And they are not happy that Barnabas's place it burned down, because they liked his curry. And they are not happy that them police are storming their corners and asking questions. And for this they blame me, and they blame Derek, and most of all they blame you."

"It's the second part of that what's really troubling, if you ask me," said Derek.

"So this is not just suggestion that you leave this alone," said Antoine.

"It's a threat," I said.

He leaned toward me, slapped a big mitt on my ear, grabbed my face, and pulled it close to his. "There you go, mon," he said. "There you go."

I grabbed onto his wrist, like grabbing onto a metal fence post. "I get it," I said. "I get it, I get it."

He gave me another quick slap and then turned around to face front again. "So now you know. You want us take you to them who are not happy? You need them to deliver the request in face-a-face?"

"No," I said.

"That was the first smart thing came out from your lips all night," said Derek.

"And you also should be knowing, Victor Carl," said Antoine, "that the bwoy assigned to enforce all this is me. So I want to be able a report back that the message it was sent and that Jamison is no longer mess up in that thing."

"Okay," I said meekly.

"You leave this alone, Mr. Victor Carl, or someone going a get a licking, that's for sure."

"Just so long as it ain't me," said Derek, "then you can do what you want."

"Understood?"

"Understood," I squeaked.

"Good," said Antoine. "Now we all be buddies again. Pull over there, D."

"Here?"

"Fine. I be back in a minute. No slip-ups, right?"

"No, sir," I said.

Antoine nodded as he opened the door, left the car, headed into an alley, and disappeared.

"You're one dumb son of a bitch," said Derek. "You just lucky I was here to save your ass."

"Funny, I don't feel lucky."

"This isn't the way they wanted to handle it, but I convinced them you were some big-shot lawyer with City Hall connections and that killing you would bring down serious heat."

"You lied for me, Derek? That's almost sweet."

"Yeah, it is, isn't it? Especially since you still haven't paid me for the other night."

"Show up tomorrow and I'll write you a check."

"No check, bo. Cash."

"Fine. Is Jamison going to be okay?"

"Thanks to you, he's on the run. But he has family in the South, and he's on his way to visit as we speak. He'll be gone a long while."

"I suppose that's good," I said. "For Jamison."

"And for you, too."

"But not for my old girlfriend."

"See, that's the beauty of old girlfriends," said Derek. "No matter how much they mean to you, everyone else just don't give a damn."

"The cops who stormed the club," I said. "Do you have any idea who they were? Were they narcotics agents, L&I people?"

"Was a mess of cops swarming the place," said Derek. "But the leader and the one asking the questions was a little guy in a flash suit."

"I get the idea," I said.

"He was handing out his card like he was looking for a date. Asking anyone who found Jamison to give him a call. He was real determined like."

"I bet he was," I said.

It didn't make any sense, I couldn't yet see the reasoning behind it, but what had happened was pretty clear. Sims hadn't just come for Jamison, he had come for me, too, throwing me head-first into deep, shark-infested waters. I couldn't tell if I was more angry or more scared, but I was sure more something.

"You know, Derek," I said, "I should be happier than I am right now, seeing as how I've just been totally screwed."

23

When I stepped into my office a few hours later, my mind thick with the syrup of sleep deprivation, it took me a moment to take in the scene.

"Oh, it was quite a night, yes it was," said Derek as he leaned on my secretary's desk. "You should come join Derek some evening. He'll show you a time. You don't know what you're missing by not partying with Derek."

"I have a pretty good idea," said Ellie without looking up from the papers on her desk. "And Ellie doesn't date anyone who refers to himself in the third person."

"There won't be no third person," said Derek. "Only me."

"Hello, Derek," I said. "A little early, isn't it?"

He swiveled his head and smiled. "Never too early for collections, bo," he said before turning back to Ellie. "So what you say?"

"I already said it," said Ellie. "You have a few messages,

Mr. Carl. And a visitor who decided to wait instead of coming back, which indicates to Ellie that there is not much going on in his life."

"Derek's got patience, is what he's got," said Derek.

"Leave her alone," I said as I stepped up to the desk to grab my messages. "I'll be with you in a minute, Derek, but I'm going to have to go to an ATM to get your payment."

"Okay," he said, backing off. "Can't blame a man for trying. But, bo, you got any new magazines or what? I already read these dogs. And you could use something with a little spice. *Maxim,* maybe. I hear all the best law firms, they subscribe to *Maxim.*"

"You read it just for the articles, I suppose."

"They got articles? By the way, if you want, I'm available for lunch."

"That's an upset," said Ellie.

"Derek likes them sassy," said Derek.

"Ellie, can you get me Detective McDeiss on the phone without telling the secretary who wants to talk to him?"

"Of course."

"If she needs a name, tell him it's Prentice from the mortuary. And if Derek keeps hitting on you, you have my permission to staple his hand to your desk."

"That's cold, bo," said Derek. "After what I done for you last night."

"Next time you visit my apartment, Derek, knock," I said as I passed Ellie and slipped into my office.

I went through the messages quickly, the usual crap, clients calling to complain about their cases, prosecutors calling to complain about my filings, copier salesmen trying to sell me copiers. Yeah, yeah, yeah. And then there was a message that pushed a shiver down my spine: "Mr. Trocek called, said he had a funny story for you." Believe me when I tell you that was one funny story I did not want to hear.

"Detective McDeiss on line two, Mr. Carl," said Ellie, standing now in my office door.

"Thank you," I said. "And if Mr. Trocek calls again, tell him I'm out of town."

"When will you be back?"

"Thanksgiving," I said as I picked up the phone and pressed the blinking button.

"Did you hear about the fire?" I said to McDeiss.

"The one at Barnabas's place?" he said.

"You know Barnabas?"

"Best goat north of Kingston. I suspected that his place was what you were talking about when you brought up the alibi. Then, when I heard about the fire last night, I figured the alibi and the fire might be linked."

"Linked absolutely," I said. "It was Sims who burned the place down while he was looking for the alibi witness."

"You sure?"

"I got word firsthand. Not that Sims has much of a chance to find him anymore."

"The witness ran?"

"He's as good as gone."

"How'd Sims know where to look for him?"

"I might have told him enough for him to figure out," I said. "He wanted me to put pressure on Julia, I wanted him to back off, so I followed your advice and gave him what I had. It didn't quite work out the way I had hoped. But I should have known better than to give Sims anything. As the old saying goes, the stupid fish should just keep his damn mouth shut. Do you have any idea what Sims is after?"

"A killer?" said McDeiss.

"Yeah, sure, and all we need is love. He's got something else on his mind that he's not spilling yet. But either way, what he did last night was strange. Why would he make so much noise looking for a witness that he ended up chasing him off?"

"Maybe he wanted to chase him."

"Why?"

"To get rid of a lie that was threatening to gum up his case."

"A lie?"

"The alibi wasn't any good, Victor. It wouldn't have held up. You said she was in North Philly buying drugs. But the toxicology reports blow that out of the water. The victim was clean, no drugs in the system, no sign of needle marks. And your old girlfriend was clean, too."

"Oh."

"If she was buying drugs, who were they for?"

"Damn good question," I said.

24

"So how much do I owe you?" I said to Derek as we walked together down the steps toward the front door of my building.

"More than you know," he said. "I did a lot of talking to save your neck. Told everyone we can't be getting rid of lawyers who actually know how to win. Even told them that you'd do your thing on their behalf."

"No thanks."

"They come knocking, you best hitch up your pants and get to working. You don't know how close both of us came last night."

"I think I do, but I'm asking how much money I owe you for your detective work."

"Is that what I was doing, taking you down to Barnabas's place?"

"Sure. Every lawyer needs a PI, and for that night at least, you were mine. We agreed on twenty an hour, I believe."

"We did, for truth, yes, but that was before I learned that I would be working as an official private detective. Got to raise my rates for that, don't you think?"

"You have a license?"

"What do you mean, license?"

"Then no." I pushed open the door on the ground floor and headed south, toward my bank on Walnut Street. Derek followed on my flank.

"Dangerous work, detecting," he said. "No telling what kind of trouble you can find yourself in. People always putting guns in your face."

"Anyone put a gun in your face?" I said.

"Not yet, but the way you making enemies by the fistful, it bound to happen if we continue working together."

"Not much chance of that."

"I figure what you get per hour should be the starting point. How much you get?"

"What I get, as a trained and experienced criminal defense attorney, trained and experienced enough to keep your butt out of jail, isn't relevant. I have to maintain an office, I have to pay Ellie, I have a lot of expenses just staying licensed."

"And I got to keep my wardrobe up."

"Twenty an hour is what we agreed on."

"Fifty."

"Should we turn around and go back?"

"Twenty-five, then."

"Because you were actually pretty helpful, and because you stuck your neck out for me, and because your doing that put your neck on the line, I'll go up to twenty-five. But that's it."

"All right, now we're getting somewhere. Let's see, we got three and a half hours the one night and then two more last night."

"I didn't hire you for last night."

"All part of it. And I don't do partial hours. You get a piece, you pay for it all, like a plumber. I did a lot of stuff you didn't see."

"And I'm glad of that. All right. Twenty-five times six is one-fifty."

"Plus expenses."

"I paid for the drinks and the goat."

"Bo."

"How much?"

"Another forty."

"What for?"

"Incidentals."

"You got receipts?"

"Do I look like the kind of man that's always asking for receipts? Got to keep up a reputation, you want to do effective detection. You should know that."

"Okay, forty for expenses, just so long as you agree to one thing."

"What's that?"

"Don't say another word, please. Just keep your mouth shut. Now, there's the ATM right across the street. Stay here. I'll go over and get the cash."

"Maybe I'll come along."

"Maybe you won't. I don't need you looking over my shoulder and stealing my code."

"You don't trust me. That hurts."

"And then, before you get the cash, we're going to fill out some tax forms."

"Come again?"

"A Form 1099."

"What say?"

"Derek, it's called a job. You get money for work, I file documents, I get a deduction, you pay taxes. Those are the rules."

"That wasn't part of our deal."

"Wait here," I said.

"I'm not paying no taxes," he called out after me.

"Say it a little louder, maybe the government cameras didn't catch it the first time."

I left him scanning the light posts for spy equipment as I crossed the street and headed to the ATM on the side of my bank.

Usually there wasn't enough money in my account to withdraw all I pleased, but lately, because of a questionable retainer I had been accepting as part of a case that most likely would never require my services, my account was flush. It was how I had redone my office, paid my secretary, bought my new pleather couch and flat-screen television, how I had paid the cable bill. I wasn't wealthy by any means, and my lack of wealth still rankled like a thorn in the eye, but for a few more months at least I could pass for a modicum of success, and a modicum was about as high as I could ever hope for anymore. No longer was I worried that the little INSUFFICIENT FUNDS message would pop up on the screen. Now I put in my card and tapped in my PIN and asked for a few hundred dollars and heard the sweet grinding of the gears as the crisp twenties were dealt out one after another after another.

It was almost pleasant, until I felt something sharp, like the point of a pen, press into my ribs.

I froze. Something moved behind me. A hot breath washed over my right ear.

"Take the dollars," said a soft, accented voice with a pronounced lisp, "and put them in your pocket."

"My pocket?"

"Your pocket."

"Shouldn't it be your pocket?"

"Shut up and do as I say."

I did as he said.

"Now turn this way, and together we walk down the street."

I turned, and as I did, I caught sight of him, and whatever fear had lodged in my ribs from the feel of that pen point blossomed like a beastly rose when I recognized Sandro, Gregor Trocek's Cadizian thug.

His left hand was in the pocket of his leather jacket now, with something very much like the shape of a knifepoint pushing out the leather. He jabbed me in the ribs again and indicated that I should walk west.

I walked west.

He followed close behind. I tried very hard not to collapse into a heap as I walked, but even so, my legs felt strangely rubbery, like the bones were melting. I thought of the fingers on ice in upstate New York, and I wobbled.

"Keep going," said Sandro. "It's over there."

And there it was, the predatory gray Jaguar, parked aslant, headfirst in front of a hydrant. As we got closer, the rear door opened, and Sandro pushed me roughly toward it. I ducked my head so as not to slam it into the roof, and there, inside the car, now face-to-face with me, was Gregor Trocek, smiling warmly.

"What's wrong, Victor?" he said. "Why you avoiding me? You don't want hear my funny story?"

Sandro drove. He drove slowly, through the narrow streets of Philadelphia, turning here, turning there, going no place in particular, which just then was about the worst place I could imagine.

"I was waiting for your call," said Gregor Trocek. "It was so lonely, waiting like that. My feelings are bruised."

"I'm sorry," I stammered. "I've been a little busy."

"And I hope your busyness was profitably spent. So what have you found for me?"

"Not much."

"Ahh, Victor, you disappoint," he said, sitting uncomfortably close to me in the rear of his Jaguar. "I don't enjoy being disappointed."

"Join the club."

It was quite a car, that Jaguar, with its new-car scent, its ivory leather seats, its burled-wood trays and flat screens in both front headrests. Even as I felt the fear he wanted me to feel, I also felt the old longing to get my piece of the pie, my seat at the table, my own damn Jaguar. Nothing slakes fear like raw greed. Gregor Trocek was leaning on me to get back his one point seven million dollars. How many Jaguars would a piece of one point seven million buy? One was enough, with cash left over for down payments on a town house here and a vacation home in Florida and half enough gas to get me from one to the other.

"So now, Victor, are you ready to hear my funny story?"

"Sure, I guess."

"Okay, so there was woodcutter in my country named Ivan. Ivan is biggest cuckold in village. Every afternoon Ivan's neighbor, he strides into Ivan's house and lies with Ivan's wife, and Ivan does nothing. Nothing, you understand. So one afternoon Ivan comes into his house with ax in hand and finds neighbor's bull in bed with his wife. Ivan, he raises ax over his head and slams it down, just missing bull and chopping bed in two. The bull, he quickly jumps out of bed and says, 'Why you get so angry? My owner, he come in here every afternoon to fuck your wife, and never from you a peep.' And Ivan, he says, 'But you I can eat.'"

A cackle came from Sandro in the driver's seat, and Gregor joined in with a hearty guffaw that sent shivers of saliva flying about the backseat.

"Yes," I said. "Funny."

"You don't like?" said Gregor. "Then how about this one? A friend, he calls me and asks me to kill you. Yes, you. You are in this joke. I ask why? He says because he thinks you are fucking his wife."

"I told you already it wasn't true."

"Yes, you did, and I chose not to believe word of it. But even if true, what does it matter? Especially when I learn that maybe he wants to kill you for different reason. Maybe he thinks you stole something from his good friend Gregor."

"What are you talking about?"

"I'm talking about money, my money, invested in partnership with some stranger and which is now inconveniently gone. I informed you already, Victor, that I am willing to kill for someone else's pittance, so don't even think of what I won't do to get back what is mine."

"I don't have your money."

"Are you sure? Or do you maybe know where it can be found? I have been told that things are going now well with you. A new flat-screen television, new paint in the office, a new couch. Leather."

"Pleather."

"All the better," said Sandro from the front seat. "Easier to care for, and if it rips, you just melt it back together."

"Thank you for that interior-decorating advice, Sandro," I said.

"So where has your new affluence come from?" said Gregor. "I wonder if it has come from my ass."

"It came from a case. And whoever's been whispering in your ear is playing you for a fool. I don't have your money. Miles Cave has it, and I'm trying to find him just as much as you are."

"With no luck."

"No."

"Convenient. Did you talk to Julia?"

"Yes. She said she didn't know him, truly. But I did find out that a great deal of money was transferred to him as Wren Denniston's business was collapsing. And I know for sure that if he's ever found, he would lose the money, either to you, through Sandro's happy knife, or to the government, through litigation. He had one point seven million reasons to run. One point seven million reasons to kill Wren to keep from being found. And one point seven million reasons to try to divert the search for him to someone else."

"Like who?"

"Like me. Which is a laugh, because if I had taken off with

your one point seven million dollars, Gregor, I wouldn't be hanging around on my pleather couch. I'd be in Belize."

"Ever been to Belize?"

"Yes, actually."

"A little boring for my taste. It is the British influence. They think violence and warm beer make a good time. They are half right."

"Who told you that I might have your money?" I said.

"A little bird."

"Probably the same little bird that's been whispering to the police and that's been trying to set me up from before Wren was murdered. What was it, a letter? A phone call?"

"Phone call."

"Did you get a name or a number?"

"Just a number on my phone. Who you think?"

"I'll tell you who I think. I think it's your boy Miles Cave. He probably heard all those Victor Carl stories that Wren was dishing and figured I was the perfect patsy. I think Miles is setting me up, I think he decided to set me up from the start. And if he can convince you and the police to concentrate on me, then he's free to flit away and live fat off your money. What do you know about the creep?"

"He was old friend of Wren. He had an in at bank, was able to handle cash payments without filing usual documents with government."

"Cash?"

"Yes."

"You gave him one point seven million in cash?"

"Why not? A small satchel is needed, that is all. I handed it directly to Wren at his house. The terms were all agreed to, including using Miles Cave's name for the investment."

"Was there a written agreement?"

"Yes, of course. We were limited partnership. Youngblood, LP. I came up with title myself."

"Why am I not surprised?"

"The agreement was written quite carefully."

"By your lawyer?"

"No, by Cave's. But my lawyer, American working in Lisbon, looked it over."

"You have a copy here?"

"Of course."

"Let me see it."

"Sandro," said Gregor with a snap of his fingers. "Briefcase."

"While I look at this," I said when he handed me the partnership agreement, "why don't you call back that number and try to find out who the hell is whispering in your ear."

The agreement was a typical partnership thing, party of the first part, party of the second part, all that legal jazz. It was dated not too long ago, which meant Miles stole the money shortly after it was placed in Wren's business. Reading through the boilerplate was like wading through a steaming pile of legal muck without your boots on. Miles Cave was the general partner, which meant his name was up front and he was liable for all debts. The investment would be made in his name only. Gregor was a limited partner, which meant his participation could be hidden, even if he supplied the cash. All pretty normal, and the language was enough to induce an insomniac into coma, but as I read through it, I noticed something peculiar.

Most contracts detail the name of the lawyer who drafted them at the end, by either name or initials. This contract had nothing to indicate the drafter. But in even the most vile examples of legalese, something of the personality of the writer always comes through: a touch of humor, a penchant for showoffy words, a strange fear of spiders. And reading through this agreement, I was getting a whiff of personality. The drafter was both arrogant and imprecise in language, was quick with the formal phrase that said nothing except to let you know it was written by a lawyer, was careful to provide for all kinds of bizarre eventualities while allowing certain obvious loopholes to remain. In short, the lawyer who drafted this partnership agreement was an unpleasant weasel.

And I had a pretty good guess who the weasel was.

I looked up from the document. Gregor was on his cell phone. "So," he said, "be nice fellow and tell me where you are."

Pause.

"No, not what you are wearing, this is not that type of call. Just where you are, please."

Pause.

"You don't say. So thank you and have nice day." He flipped closed his cell and looked at me. "Pay phone," he said.

"Where?"

"Here. Philadelphia. Thirtieth Street Station."

My eyes lit up. "Miles Cave is still in town."

"So it appears."

"Then we can find him."

"Yes," said Gregor. "The hunt is on. This will almost be enjoyable, though not as enjoyable as squeezing his head until his eyes pop out like avocado pits."

"What about me?" I said.

"Believe me, Victor. If you have my money, I will enjoy squeezing out your eyes twice as much. Cruelty is always richer when the victim is someone you know."

"That's not what I mean," I said. "What I mean is that if I find the bastard for you, what do I get?"

"I told you already. The information about Wren wanting to have you killed, it disappears. That was my promise, and I intend to keep it."

"I don't really care anymore. The way things are going, your tepid piece of information is the least of my worries. If I find Miles, I'd be better off turning him over to the government. The D.A. would have a suspect, the trustee of Wren's business would get his one point seven mil, and I'd be off the hook whatever you do."

"I sense a scheme rising. What are you proposing, Victor?"

"I want a piece of the pie," I said.

"Of whatever I recover?"

"That's right."

"Of my own money?"

"Exactly."

"Go to hell."

"I was thinking the bank."

"It is impossible."

"It is only fair."

"It is not fair, it is robbery. But if what you want is your normal fee, paid on an hourly basis, then—"

"I wasn't thinking of an hourly fee. This is a collection case, pure and simple, and lawyers in collection cases usually get a third."

"Because they are greedy bastards."

"That's my club."

"A dangerous club to belong to."

"But prosperous."

"As long as you live. But I might be able to see myself clear to giving you five percent."

"Now you are insulting me."

"That is absolutely my intention. And just so I am clear, you are ugly as well as greedy."

"Give me a quarter and we'll call it a deal."

"Ten percent."

"Not enough."

"Twelve point five, then, and that is my final offer. Only if you find him first, and only from what I actually recover from the bastard."

"Forget it. I'd rather snooze at the shore."

"I could have Sandro kill you, painfully."

I heard the sound of a switchblade opening in the front seat. *Swish-click.*

"Twelve point five it is," I said cheerfully.

"So we are agreed. Good."

The car pulled up to an intersection and stopped. "Is this all right, Mr. Trocek?" said Sandro.

"Perfect," said Gregor. "Good hunting, Victor."

I opened the door and started to slide out when he grabbed the lapel of my jacket.

"My patience is not limitless," said Gregor Trocek. "I have pressing business back in Iberia. Her name is Aitana, and she is a vision of youth. But for how long, no one knows. So know this, Victor. In exchange for your percentage, I am taking back promise of speedy delivery. Don't disappoint me."

"I'll do my best," I said.

"For sin's sake, Victor, let's both hope you do better than that."

I slid out of the car, slammed the door behind me, watched as the Jaguar slid away down the street, did the calculation even as the car slipped from my view. Twelve point five percent of one point seven mil. Something over two hundred thousand dollars. Enough for my own Jaguar after all. Sweet.

And I knew exactly where to start looking.

When the car finally disappeared, I scanned the location where I was dropped off. It was the same intersection where Sandro had picked me up. The bank where I had been shanghaied was across the street. I turned around, and there was Derek, still searching the sky as if seeking out those IRS cameras on the light poles.

"Hey, Derek."

He stopped looking and turned his attention to me. "Took your sweet time, bo."

"Did you happen to notice, with your brilliant detecting skills, what happened to me across the street?"

"Trouble with the ATM?"

"Not exactly. You see, I was kidnapped at knifepoint, forced into a strange automobile, taken on a drive through the city, all the while being threatened with bodily harm from a Cadizian assassin and his blood-soaked switchblade."

"Word?"

"Yes, Derek," I said. "Word. And all the time you were standing here, across the street, you saw nothing."

"Not nothing. I think I spotted one of them cameras right up there."

"You've certainly got eagle eyes."

"So let's get to it. You got my money?"

"Yes, I do," I said, "but first I have to catch a weasel."

The offices of Swift & Son were on Pine Street, just west of
Broad, occupying the ground floor of an old stone apartment
building. The name of the firm was printed in ornate gold leaf on
the wide plate-glass window. The gold leaf was in varying states
of peel.

"This a beat little outpost," said Derek, standing beside me.
I had come right over from the bank, and Derek, still waiting for
his money, had followed.

"I'll just be a few minutes," I said.

"What should I do in the meantime, bo?"

"Wait out here," I said as I peered through the window. The
outer office looked like it was straight out of a Hopper painting,
bare and dusty, with a few old chairs scattered across the worn
wooden floor. On a side table, a single magazine sat forlornly.
Radiators were uncovered, the walls were a faded pale blue, a
vintage ashtray stand was set beside one of the chairs.

When I stepped through the wooden door, a little bell rang.

"Can I help you?" said an older woman behind a counter so high that only the top half of the woman's head appeared. From what I could gather, her hair had once been red.

"I'm looking for Clarence Swift," I said.

"Which one, Clarence Swift the Elder or the Younger?"

I thought about it for a second. "Clarence Swift the lawyer."

"That would be the Younger, which is good for you, sir, since Clarence Swift the Elder passed away five years ago."

"Lucky me."

Just then the little bell atop the door rang again. The woman and I turned our heads at the same moment. Derek.

"You mind if I sit?" he said. "My dogs are barking."

"Just stay quiet, Derek," I said. "I won't be long."

Derek looked around, took a disapproving sniff, and then dropped into one of the chairs. He picked up the magazine on the side table, looked at it quizzically, then showed it to me. "Who's that?" he said, pointing to the man on the cover with a shock of dark hair gelled perfectly in place.

"Reagan," I said.

"Who?"

I turned back to the woman, whose gaze remained on Derek. "Is Clarence Swift the Younger in?"

"Mr. Swift is quite busy at the moment. Maybe I can help you? Is this about an overdue rent?"

"No, ma'am."

"A problem with a property?"

"Not that either."

"You are looking for insurance, then."

"No."

"Hey, lady," said Derek. "You got anything more recent than 1987?"

"No," she said.

"No *Maxim*s or nothing?"

"Maalox?"

"What say?"

"There's a drugstore on the corner." She turned her attention to me. "Are you sure you gentlemen are in the right place?"

"I'm sure," I said. "Would you tell Mr. Swift that Victor Carl is here to see him?"

There was a moment when the eyes peering above the counter appeared to fill with terror, as if I were the ghost of Clarence Swift the Elder come back to enact some terrible revenge, before they calmed again.

"Just a moment, please, Mr. Carl," she said, "and I'll see if he is available."

The woman stood, eyed me warily as she straightened her print dress, and then made her way from behind the counter to the door leading to the back office. She was taller than I expected, big-boned and sharp-faced, long past fifty but with a rigidity to her posture that made her an altogether formidable presence. And somehow she seemed vaguely familiar, as if somewhere before I had seen the form from which she had been cast. She opened the door, eyed me again, closed it behind her.

From inside the back office, I could make out a scene of riotous anxiety. The exact words were muffled by the heavy door, but there was a high-pitched shout, a loud reply in a lower pitch, the scraping of furniture, the banging shut of file drawers, more shouts in the two different keys.

Derek raised an eyebrow. I shrugged.

When the door finally opened, the secretary once again appeared, smoothing straight her dress, patting her hair.

"Mr. Carl," she said. "Mr. Swift will see you now."

She held the door open for me and stared me down as I passed on through. She kept the door open as she returned to her spot at the counter.

"Victor, yes," said Clarence Swift, waiting for me inside his office, standing before his desk, hands clasped, leaning forward, peering at me from beneath his brow. "Welcome to my humble workplace."

I looked around. "Not so humble," I said, but I was lying. It was humble as hell.

The walls were dark and scuffed, the blocky wooden furniture was ancient and rutted, the floor was distressed, not by a decorator but by time. There was a cluttered desk with a battered chair, there were dark wooden file cabinets, there was a tall slanted writing desk with a holder for a pot of ink and a worn stool before it. It was an office out of some 1940s movie, without even a hint of the modern or luxurious. No computer, no radio or television, an old manual typewriter and a phone that was bulky and black, with a rotary dial. I had the sense that except for a few silver picture frames on the windowsill, this was exactly the way the office had been set up by the elder Mr. Swift many decades before, and the son had seen no reason to change it.

"What can I do for you, Victor?" said Clarence Swift, maintaining the pose of a suspicious prelate.

"I just have some questions, if you don't mind."

"I'm quite busy."

"Working on Julia's case?"

"There is much to be done."

"Oh, Clarence, I'm sure you have the situation well in hand."

"Thank you for your confidence. But still, this is no time for letting up. I need to be sure that Julia's interests are completely taken care of. There is a surfeit of work yet to do, and your rejecting my caution and continuing to impose your presence on her has just amplified my difficulties. So if you'll excuse me—"

"Youngblood, LP."

Clarence blinked.

"You set it up," I said.

"I'm sure I don't know what you are talking about."

"I'm sure you do, Clarence. Youngblood was a limited partnership created to launder ill-gotten gains through Wren Denniston's investment company. There were two partners. One was Gregor Trocek, a shady business associate of Wren's. The other was an old friend of Wren's from their school days. You knew all of Wren's old friends, surely."

"Not all," said Clarence. "I didn't go to school with Wren. He attended Germantown Academy, I went to public school."

"That must have rankled," I said.

"Public school was good enough for a modest boy of modest means like me."

"It was Gregor's money that financed the partnership—cash, actually—but the money was earned through questionable means and no taxes had been paid, so he needed a way to turn the cash into an investment. Which is where the old friend came in. I'm talking, of course, about Miles Cave, the man you told me you never heard of. And when it came time to finalize the agreement, a document was required, and Wren came to you to draft it up, and you did."

"I'm afraid you're mistaken, Victor."

"I read the thing, every word. It's full of useless Latin and tortured legal phrases. The agreement humbly wrings its own hands even as it carefully creates a vehicle for illegal money laundering. It's got your fingerprints all over it."

"You're making this up. It's not possible to tell."

"Then let's ask the FBI what they think."

"Why would they care?"

"I could give you one point seven million reasons."

"You're guessing," he said, backing up now as his voice rose higher. "It's not true. You're lying."

"No, I'm not."

"I know your type," he hissed. "Willing to make up anything to put the likes of me down. But I deserve more than the lies of a private-school brat. Where did you go, Victor? Penn Charter? The Haverford School? In which lofty tower did you learn to make up stories about the rest of us?"

"I went to public school myself."

"In the suburbs, I'd bet."

"Yes, actually."

"That hardly counts."

"Still, you wrote it."

"You don't know that."

"Yes, I do," I said.

He pulled his outsize handkerchief from his jacket pocket, wiped the shine off his forehead. As he flicked the handkerchief back into the pocket, he collapsed loudly onto the high stool before the slanted writing desk.

Just then a voice poured through the doorway. "Anything I can do for you, Mr. Swift?" called in the secretary.

"No, Edna, we are fine, thank you."

Swift stared at me for a moment with weary resignation in his eyes. Then he propped an elbow on the writing desk and clasped his hands together.

"You are correct, Victor. Yes, I drafted the agreement. I am embarrassed to have lied, but Wren asked me to tell no one of my involvement, and so I was merely trying to accede to the request of the dear departed. But you found me out fair and square. I should have known that a poor liar like me would be found out by someone as clever as you. Is that what you came for, to humiliate me?"

"Nah, that's just a bonus. What I've really come for is Miles Cave."

"What about him?"

"I'm looking for him."

"There seems to be an army looking for him."

"But I'm going to have your help."

"Why would I help you?"

"Because if I can find him, the police will have a sweet suspect to nail Wren's murder on. Which would be a great benefit to Julia."

"Yes, it would."

"And we both are doing all we can for poor Julia."

"Yes, we are." He stared at me for a moment and then dropped his chin. "He is a frightening man, Victor."

"Then the sooner I find him, the better for everyone."

"I've never met him, of course. And so everything I know is secondhand, from Wren."

"Go on."

"Wren said he was tall, good-looking, a ne'er-do-well. He drove a convertible and wore sunglasses and dated actresses. He lived on the West Coast but was often in Philadelphia to visit family and friends."

I think it was the sunglasses that got me to thinking. The actresses, too, maybe, but really the sunglasses. I mean, where did that come from, sunglasses?

"Wren told me Miles had shadowy contacts with mobsters and drug dealers," continued Clarence. "Some of his deals had been quite questionable, and there were rumors of an incident in Fresno that left one man dead."

"Fresno?" I said.

"Yes, that's right. Fresno. Wren told me that he didn't trust Miles, didn't really want anything to do with him. But Mr. Trocek had done him a favor in the past, and Wren wanted to help him with his investment. Miles, with his contact at the bank, was perfect for that. So Wren asked me to draft the agreement quite carefully, to protect everybody in case Miles stepped out of line."

"Did you ever talk to this Miles fellow?" I said.

"Once, on the phone," said Clarence.

I watched him closely as he spoke.

"His voice was deep, booming," said Clarence. "He called me 'Clarence, old buddy,' even though we'd never met. He tried to be helpful, but he wouldn't tell me much. He said his accountant would get back to me to answer my questions, but the accountant never did."

Clarence spoke now with none of the hesitancy or meandering language that had typified his speech before then, and I let him. He tossed off a few more details, he mentioned something about a toupee. I nodded and returned his smirk when he told it, but I wasn't listening anymore. It was the "Clarence, old buddy" that did it finally, and the way Clarence Swift couldn't avoid the slight sneer that appeared on his lips when he repeated it. As soon as I heard it, I realized what I should have realized long ago. That Miles Cave didn't exist. That he had never existed. That he was a figment of Wren Denniston's imagination, and Clarence knew it.

Clarence kept on talking, telling me what he could about Miles Cave, with his convertible and sunglasses and actress girl-friends, with his life that contained everything that Clarence's did not, while I looked again around the office.

Piles of files, documents, small drawers for keeping three-by-five cards listing rentals paid. All the hallmarks of a crimped legal practice and a real estate management company barely getting by. And the photographs in their frames. Clarence with an older man, his father, maybe? Another portrait of that older man, staring fiercely at the camera. Clarence with Wren Denniston. Clarence with his secretary, Edna. And one of a woman, tall and broad. It looked like Edna in her younger years, but that's not who it was. I had seen that photograph before, Clarence had shown a copy of it to me in my office. It was of his fiancée, Margaret.

But I recognized the woman from more than her picture.

Clarence Swift again pulled out the handkerchief and wiped his brow. He had worked up quite a sweat manufacturing his Miles Cave tale. I almost felt like clapping.

"I hope that helped, Victor," said Clarence as he snapped his handkerchief back into his pocket.

"It did," I said. "More than you know. Thank you."

"Do you need something, Mr. Swift?" called the secretary again from the outer office.

"We're fine, Edna. Fine." He looked at me, pursed his lips as if at the trials he suffered at the hands of his secretary. "And I again apologize for misleading you initially."

"No harm, no foul, Clarence. Have you heard from this Mr. Cave lately?"

"No, not at all."

"You'll let me know if you do."

"Of course."

"Do you think he might have killed Dr. Denniston?"

"It's possible, maybe probable. From what Wren told me, I sensed he could be quite dangerous."

"Fresno," I said, nodding.

"Yes, Fresno. But one thing I know for sure is that Mrs. Denniston had nothing to do with the murder."

"How are you so certain that she didn't?" I said as I stood.

"Because I know her," said Clarence. "She is a unique woman, so extraordinary in so many many ways. It would be impossible for her. Just impossible. The very thought . . ."

"Yes," I said. "The very thought."

"I hope you find him, Victor. Find him and drag him to justice."

"That's just what I intend to do," I said.

So why didn't I charge up to the bastard, grab him by the lapels, butt him in the chest like an irate French soccer player, and call him a liar?

Because he would have denied it, in a whining, plaintive voice that would have set my teeth on edge and my ears to bleeding. Because I couldn't have proved it, not yet at least. Because I didn't understand what it was all about or what it had to do with Wren Denniston's murder or what happened to the money, and I didn't think it advisable to spook him before I had some answers. But I now knew one thing for sure, if I hadn't known it already.

Clarence Swift was the enemy, deadly or not, I couldn't yet tell, but without doubt the enemy.

"So we done roaming and ready to get down to getting me my money?" said Derek as I stalked away from Swift & Son while Derek followed on my heels.

"I'm going back to the office now," I said. "You can fill in the tax forms there."

"I been thinking about that tax thing, and I got to tell you, bo, it's not such a good idea. Really, why bring the tax man in on our business and get all legal on me?"

"Because I'm a lawyer, Derek. You know, if your income is low enough, you might get money back from the government. Filing your taxes could provide a financial windfall."

"But it's the principle of the thing, know what I mean?"

"Unfortunately, I think that I do. Now, could you do me a favor and let me think for a bit?"

"Sure can. I don't mean to be messing with your mind."

"Thank you."

"But what I was—"

"Derek."

"I only mean—"

"Derek."

"Okay, bo. I can take a hint."

"Good."

"It's just that . . ."

He kept talking. That was just the way he was built, but I tuned him out as I tried to figure what the hell was going on.

Why had Wren Denniston invented Miles Cave? To create a partnership for Gregor Trocek's money. Why do that? The only answer was that he had planned to steal the money from the start. I'd bet almost anything that the date of the partnership's creation was after Wren discovered the embezzlement in Taipei that killed the hedge fund and caused Inner Circle's collapse. Gregor needed a vehicle to invest his illegal cash. Wren created it, all the while plotting to steal the cash and leave Gregor searching for the mysterious Miles Cave. And how much did Clarence know about it? Probably everything.

Did the missing money have anything to do with Wren Denniston's murder? I'd bet yes—one point seven mil is a lot of motive—but then who pulled the trigger? Gregor Trocek, who put the money up in the first place? He was still searching for Miles Cave, he'd been duped, maybe he'd found out what had happened and decided to get some revenge before he found the cash. Or maybe it was someone who knew where the money had gone to. Someone like Julia? But she had an alibi. Someone like Clarence Swift? Who had created the partnership? Who was probably in on the scheme from the start? Who was lying to everyone to protect his secret?

Clarence Swift.

Right now I'd bet it was that sleazy little weasel who had tipped off the cops that I'd been out of my apartment the night of the murder when in fact I'd been in all night. Who had tipped off Gregor from a pay phone that I was the one who knew where his money was hiding. Who had created that letter from Miles Cave and then put my address and a signature that seemingly matched mine onto it. That's why he had closed his briefcase as soon as I came in my office door, he had pilfered a letter from my desk to get his specimen. And I knew just how the son of a bitch had slipped the bogus letter into the Inner Circle file.

He was setting me up, trying to deflect the blame from himself, trying to yoke a collar around my neck while he waltzed off with the prize.

There were enough permutations to give a mathematician a headache, but the whole thing made sense, sort of. I could believe I had figured it all out, sort of. Except for the part about Clarence doing the shooting. He was a small, twisted little man, but Clarence Swift, with his bow ties and dusty old office, with his diffident manner and false humility, didn't seem like the type that would kill over money. I had seen the Dylan Klebold in him and so I believed he could kill, but money didn't seem to power his engine. Then what did?

I found the answer sitting in plain sight on top of my desk.

Derek was up front, waiting as Ellie prepared the tax forms

and receipt for him to sign. I was sitting behind my desk, still puzzling over it all, when I idly started paging through a file. It was the file I had gotten from Inner Circle, the file that contained all the letters of complaint. It was a sad file, full of sad letters from those who had suffered great losses, the kind of file that lawyers find great joy in, because it contains the possibility of great profit. And I was trying to find the joy in there when Derek showed up at my office door.

"I filled out them forms," he said. "Signed them, too."

I closed the file and looked up at him.

"I still don't like the idea," he said. "It doesn't seem right somehow."

"Hand them over."

He handed them over, I gave them a quick scan. It was all official, and signed, just like he said. I took the forms and put them into my desk drawer. Then I pulled out my wallet and counted one hundred and ninety dollars. I held the bills out to him, he took hold, but I didn't let go.

"You did a good job, Derek," I said. "You earned this."

"Fine, bo."

"You can be proud of the work you did."

"Thanks."

Pause.

"You going to let it loose so I can be on my way," he said, "or am I going to have to cut off your hand?"

"It's just that I want you to know that you can do something real with your life. You don't have to dance on the wrong side with your boys on the corner."

"I told you I was just hanging."

"Maybe, but hanging often turns into something else. And then you're just being used by a bunch of creeps who don't give a damn about anything but their business."

"Is the lecture a necessary part of it? Is that another requirement along with the tax forms?"

"I'm just saying."

"I know what you're saying. But I don't think there's a great demand outside of this office for my detecting services, know what I mean?"

"You don't know, Derek. Get some training, find an entry-level job with a PI firm. I could help you get started. You just don't know."

"Yeah, you're right. I don't know."

He gave a yank. I let go. He loosed a bright smile as he stuffed the wad into a pocket. "Thanks, bo."

Just as he turned to leave, I noticed it. On the outside of the file that was sitting on my desk. The printing. Made by hand. All capital letters. "COMPLAINT LETTERS." Just two words, but they reminded me of something. And when I looked close, I could see it. The way the *L* looped. The way the *S* curved. It all came together like a thunderclap.

"Hey, Derek," I said before he was out the door. "You busy tonight?"

He stopped, leaned back into the office. "Not really."

"I might have another job for you."

"My usual rates?"

"Sure."

"Thirty an hour."

"It was twenty-five."

"But that was before I got all this detecting experience."

"Okay."

"Plus expenses."

"Fine."

"Beautiful. So what do you need from me?"

I opened a desk drawer, pulled out a small brick of electronics, tossed it to him.

"This is a mini tape recorder. I want you to go to the store and buy some mini tapes that fit. And then I want you to spend some time and figure out how the damn thing works."

It was a neat little Cape Cod, white and freshly painted, in a neat little neighborhood in Haddonfield, New Jersey. The lawn was well cared for, the perennials beneath the dogwood were neatly weeded, there was a cat in the window. The cat was gray and fluffy, and it eyed me with evident suspicion. Smart cat.

I knocked on the door.

"Not a word until I give the go-ahead, all right?" I said as Derek and I stood side by side and waited.

"I got it, bo."

"Just follow my instructions and do as we planned."

"I heard you the first three times."

"Good. This is tricky stuff. The timing is all."

"Now, don't go insulting my timing. My timing is impeccable."

"Impeccable?"

"That's what I said."

"Let's hope so."

I knocked again. We could hear footsteps from inside the house, the cat jumped off the sill, the door opened. The wide face at the door peered at me blankly for a moment and then froze with surprise.

"Hello, Margaret," I said to the secretary from the Inner Circle Investments offices, who had made the copies of the complaint letters for me. She was wearing a print dress and sturdy shoes and held a dish towel in one hand.

"Mr. Carl," she said. "What are you doing here?"

"This is my friend Derek. Do you have a moment to speak to us?"

"Not really."

"We just have some questions."

She glanced quickly at Derek and then back at me. "I'm sure Mr. Nettles can answer all your questions. He'll be in the office tomorrow morning."

"We don't want to talk to Mr. Nettles," I said. "We want to talk to you. Do you mind if we come in?"

She looked at me, then down to her cat, who was twisted within the twin pillars that were her legs and showing me its teeth. I showed mine back.

"Yes, I do mind," she said. She leaned forward and glanced up and down the street. "You shouldn't be here. How did you find my address?"

"Have you started planning your wedding yet, Margaret?" I said.

"That's none of your business."

"Does Mr. Nettles know who your fiancé is?"

"My private life is my own, Mr. Carl. Now, please leave, or I will have to call the police."

"You won't call the police, you're too smart for that. You don't want them sniffing around, asking questions. You do know that bankruptcy fraud is a federal crime, don't you?"

"I have no idea what you are talking about."

"Does Mr. Nettles know that you've been engaged to Dr. Denniston's personal lawyer all the while you've been working for him? Does Mr. Nettles know that your fiancé drafted a legal agreement for Miles Cave, the investor he has the FBI out searching for? Does Mr. Nettles know that you are slipping fraudulent letters from that selfsame Miles Cave into Inner Circle's files?"

"What do you want?" she said, her face a stony mass of anger. I'd seen softer peaks in the Alps.

"We just want to come inside," I said, "and maybe have some tea."

The house was spotless, and her knuckles were raw to prove it. While she was in the kitchen making the tea, I checked out the living room. I would have thought it would be filled with knick-knacks and sentimental doilies, but it was bright and clean and uncluttered. I stepped over to a shelf with a few photographs in frames. Margaret standing stiffly with Clarence. A young Margaret with a rather formal family. And then a few pictures of Margaret dancing, in all her finery, dipping low in the arms of some slick-haired lothario, the line of her stout body suddenly elegant and long. There was a harsh edge to Margaret, except in the pictures of her dancing, where her face was suffused with a soft joy.

"How many years have you been dancing?" I said as we were situated in the living room and she was pouring. The tea she served was Darjeeling, the cookies were sugar.

"Since I was a girl," she said. "I had stopped for years before I found the club."

"From the pictures, I can tell you love it."

"It's a place where I can forget about things."

"What things?" I said.

She looked at me levelly. "Can we get on with this?"

"Okay," I said, picking up my teacup, taking a sip. Hot, rich, and florid, like a ripe bunch of daffodils. "We only have a couple of questions."

Right then Derek took out a small tape recorder and pressed a few buttons, then a few buttons more, grunting a bit until he got the thing to work. He laid it on the coffee table beside the pot of tea.

"What's that?" she said.

"Just a tape recorder," said Derek. "I only got hold of it today, so I'm still trying to figure it out. You don't mind, do you, ma'am?"

"Yes," she said. "I do." She turned to me. "Maybe this is a bad idea. Maybe I ought to call Clarence."

"Put it away, Derek," I said. "That's totally unnecessary. We're merely having a friendly little chat."

Derek shook his head as he picked up the tape player, clicked a few more buttons, and put the player back in his pocket.

"Better?" I said.

"No."

"We were talking about Miles Cave and his money."

"Were we?"

"We are now. What do you know of him?"

She paused for an instant to bite her lip. "I've seen his name in the records."

"Did he ever come into the office?"

"Not that I remember." She scrunched her face, as if considering. She glanced at Derek and then said, "But there were letters, and he did call occasionally. I always put him right through to Dr. Denniston."

"Do you know anything about him? Where he is?"

"No."

"Anything you know of a personal nature would be of much interest. Anything?"

"No. I'm sorry."

"Yes, I'm sure you are."

"You mind if I take a cookie?" said Derek.

"Help yourself," said Margaret.

"I noticed the picture of you and Mr. Swift," I said. "You make a lovely couple. How long have you been engaged?"

"Seven years now."

"That's a long time."

"Clarence doesn't like to rush into things."

"Are you as cautious as he is?"

"I think it's wise to be sure."

"Seven years is a lot of wisdom."

"I love him very much," she said with a flat sincerity.

"That's sweet. How'd you kids meet?"

"Dr. Denniston introduced us. At the time I was working as a secretary in his medical office."

"What kind of cookie is this?" said Derek.

"Sugar."

"It's good. Can I have another?"

"Take two," said Margaret. "Clarence and I are very happy together, Mr. Carl. We're very much in love, and we've been quite busy making plans."

"For your wedding?"

"And other things, yes."

"Do you have a wedding date?"

"Not yet," she said. "But we're very close to working things out."

"And I suppose Edna is quite happy with everything."

"Edna?" She worked at a tooth with her tongue for a moment, as if suddenly in pain. "Hardly."

"No? Why not?"

"She has plans for Clarence. Plans that don't include me."

I looked at her for a moment, blankly. From the similarity in features, I had assumed that Edna and Margaret were somehow related. "I'm surprised that his secretary takes such a personal interest in her boss."

"She's not just his secretary Mr. Carl, she's also his mother."

"Ahh, yes, I forgot," I said, trying not to gag on my tea. I raised the cup to her as if in a toast. "Well, I wish you both the best."

"Thank you."

"Who deposited the checks that came in to Inner Circle? Did Dr. Denniston do it himself, or did he entrust you with that task?"

"He trusted me completely."

"And you received all the bank records."

"Yes."

"And reviewed them."

"That was part of my job."

"How about Mr. Cave's investment? Did you take care of that, too?"

"Dr. Denniston took care of Mr. Cave's investment himself."

"Did you notice the deposit on one of the bank statements?"

"I don't recall."

"It was over a million dollars."

"We had a lot of large investments."

"Not that large, I dare say, and not that late in the game. Has Mr. Nettles asked about that deposit?"

"Yes."

"And you haven't been able to find it, have you?"

"We're still looking."

"And the subsequent withdrawal."

"The company's records are all clear."

"Of course they are. But Mr. Nettles mentioned discrepancies with the bank statements, and I assumed he was referring to Mr. Cave's deposit. Was it usual for your investors to pay in cash?"

"Oh, no. There was always either a check or the money was wired."

"What about Mr. Cave's investment? Could that have been in cash?"

"I don't know. I never saw a check, but like I said, Dr. Denniston took complete care of Mr. Cave's investment."

"And if the cash was somewhere, not in the bank, you wouldn't know where it is."

"What are you implying, Mr. Carl?"

"I'm looking for Miles Cave. Actually, to be more precise, I'm looking for Miles Cave's money. Do you have any idea where I should start my search?"

"No," she said. "I'm sorry." Pause. More thinking. It was like a tectonic shift as Margaret creased her features. "But I believe I heard that Mr. Cave doesn't live here. He lives on the West Coast or something, if that helps."

"And he wears sunglasses," I said.

"How should I know that?"

"Exactly." I put down my tea, stood up. "Thank you, Margaret, I won't take up any more of your time. The tea was delicious."

Her pinched face relaxed a bit. "It was actually nice to have a visitor."

"Clarence doesn't come over?"

"Oh, occasionally. He likes when I cook him a good steak dinner. Recently I've been getting the meat delivered straight from the Midwest. I keep it in the freezer Clarence bought me." Margaret bit her lower lip. "But usually we meet for dinners in town after work, or we would go out with the Dennistons before . . . well, you know."

"Yes, I know."

"I miss Dr. Denniston, Mr. Carl. He was very good to me."

"And Mrs. Denniston, too, I suppose."

"Not really," she said.

"You don't like Mrs. Denniston much?"

"Dr. Denniston was a kind man, but his life went awry the moment he met his wife."

"And you blame her?"

"I'm just saying."

"Where's the freezer?" I said.

"Excuse me?"

"The freezer Clarence bought you?"

"In the basement."

"Big, is it?"

"Not really."

"I mean the freezer, not the basement."

"Neither."

"You mind I take another cookie?" said Derek.

"Didn't you eat?" I said.

"Not since lunch, bo."

"Then I'll drop you off at a diner."

"Just asking for a cookie."

"Take the rest," said Margaret, offering the plate, her craggy face breaking into a slight smile.

"Thank you, ma'am," he said, giving me a look as he stood.

"Did you have difficulties with Mrs. Denniston?" I said.

"She must have, bo," said Derek, cutting in as he stuffed cookies into his pocket. "Calling her a slagheap and a bangster. You don't write that to your pals. But one thing I was wondering. What exactly is a bangster? Slagheap I can figure, but bangster? That's a new one on me."

I looked at Derek for a moment like he was the biggest idiot in the universe and then turned to Margaret, who was standing stock-still with shock, her eyes staring out with the horror of discovery, our discovery, as if we had opened the bathroom door and seen her naked.

"I assume it's bad," said Derek. "Not as bad as witch's cunt, or is it?"

"Get out," said Margaret, her voice steely cold.

"I didn't mean nothing by it—"

"Get out," she said.

"Derek, why don't you leave us alone for a little bit," I said.

Derek looked hurt and hangdog. Then he reached over and took the last cookie before heading out the door. When the door closed behind him, Margaret's face seemed to crack, like a mountain collapsing.

I sat down again, picked up my teacup, took a sip, and waited.

As soon as I could dump Derek off in his North Philly neighborhood, I hied it over to the very last place I should have hied it over to. Julia's, of course. But I had to go. I wanted to see her, to talk to her, to kiss her and maybe more her. And I had great news. I had solved the mystery of those troubling letters she'd been sent. There was money somewhere, and I suspected I knew where to find it, though it was way too dangerous right now to pick it up myself. And, most crucial of all, I knew who had killed her husband, and why. The only thing I didn't know was how wrong I could be.

It had been a scene of tears and bitterness in Margaret's neat little Cape Cod. She didn't blame him. How could she? He was just being led astray by the emotions conjured by that witch. The way she swished in his presence, the way she touched his arm and lowered her voice when she spoke to him. She had bewitched Dr. Denniston, leading him into ruin, and she had done the same to her Clarence, all the time reveling in her power, the power women like that had over men, a power Margaret would never know.

"But Clarence loves me in his soul," she said, and she might have been right, but that's not where it matters.

The bitterness was etched deep into her features, as if with some brutal awl. The way the fey little girls at dance class got the solos while Margaret was pressed to the back of the chorus. The way the bright, bubbly girls in elementary school got the teachers' attention and the pretty girls with clear voices got the leads in the middle-school musicals. The designation of beauty in America is remarkably generous—so many beautiful girls walk the hallways of our high schools it can break your heart—but that only makes being on the wrong side of that line ever more painful. For Margaret, life was never so easy, expectations were lowered. The straws had been drawn, and hers came out short, and forever after, everything she held close would be at risk from those who had won the lottery.

The cat came over and nestled against one of her strong calves. She kicked it away.

"He follows her around like a pet," she said. "He does her bidding. He laughs at her jokes—not even jokes, she doesn't make jokes. She makes her world-weary little comments, and he chuckles like a fool. Sometimes he stalks after her through the night and spies on her. And other times he does whatever she asks of him. He has become her lapdog."

"So you sent the letters," I said.

"I couldn't help myself. The urge was uncontrollable. It was either write the letters or shoot her dead."

"Good choice, then. What about the drugs?"

"What drugs?"

"Clarence. How did the drugs start?"

"Clarence? Drugs?"

"No drugs?"

"Of course not. What are you talking about?"

"Nothing," I said. "I guess I'm confused. But why did you write to her, why not to him?"

"Because it wasn't his fault, Mr. Carl. She could see it happening, she could have done something about it if she wanted to. But she didn't want to. She's a siren, that's her to the bone, Clarence couldn't help himself."

"No, I suppose not."

And I couldn't help myself either, as I barreled through the dark, leafy streets of Chestnut Hill on the way to her house. There were three cars in the driveway, two I recognized: the Dennistons' blue BMW and a boxy black Volvo. I had seen the Volvo before, at that very spot. It was Clarence's car. Why should I have been surprised?

I knocked at the door and knocked some more. When Gwen opened it a crack, I pushed it open wider.

"Where is she?" I said.

"Mr. Carl, you shouldn't be here now," said Gwen in a hush, barring my way with one strong arm.

"I need to see her."

"Mr. Carl, please."

"Let him in, Gwen," came a voice I recognized from inside the house. "It's not a party without Victor."

I looked around Gwen, and there he was, Clarence Swift himself, bent aggressively forward, hands rubbing one the other beneath his insincere smile.

"It looks like I came just in time," I said.

"Your timing couldn't be more perfect," he said.

"Where is she?"

"In the den," he said. "Hurry. She's waiting for you."

"Go home, Mr. Carl," said Gwen.

I gently took hold of her arm and pushed it away. "It's all right, Gwen. I can handle Clarence."

"It's not him you should be worried about," she said, but by the time she said it, I was already past her.

"I figured out most of it," I said to Clarence, who waited unflinchingly as I approached. "The whole deal you created with your pal Wren Denniston to steal Gregor Trocek's money. Why you plotted against and killed your old friend Wren. How you've been working hard to frame me for your murder."

"I was right about you from the start, Victor. You are wondrously clever. Only a fool would underestimate you."

"But what I don't understand, Clarence, what I'll never understand, is how you figure a pathetic wretch like you will end up with Julia."

"Don't you worry, I know my place."

"And I know mine—between her and you."

"You want to know a secret, Victor?" said Clarence.

"Sure," I said as I stopped right in front of him.

He leaned close and whispered. "You're not good enough for her."

"We'll see about that," I said, and then I brushed past him, toward the den. I called out, "Julia?"

"Victor?"

I had wanted to hear that sweet lilt of pleasant surprise. *I'm so glad you came.* But that's not what I heard in the voice. What I heard instead was, *What the hell are you doing here?* But what the hell did it matter? I was there, so was Julia, and maybe, for once, a piece of the truth would be in the room with us.

"Julia," I said as I pushed open the door to the den. "I've got news."

And there she was, in her chair, in her corner, wearing pants this time, and a loose white shirt, rolled up at the cuffs. Her shirt was buttoned, her hair back, her face scrubbed, she had been crying. She stood up when she saw me and stepped forward on bare feet. So captivated was I by the sight of her that it took me a moment to register that there were others in the room, two others.

My head swiveled back and forth. Hanratty leaned against

the wall behind me. Sims was sitting on the red leather couch by the fireplace. They both seemed quite pleased to see me.

"What are you clowns doing here?" I said.

"We were invited," said Sims. "By Mr. Swift."

"I told them Mrs. Denniston was ready to talk," said Clarence Swift from behind me.

"Talk?" I said. "About what?"

"About her husband's murder, of course," said Clarence.

"I told them, Victor," said Julia as she stepped up to me. Her arms were stretched wide before she wrapped them around my neck. "I told them everything."

"You have the right to remain silent," said Hanratty.

"Really?" I said.

"No."

"I didn't think so."

We were back in the Roundhouse, back in the green interrogation room with its familiar mirror and familiar dead-rodent scent. But the room seemed so small now that I found myself struggling to breathe. It was no longer a room, it was more like a closet, or a box, and I was stuck inside, and the lid was slamming shut.

I had been driven to police headquarters from Julia's house by Hanratty, who kept his impressive jaw clenched the whole ride, but at least he didn't hit me, which was a step in the right direction in our relationship. Next we would be doing the foxtrot together on *Dancing with the Fuzz*. Sims took my car back to the Roundhouse. I expect he searched the glove compartment without a warrant while he drove. Maybe he found the twenty I'd lost in there a couple of weeks ago. If he did, that was twenty I was out, but I had more bitter things to think about, like being betrayed by the woman I thought I loved.

"Anything you say can and will be used against you in a court of law," said Hanratty.

"Brigitte Bardot," I said.

"Huh?"

"Anita Ekberg. Sophia Loren."

"He's quoting Dylan," said Sims, without looking up from the file he was staring at in that room. "He thinks he's being clever, but as usual he's being fatuous instead."

"Do you really think I'm overweight?" I said.

"You have the right to speak to an attorney, and to have an attorney present during any questioning," said Hanratty. "If you cannot afford a lawyer, one will be provided for you at government expense."

"Okay," I said.

"Okay what?" said Hanratty.

"You can hire me a lawyer."

"We are reading you your Miranda warnings, Victor," said Sims, "because we don't want you to be under any misconceptions. You are now an official suspect in the murder of Dr. Wren Denniston."

"At least I'm an official something. Do I get a badge?"

"Shut up," said Hanratty.

"Now, see," I said, "why do you need all this Miranda stuff when that's the only advice a suspect really needs. Shut up. Thank you, Detective, for that sage advice. I think that's just what I'll do."

"Gregor Trocek," said Sims.

I rubbed my tongue hard across the inside of my cheek, thought about what Julia could possibly have told them. She'd said everything. And more, I'd bet.

"What about him?" I said.

"What is your relationship?"

"We don't have a relationship."

"Early supper at an exclusive Spanish restaurant. Friendly drives around town. Let me show you this." He picked a photograph out of his file and tossed it to me. Gregor and me in the backseat of Gregor's Jaguar.

"Nice car," I said.

"Looks like a relationship to me."

"I'm not that easy."

I looked at Sims for a moment and tried to think it through. I had three options to deal with what Julia had done to me. I could lie, I could obfuscate, or I could tell the truth. As a lawyer, of course, I was partial to the first two. Lying and obfuscating are crucial tools of the profession, along with a shameless ability to overcharge. But in that room, with my neck suddenly on the line, I sensed that something else was required, something closer to the third option, maybe not the whole third option, but the third option nonetheless.

"Gregor Trocek is looking for a large amount of his money that is missing," I said.

"How much?" said Sims.

"One point seven million dollars."

"In what form was the money?" said Sims. "A check? A wire?"

"Cash," I said.

"Cash," said Sims, nodding, as if none of this was a revelation, as if one point seven million dollars in cash floating around was as natural as the sunrise. Hanratty looked at me and then at Sims with a puzzled expression.

"Trocek thought I could help him find the money," I said. "That was why he treated me to dinner and drove me around town. The latter at knifepoint, I might add."

"Why would he come to you?" said Sims.

"First, he thought I had an in with Mrs. Denniston and that she might know something, but he was wrong. Whatever she knows, she won't tell me. Then, because he had received a tip that I might be the guy with the money."

"And are you?"

"Would I be here if I was? The tip was as bogus as the ones you've been receiving about me. But I know where they're coming from now."

"From who?" said Hanratty.

"Clarence Swift."

"Mrs. Denniston's lawyer?"

"That's right."

"What are your future plans with Mrs. Denniston?" said Sims.

"I don't know. Before, I hoped things would work out between us."

"Before the murder?"

"Before that, yes. And before tonight, when she betrayed me like a snake."

"Again," said Sims.

"Thank you for that, Detective. Before she betrayed me like a snake again."

"Did you ever tell Mrs. Denniston"—he looked at a notepad sitting flat on the desk and then read the words—"that 'if it wasn't for her husband, everything could be perfect'?"

"I might have. I said a lot of things. I was trying to get her pants off."

"Did you ever tell her you both needed to get him out of your lives?"

"I was thinking more in the way of divorce."

"Do you remember when we mentioned a Miles Cave to you?"

"Yes."

"Have you ever met him?"

"No."

"We're not surprised. As best we can tell, he doesn't exist."

"Exactly."

Sims glanced up from the file and smiled. "There was apparently a partnership between Gregor Trocek and Miles Cave. But it appears that Miles Cave is a pseudonym for someone else. Do you have any idea for whom?"

"I don't think it was a pseudonym for anyone. I think he never existed in the first place. It was just a way for Wren Denniston to steal Gregor Trocek's money."

"Cash money," said Hanratty.

"Yes. Doesn't the word 'cash' make it sound that much more juicy?"

"Interesting theory," said Sims as he took out a paper from his file and slipped it across the table to me, "except for this."

I felt the shivers even before I saw it, because I knew what it was. The letter. From Miles Cave. A copy, of course, because the original I had stolen from the file and burned in my sink. But a copy in the hands of the cops was enough. I hunched my shoulders as the room grew smaller.

"It has your address," said Hanratty. "And the signature looks suspiciously like the signature you put on your affidavit the first night we met. And funny thing, the original is missing."

"It seems," said Sims, "that the original was in a file you were examining at the Inner Circle offices. It's a good thing they made this copy, isn't it?"

"Good thing," I said.

"Do you know what happened to the original?"

"Yes. I took it."

"So you admit it?" said Hanratty.

"Yes."

"Do you know what obstruction of justice is?"

"Trying to keep a lie from infecting an investigation is obstruction of something," I said, "but not justice. I'm being set up."

"You didn't steal the letter because you wrote it," said Sims. "You stole it because someone else wrote it."

"I took it because I knew I was being framed and I wasn't sure you guys were sharp enough to see the truth."

"That's a nice argument for the judge," said Hanratty, "but it won't stop us from banging you away right now until everything else is cleaned up."

"You're looking in the wrong direction," I said. "I'm just an innocent dupe."

"I buy the dupe part," said Hanratty.

"You need to find the guy who drafted the agreement between Gregor Trocek and the mythical Miles Cave, the guy who has been throwing out false tips and manufacturing false evidence, the guy who had the most to gain from Wren Denniston's death, the guy who committed the murder."

"And who is that?" said Sims.

"Clarence Swift," I said.

"He is so full of it," said Hanratty. "Look, his tongue is turning brown."

"Why would Clarence Swift kill his best friend?" said Sims.

"For love," I said. "He's got the hots for Mrs. Denniston, always has. And for money, Gregor's money. He knows where it is and had to get rid of Wren Denniston to keep it."

"Love and money," said Sims.

"That's right," I said.

"Love and money. That's your answer."

"What, you don't like it?"

"No, we like it fine," said Sims, closing the file and smiling up at Hanratty. "It's like clockwork, isn't it?"

"Happens every time," said Hanratty.

"What happens every time?" I said.

"A little psychological tic," said Sims. "In the distorted mind of a murderer, the reason for the killing becomes so prominent he can't imagine any other. So whenever be tries to blame someone else, he always imparts the very motive that drove him to kill."

"Love and money," said Hanratty. "That's why you did it, isn't it, baby?"

"I didn't do it. Clarence Swift did it. I'm sure of it."

"He's sure of it," said Sims.

"He's a sure one, he is," said Hanratty.

Sims took another photograph from the file and spun it toward me. It was grainy, black and white, a distorted picture of Clarence Swift, with his high forehead and bow tie. He was looking down, fiddling with something. It was a photograph from an ATM, with the date and time imprinted. The date was the very date of Wren Denniston's murder, the time was 8:37 P.M.

"This was taken in Center City. Based on what the medical examiner concluded as to the time of death, there wasn't enough time for Clarence Swift to have made it from the ATM to the Denniston house to have committed the murder."

I stared at the photograph, at the date and time. "There must be something wrong. This can't be right."

"Oh, it's right, baby," said Hanratty. "We checked and double-checked. The bank's records are precise."

"He's in the clear," said Sims. "Which leaves us with you."

"Love and money," said Hanratty.

"When you get right down to it," said Sims, "what else is there? Except maybe just money."

The photograph didn't make any sense, it couldn't be right. Clarence was the enemy, I knew that with complete certainty, which meant he must have killed Wren Denniston. But if the picture was true, then it hadn't been him. So who could it be? Not Julia, she had an alibi. Not Margaret, because the motive was all wrong. Not Clarence and not Gwen and not me. So who?

I didn't have an answer, but suddenly I realized I had a clue. And a question. And someone who might have an answer, if I could only get out of that damn closet so I could ask him.

"Let me book him now," said Hanratty. "He admitted to taking the letter. That's clear obstruction. We can hold him forty-eight hours just on that. It will keep him from slopping around in our evidence until we get enough to finish him off."

Sims looked back at the file, rearranged some papers, closed it, gently clasped his hands together. "That's all, Victor," he said. "Thank you for coming around."

"That's it?" I said.

"That's it," said Sims.

"As always," I said, standing quickly, "it was as pleasant as a root canal."

"What are you doing?" said Hanratty.

"Keep out of trouble, Victor," said Sims.

"Wait a second," said Hanratty. "This isn't procedure."

Sims reached into his pocket, pulled out my jangle of keys, slid it across the table. "Your car's parked in the back lot."

Hanratty strode to the table, leaned over Sims like he was leaning over a suspect. "You're making a mistake," he said. "Either he mucks up the evidence or he runs. My bet is he runs, but either way we're screwed."

"You're not going to muck up the evidence or run, are you, Victor?"

"No, sir," I lied.

"Let me talk to the captain before we let him walk," said Hanratty. "Give me a few minutes at least."

"Toodle-oo, Victor," said Sims. "Don't leave town."

I didn't hear what Hanratty said next, because by the time he could continue his angry complaint, I had grabbed my keys and was out the door.

31

FRIDAY

This is how you get to Washington, D.C. Scrounge around for signatures on your nominating petition, suck up big-time for money, hire a consultant to tell you what to believe, film yourself walking the street among a crowd of actors, declare your belief in God, hire a detective to catch the incumbent fornicating. And then, if your moral fiber is determined to be deficient enough and the national trend breaks your way and the detective catches the incumbent fornicating with a goat, maybe, just maybe, you might make it to our nation's capital.

Or you could just take I-95 south.

I was scrunched down among the candy wrappers and empty cans in the backseat of a 1973 Camaro, taking the easy way into Washington, D.C. Or what would have been the easy way had the Camaro in which I was scrunched down contained a working set of shock absorbers. It was dead early in the morning, the radio was blasting hip-hop, the car smelled of reefer and spilt beer, Baltimore was in our rearview mirror, and we were going way too fast down the Baltimore-Washington Parkway.

"You want to slow down a bit?" I said.

"Just shaking the tails, bo," said Derek, in the front passenger seat. "It not just your ass on the line on this one, it my ass, too, this don't work out slick and easy."

"But getting stopped by the cops on the expressway won't help the cause," I said.

"Don't be worrying about that. They won't be catching us, not with a 355 under this hood."

The car lurched forward as it raced south.

"We're not going to outrun the cops," I said, "not with me in the car."

"You're not that heavy. And things work out, we won't have to," said Derek as he lifted a small black box with a wire and a stand. "We got radar."

"I feel so much better," I said.

It was no mystery how I ended up in the back of that Camaro. As soon as I got out of the Roundhouse, I had called Derek on his cell. "I need to talk to Jamison," I said. You remember Jamison, the drug dealer who had been selling to Julia the night of her husband's murder. Why did I need to see Jamison? Because suddenly, in the midst of my betrayal by Julia, I started wondering whom she had betrayed me for.

With the normal vixen, in penal danger for the murder of her husband, you'd expect any betrayal to be for the purpose of saving herself. But, though you might call me a fool, I couldn't believe it about Julia. She simply wasn't built like that. I first thought she might have been manipulated into it by Clarence Swift, and though that still might have been what happened, it wasn't to protect Clarence. No, she was betraying me to protect someone else. But for whom would Julia throw me splat under the train? That was the question. And I didn't have an answer, but I did have a clue.

What had she been most anxious to hide when the police first came looking for her? What piece of information had she been adamant that I keep secret? She'd been buying drugs from Jamison, but not for herself and not for her husband and not for Clarence Swift. Then for whom? I wondered. And the only one I knew who might have an answer was Jamison.

So I had called Derek and we had arranged things. First, so late at night it was early in the morning, I had picked up Derek in his neighborhood. Then, as I drove down a narrow street in North Philly, a van had pulled out right behind us. The van veered left and stopped quickly, blocking the roadway, as I kept going. I followed Derek's directions right and then left and then right again, until I pulled the car into a rather deserted back alley.

"Park in there, bo," said Derek.

"Next to the Camaro?" I said, indicating a sharp blue muscle car with broad white stripes on the hood.

"That's the one," he said. "And whatever you do, on fear of your life, don't scratch it."

I parked next to the Camaro. Derek climbed out of my car, and so did I.

"What now?" I said.

"Get in," he said, pulling open the Camaro's passenger door.

"I only want to talk to him, Derek. The hell with all this cloak-and-dagger stuff. What about a phone call or something?"

"You said you just got out of the Roundhouse, right?"

"That's what I said."

"And you think they been following you."

"That's right."

"And they might be following you now."

"Okay, I get you. I'll get in the Camaro."

I was about to slide into the front seat when Derek leaned

down and pulled a lever, which collapsed the front seat forward. "In the back, bo."

"I'm the client."

"The detective is always in front. That's the first thing they teach you in detective school."

"You haven't gone to detective school."

"What does that matter?"

I thought about that for a moment and then climbed into the back. Derek released the seat, slid into it, and closed the door. Together we waited. And waited. Waited until I saw the belt buckle of a giant in the side window. Then the giant leaned down to look in the car. Huge shoulders, tattooed arms, porkpie hat.

Antoine.

"You don't follow no hint, now, do you?" said Antoine before he opened the door and climbed into the car. He turned around and leaned menacingly over the bucket seat. "What the blazes I tell you, mon?"

"To leave it alone," I said. "But I can't, not anymore. I need to talk to Jamison."

"You were being followed, for sure."

"I figured."

"Same Johnny Crow who came to Barnabas's place. What he want?"

"He wants me. Wants to slam me in jail for the rest of my life."

"And that is our problem why?"

"Because I still owe Derek money."

"He's got a point there," said Derek. "He does owe me money. More after today."

"I been given the all-okay for you to see that bwoy. And I got something myself I need be telling him, too. But no calls, no numbers. We'll meet him in person. I'll take you."

"You will? That's actually nice of you, Antoine."

"Nothing nice about it," said Antoine, turning around to face forward.

"Remember our arrangement?" said Derek. "Forty an hour?"

"It was thirty."

"It was, but not no more. This be dangerous now, running from cops, dealing with fugitives. I've had to jack the rates. Forty an hour."

"Okay."

"Plus expenses."

"Right."

"Well, Antoine here, right now he's the expense."

"I get the feeling this is going to be a costly trip. Where are we going?"

"You hungry, mon?" said Antoine.

"Not really."

"It don't matter," he said as he fired the ignition. "You still buying the breakfast. I know a wan irie place. You like grits?"

"No."

"You'll be liking these."

It was a long drive for a plate of grits, but Antoine was right. I did like them, lighter than I would expect, thick with butter. And I liked the biscuits with gravy and the spiced stewed apples that went along with my two eggs over. The place was narrow and old, built of stone, with open ductwork on the ceiling, steam sweating off the windows, and hot sauce on the tables. There were four of us sitting at a small booth with a rickety Formica table between us, the table laden with plates smeared with grease and filled with our breakfasts.

The waitress in her maroon apron ambled over with a pot. "You boys want more coffee?"

"Sure we do," said Derek. "Hey, this place is famous, isn't it?"

"Didn't you see the sign outside?"

"I did, yes, but just because the sign says it, don't mean it's so."

"Look around," she said, pointing at the photographs that ringed the diner. "We get politicians here, singers, movie stars."

"And now, best of all, you got Derek," he said.

"Who is Derek?"

"You're talking to him."

"Now, ain't that special?" said the waitress as she poured coffee into one of the purple plastic coffee cups. "Tell the *Post* to hold the presses."

"You want to take my picture, put it up with the others?" said Derek. "I'll sign it and everything."

"Your face is going to have to stay right where it is, honey," she said. "We can't be scaring the customers' appetites. You boys need anything else, just give me a holler."

"She wants me," said Derek after the waitress had left.

Antoine shook his head and turned to Jamison, who was sitting quietly beside him. "When you coming back, bwoy?"

"Don't know," said Jamison. He was dressed in baggy jeans and a T-shirt, more skateboarder than gangster. In the bright lights of the Florida Avenue Grill, he seemed younger than I had remembered. "My aunt's been bugging me to come down and live with her for a while. And I didn't like the cops sniffing for me like that."

"Take your time," said Antoine, "but J.T. wanted me a tell you them dues is up."

"I'm not paying my dues, me having to run like that."

"He says you still under his right arm, so you got to still be paying."

"Hell if I'm paying. Tell him I'm out. My aunt wants to put me in the school down here. Says it's a pretty good school, they got computers and stuff."

"J.T. don't want to hear about school."

"I knew something like this was going down. That's why I met you here and not at my aunt's house." He balled up a napkin, threw it atop his eggs, stood. "You're a message boy now, Antoine? After all the crap you been blowing out your ass, that's what you become? Well, here's a message back to J.T. Tell him I'm out. Tell him if I'm paying dues, I'm paying them local, and he'll have to fight through the protection I got wrapped down here to get to me."

"Well, lookie this," said Antoine, a smile breaking out. "Bwoy's all grown up. Sit down and finish them eggs. Victor's got some questions."

"What are you going to tell J.T.?"

"I'll tell him what you say. That you off to school and giving up the business. Don't make a liar of me, now, or it won't be J.T. you be worrying about."

Jamison bobbed his head a bit and then sat down again. He took the napkin off his food, shoveled a forkful of eggs into his mouth. "All right," he said to me, "what the hell do you want to know?"

"Remember the woman whose picture I showed you? The one who you said was buying heroin from you?"

"Course I remember. That's the reason I was chased down to here in the first place."

"So the question I have, Jamison, is this. Do you have any idea who she was buying it for?"

He looked at me for a moment, then down at his eggs.

"Go ahead and tell the mon," said Antoine.

"Another one of my customers," said Jamison. "A pretty boy with a ferocious habit. Whenever she came, she bought some for him and paid what he owed. We would sell him on credit whatever he wanted, because she was always good for it."

"Do you have a name?" I said.

"We called him Sweets," said Jamison, "because of the way he looked, but that wasn't his real name."

"What was his real name?"

"Terry," said Jamison. "His name was Terry."

We were back on the road, Antoine and Derek and I, heading farther south on I-95 in that blue Camaro, driving deep into Julia's past. What was going on was so obvious I should have figured it out before. It wasn't like she hadn't been telling me over and over what she was doing and why. She was begging me to understand, but I guess I was so blinded by my own lost love that I hadn't been able to see hers.

Terry. As in Terrence. *You should have seen him then,* she had said. *He was Romeo in his bones,* she had said. Now all I had to do was find him.

We were still about thirty miles from where we were headed, just rounding Fredericksburg, when my phone rang. It was noisy in the Camaro—a car built for speed, not comfort—so I pressed the phone hard into my ear.

"Victor, where are you?"

It took me a moment, within the din of the backseat, to identify the voice, but finally I did. Sims.

"What do you want?" I said.

"We need to talk."

"I think I've talked enough. You've had me down to the Roundhouse three times. Next time you want to chat, bring a warrant."

"That can be arranged, I assure you," said Sims. "But maybe we should talk in an unofficial capacity. Where are you?"

"You tell me. You're following me, aren't you?"

"I was, until you arranged to lose me. Not the most innocent of actions. You are the chief suspect in a murder case. And I must say the evidence is lining up quite neatly against you."

"I'm being framed."

"Yes, you've told us. By Mr. Swift, who I don't think could frame a poster, better yet a cookie as smart as you. But I could be convinced to see it your way, Victor. I could turn my attentions in another direction. I am more flexible than you might imagine."

"Oh, I doubt that. I think this—" I stopped talking. "What is best is—" I stopped talking again.

"Victor, you're breaking up."

"Am I? That's a shame because—"

"Remember that I told you not to leave town."

"I remember."

"There will be costs if you have discarded my advice."

"I'll be in touch," I said. Then I hung up. Then I turned off the phone.

"Who was that?" said Derek.

"Johnny Crow," I said. "How much longer?"

"About twenty minutes now," said Antoine. "Then we have to ask."

"Won't be a problem," I said. "Everyone knows where the high school is."

Just north of Ashland, Virginia, after we had left the interstate, Antoine pulled us into a convenience store. The Sav-A-Minit. Which looked amazingly like a Git-n-Go, or a Loaf 'N Jug, or an

XtraMart, not to mention the famous K collection of the Kuik-E-Mart, the Kum & Go, and the Kwik Trip. They must pay people to come up with names for these things, but they don't pay them enough. What they should call them is the Over-Priced, or the Beer 'N Bellies, or the ever popular Krap-to-Go.

"Let me get out," I said. "I'll ask."

"Nah, mon, I take care of this," said Antoine. "You-all want anything?"

"We-all?" said Derek.

"Need to be speaking the patois down here, you want a be getting anywhere."

"I wouldn't worry about the patois, I was you."

"You don't think I can fit into this cracker town, mon?"

"Hardly."

"Just be giving me some money," said Antoine.

"Are you rehearsing your lines?" said Derek. "What, you going to rob the Sav-A-Minit, get away with a buck and a half?"

"Be quiet, Derek," I said as I pulled out my wallet and handed Antoine a twenty.

"Back in flash," said Antoine as he climbed out of the Camaro.

"They're going to be chasing him with pitchforks and torches," said Derek.

"You ever been out of Philly, Derek?"

"I got a cousin in Chicago."

"You visit him?"

"Why would I want to do something like that?"

"You should maybe travel a bit, see the world, broaden your horizons."

"My horizons, they broad enough."

"I don't think so. Things aren't what you might imagine outside of the city. People are pretty much okay all over."

"For you, maybe, with your suit and all."

"If that's what you think, then get one of your own. Probably cost less than those sneakers."

"Yours, maybe. But nah, man, can you see me in a rig like that?"

"Sure. Why not?"

"Because I got style," he said.

Antoine came ambling out of the Sav-A-Minit without pitchforks and torches in his wake. He held a plastic bag loaded down with cans and junk. He climbed into the Camaro and tossed a Coke to me in the backseat and another to Derek.

"We need a keep going straight and then turn to the right," he said. "It not so hard. John Paul Jones High School. Strange territory, hey, Derek?"

"I got my degree," said Derek as he popped open his can. "Still, I didn't need to show up every day to know they wasn't nothing there they could teach me. So what we doing in a high school, bo?"

"Not we," I said. "Just me. I'll take care of it from here on in. You guys can head out to the park or something. I'll call you when I need you."

"What are you going to be doing?"

"First I thought I'd pee, seeing as sitting in the back of this car has near ruptured my bladder," I said. "Then I'm going to start a discussion about Shakespeare."

"You just can't wander the halls of a high school willy-nilly anymore," said Mrs. Larrup, vice principal for discipline at John Paul Jones.

When she had discovered me in the hallway on my way to the library without a pass, she hauled me off to her office. It made me feel seventeen again. And with her short gray hair and meaty forearms, Mrs. Larrup had my full attention.

"I don't care if you are a lawyer," she said. "In fact, that's a strike against you in my book."

"You've had a bad experience, I expect."

"More than one lawyer has tried to tell me how to do my job. Let's see them handle fifteen hundred teenagers and their dramas."

"Which is precisely why I'm here. I represent a student."

She pulled back at that, her lips setting into two sharp lines of discontent.

"A former student," I said. "One who only has wonderful memories of John Paul Jones High School and the sterling faculty and administration that work here."

"Really," she said, brightening considerably.

"Yes. Her name is Julia Denniston, but that's her married name. As a student she was Julia Crenshaw. She graduated about twelve or thirteen years ago."

"I remember Ms. Crenshaw," she said. "How could I forget, after what happened?"

"What are we talking about? What happened, exactly?"

"Oh, I'm sorry, Mr. Carl, I'm not at liberty to disclose these things."

"That's all right, I'll just ask Julia. What I've come for, actually, is to find someone else. A classmate, I believe. He was in the school play with her. Do you remember when they performed *Romeo and Juliet*?"

"Oh, yes," she said, with a heavy sigh. "That was it. A disaster."

"Really?"

"Sometimes, in the midst of great challenges, our students rise to the occasion. And sometimes, I'm sorry to say, they do not."

"I'm looking for the student who played Romeo. His name was Terrence, I believe."

"Terrence Tipton."

"Yes, that's it. Terrence Tipton. Do you have any idea where he might be?"

"No. None."

"Does his family still live around here?"

"I don't know. He had a brother who went through here before him, but Terry was the last of the Tiptons in this school, which was a relief, actually."

"Really?"

"Yes. Franklin Tipton was just your basic troublemaker, problems with his studies, fights, drinking, the usual hardhead who is just putting in time. But Terry was a—" She stopped her reverie, looked at me with the steely gaze one gives to a student about to pick up a week's detention, or to a lawyer asking one question too many. "I don't think there is anything more I should say, especially since, by your own admission, you don't represent Mr. Tipton."

"You're right, and you're being quite prudent. The drama teacher who put on Julia's play, is she still around?"

"That was Mr. Mayhew's production. His only one, thankfully. He retired a few years ago."

"Do you know where he lives?"

"I'm not prepared to disclose that."

"That's fine, ma'am. Thank you for your time."

"You're going to find him and talk to him anyway."

"That's right."

"I'll tell him you're coming. You know, we're very proud of our alumni. We have state senators, authors. One of our students played for a few years in the NBA. How is Julia doing?"

"Not so well," I said.

———

"It was a disaster," said Jeremiah Mayhew. "I should never have gone ahead with it. I always hated that play. Too tricky."

"What do you mean, tricky?" I said.

"If I had to do Shakespeare, I would have done *Henry IV, Part One*. The fight at the end, big cheers when Prince Hal rams Hotspur through with his sword. Blood and gore and victory, that's what the people want. But Mrs. Pincer had already decided on *Romeo and Juliet*. The booklets had been ordered and construction on the scenery begun. And so *Romeo and Juliet* it was."

"Then what went wrong?"

"Everything," he said. "Every damn thing. A play like that, with a romance at the core, it all depends on the chemistry. You got to have chemistry. And you can't fake it. It's either there or it's not. And with those two we had it. But when you get down to it, last thing you want with kids like that is chemistry. What else could you expect but trouble?"

Jeremiah Mayhew was not what I expected of a drama teacher. He was burly and bald, he wore a T-shirt and shorts and sneakers with his sanitary socks pulled high. I was surprised there wasn't a whistle around his neck, and I suppose he was, too. He had been the football coach at John Paul Jones High School and a health teacher at the time of Julia's *Romeo and Juliet*. But he'd acted a bit in college, had made that known to the principal, and so when Mrs. Pincer, the regular drama teacher, took ill, he was recruited to take over the spring production.

"Against his will," said his wife, sitting demurely beside him on the sofa. "But the team didn't have a very good season that fall."

"We stunk," said Mayhew.

"And there was rumbling about maybe getting a new coach."

"Like Vince Lombardi would have made a difference. We were small but slow. Marshall, Lee-Davis—they all ran right over us."

"And so when they asked him to take on the play, he thought he had no choice but to step up."

"I wanted it to be the best damn production Ashland had ever seen," said Mayhew. "That's just the way I am. And we had a chance. Right away I saw it. In football one great player can make a team, and it's the same in the theater. And we had the one great player. The Crenshaw girl. When she was onstage, you couldn't take your eyes off her. It was just a matter of finding the chemistry. I wanted Sherman, my quarterback, to be Romeo. He was handsome enough, but there wasn't an ounce of chemistry between our Juliet and Sherman. The truth was, Sherman was an oaf, on and off the field. But we found our chemistry, yes we did. With Tipton."

"Terrence Tipton," I said.

"That's right. I didn't like him much, one of those sensitive types, you know what I mean. He was too good for the school or the town. Let his hair grow and pouted all the time. Like he knew something the rest of us didn't. But when he read with her, there were sparks. Undeniable. So I made a mistake and I cast him."

"In the rehearsals they were quite wonderful," said Mrs. Mayhew. "The rest of the show, well, they were kids. Do you remember Sherman as Mercutio?"

"It was like the words turned to fudge in his mouth."

"With the rest you could see the seams. But whenever Romeo and Juliet were onstage, there was magic. It was so touching. Young love."

"That was the problem," said Mayhew. "The fools fell in love. And that always screws up everything."

"Jeremiah."

He reached out a hand to his wife, gently cupped the back of her neck. "Almost everything," he said.

"So what went wrong?" I asked again.

"They did."

"For a while you could see the sparks," said Mrs. Mayhew. "And then something happened, and they could barely look at each other. Something had gone drastically wrong, and it showed. In every gesture, every word."

"I took them aside, both of them, and told them to suck it up. To make it work. It's called acting, I told them. For the good of the play, they had to make it work."

"They tried," said Mrs. Mayhew. "Things seemed to get better, until opening night."

"Worst night of my life," said Mr. Mayhew.

"Oh, Jeremiah."

"It was. If I had to do another, it would have killed me. Thankfully, Mrs. Pincer returned in the fall, and I went back to teaching health. But that wasn't the end of it."

"He still blames the play," said Mrs. Mayhew.

"Course I do. First comes the losing season, then that disaster of a play, and next thing you know, they hire a new football coach up from North Carolina and I'm coaching weight football at the junior-high level."

"*Romeo and Juliet*," said Mrs. Mayhew. "I suppose there's a reason it's a tragedy."

"Left with nothing but to teach string beans how to block. Damn," said Mr. Mayhew. "I always hated that play."

"God, it was funny," said Frankie Tipton. "I didn't want to go, actually. It was our mom made me, but I'm glad she did. Funniest thing I ever saw. I still wake up in the middle of the night laughing about it."

Frankie Tipton was a hard-lived thirty-five, sitting on a lawn chair atop a cement slab behind his house. He wore jeans and boots, a black T-shirt, a trucker's hat with a logo that matched the beer in his right hand. He lifted the can, sucked down half, showed me the label. "You want?"

"No thanks," I said.

"Too early for your kind, I suppose." I was sitting on a chair beside him. We were both facing the long weeds in his backyard. He turned his head and eyed my suit. "Where'd you say you was from?"

"I didn't, but I'm from Philadelphia."

"Ah, sure you are. What kind of trouble is he in now?"

"I don't know."

"That's convenient, because I don't care."

He took a sip of his beer, looked at it, took a longer draft.

"I never liked the son of a bitch," he said. "Even when he was a baby. He was sick when he was born, the doctors were running back and forth, Mom was crying on and on. He was grabbing all the attention even then. I could tell right there he was trouble. And I was right, wasn't I? He killed our mother. The worrying about him after he left, the asking for money. And she always gave it, like a fool. I told her it wouldn't do no good, but she couldn't help herself. Every time the phone rang, she was afraid to answer it. Thought it would have been word that he was dead. Too bad it wasn't."

"Was this your mom's house?"

"Yeah."

"It's nice."

"It's a shithole, but I've been fixing it up some, when I can. Putting in a new bathroom upstairs. The kitchen needs something, too."

"You might want to mow the lawn."

"Yeah, as soon as I fix the mower, which I got to tell you is not next on my list."

"So tell me about the play."

"Well, it all come about because he was in love, he said. Love. It was that skinny little dark-haired girl in the play he was all mooning over. Writing poetry, singing sad songs with that guitar. Love. Like that was ever going anywhere, the way he was. But first things was working out and then they wasn't. He never said what had happened, but it wasn't no mystery. And the story was out about the girl and that quarterback and what they was doing backstage."

"Sherman?"

"That's the one. Hell, it wasn't going be the last time he lost a girl, I tell you that. But still, the sadness, it was coming off him in waves. Far as I was concerned, she didn't have tits enough to get so cut up over, but that might have been the thing he liked, the way he was."

"You said that twice," I said.

"What?"

" 'The way he was.' What do you mean, the way he was?"

He eyed me a bit. "That's family business, isn't it? And no damn business of yours."

"Okay. You were telling about the funny play."

"Right. So the day of the play, he comes to me and tells me he can't do it. I didn't think nothing of it, you know, it was just a stupid play, but Mom was so looking forward to it. So I told him, hell, just drink a few beers and it won't be no problem. I set him up with a couple six-packs and that was that. I done my brotherly duty.

"So it's showtime, right, and I'm sitting there next to my mom, and he comes on, and there's all this applause, and he starts talking this nonsense, and I got to tell you, he didn't look so good. He didn't look so good at all. Like they had put green makeup on him. And then, not too far in, there's the dark-haired girl on this balcony. She's in this pretty blue dress, and there's a ladder leading to it. So she's talking to, like, no one, and he's talking from behind this bush, and then he starts climbing the ladder. But not so good. Halfway up, his foot slips, and he bangs his head, and everyone starts laughing. Like it's part of the play. Though it's not, I can tell. But he keeps climbing. And she says something, something about stumbling, and everyone laughs again. And he says something about love and wings or something stupid like that, and they lean forward to kiss. And they do. And then he stops. And pulls back and wavers. Like a thin stalk in the wind. And then he leans forward over the balcony, and the son of a bitch, he throws up, on her, yes he does, pukes right onto her fancy blue dress."

"Jesus."

"Yeah, I told you it was funny. Best play I ever saw. And she can't help herself—what's she going to do—she pushes him away. And he loses his balance, and his arms are swinging in these crazy big circles, and next thing you know, he's falling backward. In the air. Falling, falling with a thud right onto that fake bush.

"Everyone is just stunned for a bit, and then they all start laughing again. And I'm laughing, laughing so hard the tears are coming. And next thing you know, he's up and jumping off the stage and running right down the middle and out of the auditorium. And then the curtain, it just drops, right on top of some people who come out onstage to make sure he's all right. And that was the play."

"Did they stop it?"

"No, they finished it, with that stupid football coach reading out of the book with his shiny bald head while the Juliet said her lines with a T-shirt over her dress. From what I hear, first there was laughter, then silence, and then the place emptied out. But I didn't see it, because when Terry left, I went out with my mom to try to find him."

"Did you?"

"Sure. Right here. Sitting outside, staring. Like a zombie. He wouldn't say a thing. Mom tried to talk to him and gave up, went inside. I just laughed and told him to forget about it, that it was nothing to get shook about. And then I lit up a bone and handed it to him."

"He take it?"

"What do you think?"

"What happened afterward?"

"Nothing, really, he just kept smoking. And not only that night. It was every night. But he was mainly stealing from my stash, so I had to cut him off. Told him to buy his own, which he did. I even set him up with Rupert, who'd been selling to me. So he was taken care of. And he actually got back together with that girl for a while, believe it or not. But it didn't stop him smoking, or from drifting away. He would disappear for a few days, and then a few weeks, and then he disappeared altogether. Just up and left. Never did finish school. A little later the calls started coming, from all over, California, Arizona, all the time hitting Mom up for money."

"And now he's in Philly."

"Did I say that?"

"Pretty much. You got an address?"

"Something someplace, I don't know. He stopped calling after Mom died, but he sends me a card every year on the anniversary of her death."

"Really?"

"Yeah. And then I send him a check."

"I bet you do. Can you get that address for me?"

"Why?"

"Maybe your brother won the lottery and I'm trying to find him."

There was a chuckle. "That loser?"

"Or maybe I might just head over to the county courthouse and check out your mother's will. See if half this house belongs to Terrence. We can have the sheriff sell the thing right from under you, split the proceeds. Wouldn't that be fun?"

"Who the hell are you?"

"An only child," I said, "and suddenly damn glad for it. Let's go get that address, shall we?"

a killer's
kiss

34

The address Frankie Tipton gave me was about 250 miles north of Ashland, Virginia, in a ragged part of industrial Philadelphia called Kensington. I could have given the address to the police, left it to them to roust Terry and ask him the questions, but the task would then have ended in Sims's hands, and I held no confidence that he wouldn't scare off Terry like he'd scared off Jamison. Whatever angle Sims was pursuing, it wasn't designed to be beneficial to my health. So no, this I would have to do myself. I figured I'd slip into the house, grab hold of Terry, shake out the truth, and bring him and it to my pal Detective McDeiss, along with any evidence I could grab. But as soon as I got a gander of the row house that sat at the address, I revised my plan.

"Squatters," said Antoine from the driver's seat of his Camaro.

We had made the drive in a straight shot, and now, in the

ill-lit darkness of Kensington, we could see a swarm gathered on the front stoop of the house as we passed it slowly.

"Does that mean it's abandoned?" I said.

"It mean anything, mon," said Antoine. "Maybe the owner's renting space cheap for a few dollar here and there. Or maybe he being generous, who knows? But I can tell you just by looking, there be a crowd inside."

"Park here," I said.

"What you doing, bo?" said Derek.

"I'm going to find out what's going on."

"How?"

"I've got a source."

About fifty yards down from the house, on the opposite side of the street, an old man sat flat-footed in a lawn chair set up on the sidewalk. He wasn't smoking a cigar or drinking a beer or discussing the state of the union. He was simply sitting, still as the earth, as if he had been planted in that very spot a century ago and grew up and old with the neighborhood, sitting there, losing teeth as the block lost buildings, letting time wash over him. The perfect spy. In Philadelphia there's one on every corner. I knelt down beside him. He didn't turn his head a degree.

"You see that house over there?" I said. "The one with all the folks milling about in front?"

"I see it."

"You know who lives there?"

"A bunch of fools."

"You know their names?"

"Don't want to know their names."

"Who owns it, do you know that?"

"The king of fools."

"A white guy, dark hair, about my age?"

"He don't dress as good."

"You like the way I'm dressed?"

"Except for that tie."

"Yeah, I get that a lot."

"And the shoes ain't nothing to write home about neither."

"What are all these other people doing there at that house?"

"They do errands, keep intruders out. But mostly he lets them stay to up and rile the block."

"Tough crowd?"

"They too drugged out to be tough. Back in the day, I would have cleared them out myself with but a baseball bat."

"I bet you would have. Ever see a woman show up, dark hair, well dressed?"

"Pretty?"

"Oh, yes."

"I seen her. Seeing her always cheered up my day."

"How often she show up?"

"Once or twice a week."

"Have you seen her in the last couple of days?"

"Come to think of it, no."

"You see anyone peculiar show up instead of her?"

"You mean other than you?"

"Yes, other than me."

"Bow tie."

"You don't say."

"Little man, near bald, in a black Volvo."

"When?"

"Couple times."

"How long you been sitting out here?"

"How long you been breathing?"

"That's what I thought," I said. "Thank you."

"Good luck to you, young man."

"Yeah," I said. I stood up, patted the old man on the shoulder, went back to the Camaro, where Derek and Antoine leaned against the hood, their arms crossed.

"What's the word, bo?" said Derek.

I thought about it for a moment. I didn't like the crowd of

squatters we'd have to wade through to get inside, I didn't trust that things wouldn't spiral way out of control. But then I didn't like the crowd behind me either, Trocek and Swift and Sims and Hanratty, a vicious gang of cutthroats and cops that all seemed to be aiming their malevolence at me.

"The word is," I said, "that we're going in."

"Then let's do it," said Antoine.

I took the lead, Antoine and Derek walking on either side of me. I was like a Piper Cub with an undersize fighter plane off one wing and a Boeing 757 off the other. On the porch of the house, five or six of the squatters were lounging on a bench or on the stoop, eyeing us suspiciously as we made our approach. Let's just say the welcome mat wasn't being cleaned and pressed for our visit.

"What you want here?" said a woman sitting closest to the door. She had short hair and a wide jaw, and her arms were crossed.

"We came to see the owner," I said.

"You from the city?"

"No," I said.

"You're not here about them back taxes? He been getting letters."

"No, we're not from the city."

"You cops, then?"

"Not that either," I said. "I'm simply a friend of a friend. And these are my friends. We came to say hello."

"In a suit?"

"I like to play it formal. My name's Victor Carl."

"I got to check with Romeo afore I let you in."

"Romeo, huh? Is that what he's calling himself? That's almost sweet. Well, then, by all means check with Romeo. Tell him Victor Carl is here to see him. I'm sure Romeo will think it's time we met at last."

The woman eyed us for a moment longer and then pushed

herself off of the bench, pulled open the screen door, and slipped into the house. A moment later she came back through the doorway, the screen door slamming behind her.

"Romeo'll be out in a minute," she said.

"Thank you."

"Maybe you should wait on that," she said before sitting down again.

When the screen door opened once more, standing there wasn't a dissolute drug addict with curly dark locks and a pout as I expected. Instead it was a giant of a man, with no neck and a shirt that hung over his belly like a curtain. A man to make Antoine look small.

"Where's Romeo?" I said.

"I'm Romeo," said the man, his voice deep enough to send wild dogs scurrying.

"You got to be kidding," I said.

"Time to go," said Romeo.

"I'm here to see Terry," I said.

"That too bad," said Romeo, " 'cause Terry told me he don't want to see no one."

"But he'll want to see Victor here," said Derek. "We've traveled five hundred miles to find him. Why don't you let us in there, Romeo? We're just a friendly little crew. No reason to make a fuss about this."

"There isn't going to be no fuss," said Romeo.

"You right about that," said Antoine, taking a step forward.

"Antoine?" said Romeo, squinting down at him.

"Hey there, Bradley," said Antoine. "You look like you eating at least."

"You not starving yourself neither."

"What the hell are you doing here, bwoy? Last time I saw you, there was work in Boston you were headed to."

"It didn't pan out."

"So now you hanging out here with this motley bunch."

Romeo shrugged. "It's a place."

"This is step back, bruddah."

"I'm doing the best I can."

"Well, bwoy, that's just sad, that is. Now we're going inside to talk to this man. And, Bradley, you don't want to be getting in our way."

"I'm not afraid of you, Antoine."

"It's not me you should be fearing, bwoy. Step aside, or I'll tell your muddah what you're up to, and she'll tell Earl, and then Earl, he will lick you for sure."

"Not from where he is."

"Stop playing the fool, mon. You think he can't reach out from lockup to take care of his likkle bruddah?"

Romeo stared at Antoine for a moment, licked his lips, and then stepped back, keeping the screen door open.

"Up the stairs," he said, "room at the back."

"You done right, bwoy," said Antoine, brushing past Romeo to step inside the house. Derek and I glanced at each other nervously and then quickly followed.

The inside of the house was dark, filthy, a fetid swamp covered with a foul mist of smoke and despair. The living room, if it could still be called that, was crowded with mattresses and sleeping bags and dazed humans lounging lethargically as a large-screen television flickered. It smelled like feces and sweat, laced with marihuana. Two dogs yapped at us and snarled before someone threw a shoe. I started itching just being in there. On the far side of the room was a narrow staircase. We picked our way past the mattresses and sleeping bags. A hand grabbed at my ankle, and I kicked it off.

A few ghosts, languid and vacant, drifted down the stairs. As we rose past them, the sounds of a rock 'n' roll band and a plaintive male voice climbed above the noise of the television. A whining, complaining voice wailing about bitter pills and love and loss.

On the second floor, there were four doors closed, the sounds of slow shuffling movement coming from within one, from another a groaning. And then the music, sad and angry and wistful all at once coming from the rear room, the front man not really singing, more howling out in desperation. Follow the voice, I figured.

A girl was sitting on the floor in front of the door, picking at a thumbnail.

"Terry in there?" I said.

She looked up at me, a pretty girl, young and thin, her face a terrifying blank.

"Let's go, sister," said Antoine, putting out his big mitt.

She placed her tiny hand in his and stood up slowly, swaying once before she moved away from the door.

I gave her a long look and then said to Antoine, "Wait out here. Make sure we're not disturbed."

"Not a problem, mon."

I turned to Derek, nodded once, and pushed the door open. A waft of sickeningly sweet smoke tumbled out of the doorway along with the earsplitting music.

Together we pressed inside.

We entered a room so out of place in the middle of that crack house that my breath caught in my chest.

It was like a gentleman's room from centuries past, or a whore's boudoir, with blood-red curtains and gold flocked wallpaper. There was a huge, ornate bed in the middle of the bare floor, its carved posts reaching almost to the ceiling, its velvet bedspread mussed, its brown paisley pillows awry. The windows were closed, the curtains drawn, the room ill lit and smoky. In the corner sat a broken guitar, the neck detached from its body.

A cone of light fell from a lamp to illuminate a small desk set against one of the walls, where a man, with his back to us, was bent over, writing, writing away, scribbling with a great urgency, as if the true meaning of the world had just been passed to him in a whisper. He was wearing a jacket, jeans, no shoes, as the music poured out around him. Beside him on the desk was an ashtray with the stub of a dead joint perched on its edge.

I softly closed the door behind Derek and me, stepped over to the stereo. The band's front man was now raging in compressed anger, a soul-shattering blast of teenage angst. In the middle of the howl, I punched the power button. The music died.

"Romeo," the man at the desk called out sleepily, dreamily, even as he kept with his scribbling.

"Romeo's busy," I said.

Without moving his body, he tilted his head and held it for a moment, then turned around. He had a pale, handsome face, so classical in its features it was like a painted Greek statue come to life, cleft chin, thick pouting lips, cheeks smooth as alabaster, their highlights red as rouge. His curly black hair fell carelessly across his forehead, so perfectly carelessly that you could tell it wasn't careless at all. I would have expected a shock of surprise on that strange mask of a face, but there was none. It was as if nothing could surprise its owner.

"Ah, so it's you," he said leisurely, through a blurry smile. "I wondered when you'd come."

"And here I am," I said.

"What's the matter? Didn't you find the music soothing?"

"More like a pick in the eye," I said.

Terrence Tipton's own eyes, red rimmed and blue irised, squinted in stoned amusement. But it wasn't his eyes that drew my attention, it was his chest. He was wearing a suit coat but no shirt, and his chest was a gory thing, pustuled with welts and boils, striped with scars.

"Maybe you could come back later," he said. "I'm working."

"On what? A suicide note?"

"No, but keep hoping. Poetry. I dabble. 'Such is the refuge of our youth and age.'"

"Sorry to interrupt your great work, but we need to talk."

"Do we?"

"Oh, yes."

"How did you find me? Julia?"

"Your brother."

"My dear brother," he said. "I should have guessed. Franklin never could keep a confidence." He reached for the stub of the joint in the ashtray, stared at it for a moment, offered it up to me.

"No," I said.

"So you're like that, are you?"

"Yeah, I'm like that."

"Is that what Julia sees in you? The utter straightness, the complete lack of any coil in your spine? I suppose it's a nice counterpoint to my own."

He popped the roach into his mouth and swallowed it. Then he leaned over, opened one of the desk drawers, pulled out a cigarette and a lighter. He flicked the lighter to life, took the page he'd been scribbling on and set it on fire. As it burned down, he lit his cigarette on the flame, before dropping the burning page onto the floor. As the paper flamed out among the charred remains of scores of other pages, he took a deep drag from the cigarette. He leaned his elbow on the desk, propped his head languidly on his hand, exhaled a plume of smoke.

"I guess it wasn't much of a poem," I said.

"I burn them all," he said, looking down at the smoldering paper. " 'The dying embers of an altar-place where had been heap'd a mass of holy things.' " He lifted his head to stare at me with lidded eyes. "So, Victor, I suppose you're here to thank me."

"Why the hell would I thank you?" I said.

"Because now your love has a chance."

"You killed Wren Denniston for me, is that your story?"

"I wouldn't cross the street for you. But for my Julia, who 'walks in beauty like the night,' I would do anything."

"Including murder?"

"Especially murder. But true love demands nothing less, don't you think?" He pushed himself out of his chair and began to walk slowly toward the bed. He had a pronounced limp, and I noticed only then that his right foot was badly swollen. "I'm not talking lust here, Victor, though I have nothing against lust per se. I'm talking love, the kind that bites into your bones and never lets go. The kind that grows up with you, that grows old with you, that stands the test of your aging because time fails to blunt its sharpest edge."

"And that's the way you feel about Julia?"

"No, Victor, that's the way you feel about Julia."

I stared at him without responding. He sat on the edge of the bed, winced as he lifted his purpled foot onto the dark maroon bedcover, and then leaned back dreamily on a mound of paisley pillows.

"It is over for me," he said. " 'The hope, the fear, the jealous care, the exalted portion of the pain and power of love.' "

"Who is that you keep annoyingly quoting? Shakespeare?"

"Byron."

"Byron, huh?" I looked around at the extravagant room, the burned poetry. "Wasn't he a self-dramatizing fop who screwed other men's wives, wrote scads of overwrought romantic verse, and had wanton sex with his sister?"

He took a long drag from his cigarette, exhaled, raised an eyebrow. "Half sister," he said. "Do you like my room?"

"No."

"Neither do I. Julia did it. She is always bringing me something, fixing the place up, trying to make me comfortable."

"Trying to make you something, all right."

"This fits her image of me."

"Was this ever you?"

"No. Even when we were young, she had me wrong. I suppose that's the true nature of love. I only play the part these days because it makes her happy. But now, with the ogreish Wren Denniston off to 'the vanished hero's lofty mound,' there is nothing to stop Julia from finding her happiness with you."

"Except you," I said.

"Well, yes, true, there's always me. But I don't take up much space."

I pulled a chair next to his bedside and sat down. I now had a clearer view of his ravaged body, and it was a brutal sight. Yes, his face was smooth and perfect—Dorian Gray came to mind— but it was clear from his chest and foot that he was being devoured by some virulent disease, something that infected him blood and bone. Above the tobacco smoke, I picked up a faint whiff of rot.

"What's with your foot?" I said.

"It's nothing. I stubbed my toe on something."

"It smells bad. Like it's gangrenous. You need to get out of this sepulcher and get it looked at."

"I don't want it looked at. 'The worm, the canker, and the grief are mine alone.'"

"Stop acting like an idiot. Do you have a doctor?"

"Do I look like I have a doctor? I subscribe to the Doris Day health plan. What will be will be."

"Let me get you out of here. The emergency room at Temple is not too far."

"Is that why you came? To save me?"

"No," I said. "But I'm willing to do that in addition."

"Who is he?" he said, indicating Derek.

"My investigator."

"He doesn't say much."

"Miracles happen. But he helped me find you, and now he's here to listen to your confession."

"Is that what I'm going to do? Confess?"

"That's right. You're going to tell us everything. How you showed up at the Denniston house. How you got hold of the gun. How you shot Julia's husband in the head. And then we're going to the emergency room."

"You sound so sure of yourself. Is your investigator going to beat the truth out of me?"

"He won't have to."

"Going to ply me with drugs? Please say yes."

"You're floating already."

"No more drugs?"

"No."

"Pity. But then how do you intend to get me to talk?"

"I'm going to wait," I said. "You want to tell me. You're so proud of yourself you can't help but tell me."

He laughed. Then he snubbed dead his butt, opened the drawer of his bed table, pulled out a full joint, licked it, lighted it. He sat on that bed, leaned forward to prod his bad foot with a finger, leaned back, stared at me while he sucked in and held the smoke.

I watched him in silence.

It had been an astonishing performance, Terrence Tipton's little show, with its burning poems and slurred voice and incessant quotations from a long-dead libertine, but that's all it was, a show. It hadn't taken me more than a moment to realize he was a dramatic little snit, still on the stage all these years after his vomitous failure as Romeo, still playing the melancholy young man brooding on some mysterious, unforgivable event in his past, still waiting for the spotlight to come his way and give him another chance.

And now here I was, at last, his opportunity.

So I wasn't worried that he was apparently turning me down. I stayed quiet, and I waited. He wasn't made for Beckett and his cold silences, no. He was made for Shakespeare and all that ripe verbal excess, for Byron's fatal romanticism. He would soon take his place behind the footlights and begin his grand soliloquy. He couldn't help himself.

I waited, and I waited some more. But I didn't have to wait too long.

I had plenty of time to think it through later that same night while I sat in the dark in my apartment.

I sat in a chair in a corner of my living room and stewed in a simmering pot of bitterness. She had betrayed me, not just once with the police at Clarence Swift's urging but repeatedly, overtly, time and again. Terrence Tipton hadn't let me take him out of that house to treat the disease that was ravaging his body, but he had told me a story, and its clearest message was that at every turn in my tortured relationship with sweet Julia she had betrayed me.

To hear Terry tell it, Julia broke off our engagement because she feared I couldn't support both her and his drug habit in the manner in which he wanted to be accustomed. She married Wren Denniston because Wren could and was willing to, and look where it got him, the sap. She confessed the details of our old-lovers' tango to Terry, even as she told me that what was going on between us was ours and ours alone. In my apartment, when she learned of the murder, she collapsed under the weight of her intuitive knowledge that sweet little Terry had shot her husband in the head to allow our tango to reach some heated fruition. And when she rose again, she gathered her senses and did everything she could to protect Terrence Tipton from the just consequences of his brutal act, even if it meant throwing me beneath the train.

I suppose I could have taken this with a certain grain of equanimity in and of itself. Duplicity might simply have been an integral component of Julia's character, and not the least alluring component at that. Who is ever sexier than a woman on the cusp of a betrayal? But she had betrayed me for a drug-addicted piece of putrefying flesh lost in a haze of posh, romantic, adolescent angst. She had betrayed me for the likes of Terrence Tipton, and that was almost more than I could handle.

Still, amidst all this, I wondered if we had a future. Now who was the sap?

But there was a foundation to my madness. Suddenly it was as if I could peer through Julia's shields and glimpse her inner life for the first time. She had been twisted around by a twisted love. Something had happened between Julia and Terrence in their desperate youths that had left scars evident in her psyche and upon his flesh. And I now knew what it was. And maybe my love was exactly what she needed to salve the wounds and save herself. The possibilities gleamed. All they required, of course, was to rid ourselves of that murderous piece of human excrement. And right there, sitting on my coffee table, I had the key to his riddance.

"Did you get it?" I said to Derek as soon as we left Terry Tipton's room.

"Sure thing, bo." He reached into his pocket, pulled out the miniature tape recorder, clicked it off. "I learned my lesson from last time. This time I pressed the damn buttons before we started."

"Let me have it," I said.

"You sure?"

"Sure I'm sure," I said.

"You really sure? I mean, how you think she'll feel about you if you turn that freak in?"

"She'll never forgive me," I said.

"So is this tape going to end up in the grip of the police," he said as he tossed the recorder to me, "or is it going to disappear to keep that girl happy?"

"Don't know yet," I said.

And I didn't, but I intended to find out. So I sat in a dark corner of my living room, staring at the miniature tape recorder glowing dully on the coffee table. I sat there stewing and waiting. Waiting for the knock at the door. Waiting for the ring of truth.

That day I had run from Philly to Washington to Ashland, Virginia, and then back again. I had run around like a fool looking for answers. But I wasn't running anymore. Whatever was going to happen was going to happen tonight, and it was going to happen here. The players would come to me to figure it all out. How did I know they would come to me? Because I had spent the whole day looking for answers, and now I had them. I knew who had killed Wren Denniston. I knew where the money was. I knew what each player was after, each player but one. All I didn't know for sure was what my future would bring. But that I would find out with the first knock on the door.

And then it came.

Knock, knock.

"Come on in," I called out cheerfully. "The door's open."

"Victor?" said Julia, peering into the glum darkness. "Is that you?"

"It's me, all right," I said.

"I'm so relieved," she said, stepping into the apartment. "Where have you been all day? I was so worried. I wanted to explain."

"I bet you did."

"Victor?"

"I've been waiting," I said. "Waiting for your explanation."

She must have caught something in my voice because she hesitated at that instant, turned her head to see if someone else was hiding in the apartment, which told me all I needed to know about whose room she had come from.

"I didn't mean to get you into trouble," she said. "I just told the truth to the police, that's all. About us. Just like you did the night of the murder."

"That's not what I wanted explained," I said. "I want to know the truth about why you left me. The truth of why you married Wren. The truth, for once, about us."

"I told you that already. You were pulling away, Wren stepped in, I was feeling vulnerable."

"But you left out one last player."

She stepped forward and tried to stare into my eyes through the darkness. Discouraged, she dropped onto the couch, one leg crossed beneath her.

"I knew you'd find him eventually," she said, her voice carefully calm. "He said he told you a story to get you to leave him alone, a story full of lies."

"He told me a story, all right, but it wasn't full of lies. And there it is, right on the coffee table. His story."

"You taped him?"

"You bet I did."

She leaned forward, picked up the recorder, pressed play. For an instant, Terry Tipton's slurry voice filled the room. *"—had been sending me money since before their wedding. That was his agreement with Julia, the way he got her—"* She clicked him quiet.

"He's sick," she said. "He's not in his right mind. He's an addict, addicted to lies as much as to the drugs. And you taped him without his knowing?"

"I taped him without his knowing."

"That was so unfair."

"Unfair is the way I play it when my neck is on the line."

She clutched the tape to her chest, leaned back, let her head loll on the sofa. "Let's just go away, let's just go someplace else. Let's get on a plane and get the hell out of here and start over. Just you and me."

"And the tape."

"Stop it."

"And Terry, too, when he decides to show up again and infect your life."

"He won't. I'll make him promise. That will be the price for leaving him out of it."

"There's no leaving him out of it, and there's no running away. They'll grab us as soon as we hit the airport. Our attempted escape will be Exhibit One at our trial and add years to our sentences. We have to stay and fight. And the tape is all we have to fight with."

"We can stonewall."

"That's what they want us to do. So they can pile accusations on our heads, one after another, while we sit quietly and take it. Pretty soon the pile will be too high to shovel our way out of."

"We can find someone else to blame. What about that Miles Cave? I thought we agreed. Why didn't you tell the police about him? Why can't he be the one?"

"Because he doesn't exist."

"All the better."

"Except that your lawyer has set up a frame of his own so it looks like I'm Miles Cave."

"Why would Clarence do that?"

"To get me out of the way. Because he loves you."

"Oh," she said, not at all surprised.

"I'd set up Clarence, and enjoy doing it, but he has an alibi. At the moment Wren was killed, he was at an ATM, getting cash to pay off Terry."

"We have to do something, Victor."

"Yes, we do. We have to give the tape to the police. On it Terry admits to coming to the house, to demanding money, to being shown the open and empty safe by Wren. He admits to taking the gun and shooting Wren in the head and then dropping the gun on the floor and fleeing. And you know why he did it?"

"Stop this."

"For you. Because he loves you and he wanted for you to be happy. With me."

"He's insane."

"Yes, he is. And it's all here, all his insanity, on the tape. You have to give the tape to the police."

"I can't."

"Sure you can."

"You don't understand. I don't even understand it myself. I loved him so much. With a pure adolescent love that never leaves, that remains like a jagged diamond in the heart. Shakespeare's poetry seemed to come as naturally to us as our breaths. I would hold him, and he would kiss me, and the words just appeared. 'My lips, two blushing pilgrims, ready stand to smooth that rough touch with a tender kiss.' Just to think of him then can still draw out tears. You don't know what it's like."

I didn't say anything to that, I just stared at my own jagged diamond in the heart.

"He was so sweet, so sensitive. The part of myself that loved him was the best part of me," she said. She wasn't really talking to me anymore, she was talking to herself, her younger self, trying to justify all that she had given up. "When I hear the word 'love,' it's his face that comes to mind."

"Then why aren't you together forever and always?" I said, interrupting her reverie.

"You sound so bitter."

"I've been here before," I said. "I've heard the violins."

"If only you knew the truth, you wouldn't feel that way. You wouldn't act so threatened. He's not like other men."

"He showed me."

"What?"

"I asked him what was keeping you two apart. Why you didn't just be with him. I asked him if he was gay, and he laughed, and then he asked me if I wanted to see."

"So you know."

"It's not that big a deal."

"To him it is. And it was to me, then. And the way I re-acted."

"You were sixteen."

"And so was he. Imagine what it did to him. What I did to him. When he wouldn't do anything, no matter how forward I was, I did something terrible. To push him to action, to make him jealous."

"You screwed Sherman, the quarterback," I said, my voice flat with the matter-of-factness of it all, "and Terry found you backstage before rehearsal."

"I wanted him to find me. And he did. But I didn't know about his condition then. You should have seen his face, Victor, cracked in pain. I can't forget it. Ever. I can't stop imagining it. Our love was real and impossible at the same time. I suppose that's what made it so perfect."

"Worth lying for? Worth betraying me for?"

"Worth everything," she said. "Still. I have no choice but to save him."

"You can't."

"But I can't stop trying either, don't you see?"

"No," I said. "I don't. Listen, Julia. That tape is our last hope. I don't know if we could ever make each other happy, but that tape is the only way to find out. Since you've come back into my life, we've been bouncing like Ping-Pong balls from emotion to emotion. Bitterness to lust to suspicion to fear to paranoia. But now there's hope, it resides in the truth, the truth on that tape."

She tossed the tape player back onto the table. "I don't want it," she said.

"If I turn it in, you'll hate me forever. If you turn it in, our future opens wide."

"Don't make me."

"I could never make you do anything. But I can make you choose."

A slight sneer stained her lips. "Between you and him?"

"Between truth and nothing. From the moment you stepped

in this door, you've been lying. You're pretending to care about us, but it's an act. All you care about is saving him."

"That's not true."

"Another lie." I stopped for a moment, thought about that strange room in which Terrence Tipton now lay, that tomblike room concocted solely out of Julia's fantasies. "In fact," I said, slowly, as revelation dawned, "everything we ever had was a lie, because the biggest truth, your love for Terry, was always hidden. But now there's a line. On one side is the end of lies. On the other side is the end of hope, any hope you might have for something, anything, that's worthwhile in your future. Because if you can't face the truth now, that hope is dead."

"It died fifteen years ago."

"Stop it. You and he are both blathering idiots. So he's got no cock. Find a surgeon, for God's sake. You screwed the quarterback to get him jealous. It happens every day—why do you think high school quarterbacks are always smiling? And the tragic dénouement was a stupid high school play, nothing more. Shakespeare being mangled by high school kids is bad theater, but it's not a tragedy. Get off the damn balcony and move on."

She looked at me with something implacable warping her features. Then she stood up and grabbed her bag. "I need to use your bathroom."

I waited for her to desperately snatch the tape recorder from off the table. I expected that she would take it to the bathroom, pull out the cassette, yank the tape free, and flush it down the toilet. She eyed me for an instant as if she were calculating the odds of her actually getting her hands back on the tape before I grabbed it. But if she wanted to destroy the tape, I wasn't going to stop her. All I really wanted was an answer, finally, and her grabbing the tape like that would ring as clear as I could hope for. But she didn't grab the tape. Instead she glanced at it, glanced at me, and then went off through the bedroom door, leaving me both confused and just the slightest bit optimistic, which in my experience has always proved to be fatal.

It took her a long time to return. She was thinking it through. I sat in the darkness and thought it through myself. I wondered if possibilities still existed. I wondered if we had a future. I wondered if that's what I really wanted. As the minutes ticked by, my neck tensed, my heart beat a little faster. What had I gotten myself into? I had been fighting all this time to keep something alive, and suddenly, with the tape still on the table and the possibility for survival rising all the while, I began to think it would have been better to let it die, long ago. Better had it shriveled like a leech covered in salt and suffered an excruciating death than to let it attach back onto my heart.

I'm not much good at romance, I'm afraid, but I am the master of ambivalence.

"Okay," she said, back now, her face clean, her brow strangely untroubled. "What am I supposed to do?"

"Take the tape player," I said. "Go to the Roundhouse. Ask for Detective McDeiss. He'll probably be at home, but they'll find him for you. Give him the tape, along with the address in Kensington where Terry can be found."

"McDeiss?"

"That's right. He'll make sure the arrest is done clean, by the book and without any shooting."

"And what happens to Terrence?"

"I'll find him a lawyer. He'll make a deal and will have a chance to clean himself up in prison."

"You make it sound like I'll be doing him a favor."

"Buying drugs for him, shooting him up when you visited, letting him live like a tick sucking off Wren's wealth, enabling his self-destruction, and protecting him every step of the way, that was no favor. There is an infection in his body that is chewing him to pieces, and he's doing nothing about it. He's killing himself. Prison might be his only chance."

She looked at me for a moment, a harsh emotion rolled across her features like a rough ocean wave, and then she smiled wanly. "You're a bastard."

"Yes, I am."

She stared down at the tape player on the table, as if she were staring at betrayal itself, and then she picked it up, dropped it into her bag, whirled around.

"Call me when it's done," I said to her back.

"One step at a time," she said, and then she was out the door.

I gave her a minute, in case she quickly changed her mind and came back in, and then I rushed over to the window and watched her leave as I took out my cell phone and made a call.

"I see her, bo," said Derek from the other end.

"Don't lose her. She'll be in a dark blue BMW."

"She got the tape?"

"Yes."

"What she going to do with it?"

"Call me when she gets to the Roundhouse."

"And what if she goes the other way?"

"Then keep following."

"Just so you know," said Derek, "I think you got some visitors."

"Who?"

"Two men. They was waiting for her to leave before they popped in."

"Okay, thanks for the heads-up. I was expecting them anyway."

And I was. Sims and Hanratty, I figured. I had dropped their tail, I had slipped out of town, I had pissed them off. At least I was being consistent. Now they were coming for answers, which worked out just fine, because answers were what I had for them.

I again took to my chair and waited in the darkness for the knock at the door. And then it came.

Knock, knock.

"Come on in," I called out cheerfully. "The door's open."

And in they came. Not Sims and Hanratty.

Damn.

"Where is my money, Victor?" said Gregor Trocek.

The question was rhetorical, I supposed, what with me flopped on my back and the point of Sandro's switchblade digging into the soft flesh beneath the point of my jaw. If I had tried to answer, my flapping jaw would have been impaled like a speared fish. So I kept quiet as Gregor wandered around my apartment, raising his hands in mock exasperation.

"Where could it be? Where, where, where? What?" he said, turning to stare right down at my face. "No answer for me?"

I guess the question wasn't so rhetorical after all.

"I don't have it," I tried saying through gritted teeth, my words sounding less like English than a Neanderthaloid grunt.

"But, Victor, how can I believe anything you say?"

"I'm telling the truth," I tried again.

"Speak more clearly, please," said Gregor. "I can barely understand a word."

"There's a knife."

"Yes, I've had enough, enough of your lies, your thievery, the baubles in your apartment." He walked up to the flat-screen television bolted onto my wall. "Nice. High def?"

"Yes," I said.

"It is quite gratifying to know my money paid for such quality merchandise. I would have hated for it to be wasted on junk."

"I didn't buy it with your money."

"What? I still can't understand you. Maybe a little more persuasion will clarify your words. Sandro, cut off his nipple."

This wasn't going well. This wasn't going well at all.

When I realized that it was Gregor and Sandro coming through my door instead of two cops, I figured I was in trouble, and I became ever more certain when Sandro, instead of hesitating tastefully once inside, charged right at me while Gregor locked the door behind them both.

I grappled to my feet. Sandro socked me in the eye with a forearm shiver. I reeled from the blow and slammed into the floor.

Swish-click.

And just like that, Sandro was on top of me, the point of his switchblade pricking my flesh.

That was bad enough, that was enough to swell my eye and roil my stomach and leave me clenching my teeth to stop from being impaled. But now, with a simple imperative from Gregor Trocek, it was getting far, far worse.

Sandro began undressing me with his knife.

"Such an ugly tie," he said as he looped the blade between the knot of my loose red tie and my shirt. With a jerk of his wrist, the tie was sliced in two.

I tried to scuttle backward, but Sandro grabbed my shirt.

"And now these annoying buttons," he said.

A flick of the knife and a button flew off. Flick went another.

I let out an involuntary wail of fear.

Flick, flick, flick. The front of my shirt drifted open.

I tried again to get away, but he grabbed my T-shirt, pulled me forward, and in a quick move plunged the knife into the fabric, ripping upward with the blade until the metal edge snapped by my cheek and nicked my ear. As he jerked the shirt once more, it ripped in two, leaving my chest bared.

I stared up at Sandro's face as he grabbed my hair with one hand and pointed his knife at my chest with the other. His eyes were bright, his lips twisted somewhere between anger and delirium. He was enjoying this entirely too much. Yet another lesson that I was not made for prison.

"Oh, look," said Sandro. "A tattoo. Is that your lover's name? Maybe I deal with her after I deal with you."

"She's already dead," I said.

"Too bad."

On the coffee table, my cell phone rang. Sandro stopped and turned his face toward it. It rang, rang again, and then went to voice mail.

"Enough of your games, Sandro," said Gregor, standing to the side of us, his hands behind his back as if examining nothing more alarming than a mediocre piece of art. "Make your mark."

"Can I take the tattoo?"

"As you please," said Gregor.

"*Gracias,*" said Sandro as he used the point of the knife to painfully scrape a wide circle around my left nipple, which included the tattoo. I tried to pull away, but Sandro held me tight as he worked. Blood began rising through the slices, welling and dripping down my chest, across the shallows of my abdomen.

"What is he doing?" I yelled.

"Marking where he will slice when he cuts off nipple. He needs be sure there is enough flesh, so after shrinking in smoke, it will still look like something."

"What are you talking about?"

"Sandro saves pieces he cuts off. He has quite lively collection. Fingers. Ears. The nipples dry nicely with smoke and turn same brown as tobacco."

I fought to catch my breath. "Sick" was the only word I could grunt out.

"Agreed, but I don't value Sandro for his sanity. We could end this right now, Victor. You could emerge with your measly chest intact, right now. If you are ready to tell me what I need to know."

"We made a deal," I whined as I stared at the blood. "We had an arrangement. Twelve point five percent."

"That was before I learned that you have it all. All is better than an eighth in everything but shrapnel."

"I don't . . . No . . . I don't have . . . your money."

"Ah, Victor, you are making Sandro very happy."

The knife dipped down, the edge pressed into the bloody circle.

"But I know who does," I said hastily as I tried again to pull away. "I know who has it."

Gregor tapped Sandro on the shoulder. Sandro dug the knife in deeper and then, with a sigh, lifted it from my chest. He wiped it on my pant leg, one side, then the other, before snapping it closed and rising to his feet.

I shut my eyes, opened them again. The pain was still there, along with the blood. I touched the wound, the red smeared sickly.

"Get up now," said Gregor. "No need to wallow."

I pushed myself to a sitting position and then stood, unsteadily. My chest burned, my stomach shifted, a line of vomit climbed up my throat and burned its way down again. I staggered a bit before collapsing onto the pleather sofa. I put the remnants of my T-shirt against the bleeding wound and then modestly clutched my buttonless shirt closed. I might have sobbed.

My cell phone rang again. Derek, I assumed, calling to tell me where Julia had gone, calling to read to me my future.

"You want to pick that up?" said Gregor.

"No," I said, and the truth was that I really didn't. In the midst of the blood and the torture, I didn't need another blow.

"Okay, Victor. Now tell me what you know."

My breathing was crazed with fear, like a raccoon on the run. I took a moment to try to get it under control.

"Come, come," said Gregor. "Don't leave me hanging."

"Remember how we were on the track of Miles Cave?" I managed to say. "Well, he doesn't exist."

"Really," said Gregor. "No Miles Cave. Interesting. He's ghost, but ghost who writes letters." He reached into his jacket, pulled out a folded piece of paper, and began to read in his dark Russian voice. " 'Dear Wren, As our recent conversations have not gone well, and you have lately been refusing to take my calls, I am having this letter hand-delivered in hopes—' "

"It's a fake," I said.

"But of course you would say that. It has your address. And it looks like your signature. And I have it on good authority that you wrote it."

"Whose authority?"

"Someone I trust."

"He's lying."

"It's not a he."

"Who? Julia?"

"Victor. Let us start again. Where is my money?"

"I don't have it. And I didn't write that letter. I am being framed. By the very person who does have the money."

"So talk."

"Wren Denniston was broke. He saw a way of getting out of the Inner Circle disaster with some money in his pocket by playing his old business associate for a sucker. So he concocted a way for you to invest with an imaginary partner. He took your cash and credited the investment in the books, but he never put the cash in the bank. Instead he gave it to someone to hide, in case you or the feds came looking for it. Then, later, he credited the withdrawal and, wallah, one point seven million in cash ready to soften his fall. His golden parachute."

"So Wren has my money."

"He did, but he was murdered, murdered for reasons that had nothing to do with the money. By an addict named Terrence Tipton, whom Julia has been in love with since high school. But the murder left the cash with the person Wren had hidden it with. The person who had been involved with Wren in the plan, the person who had drafted up the partnership agreement between you and the fictional Miles Cave. When you showed me the agreement, I thought I recognized the author."

"And you didn't tell me? I am hurt."

"I wanted to be sure."

"And are you?"

"Yes."

"So, Victor, who is this man who conspired with Wren, who took advantage of his murder to steal my money, and then who framed you? Who is this mastermind of crime?"

"You're not going to believe this."

"You better hope that I do."

And just as I was about to tell him, there was a scrape of feet at my door.

Knock, knock.

Gregor's head whipped around. Sandro bolted to standing as he straightened his arm. *Swish-click.*

I clutched my shirt tighter.

"Victor Carl," came a voice I recognized from the other side. "This is the police. Open the door. We have a warrant."

Click-swish. Sandro put his hand in his pocket.

Gregor turned his face from the door, grabbed hold of my head with both hands, pulled me close enough so I could smell the cumin on his breath. "Who?" he said, quietly but urgently.

I thought it through as quickly as I could, thought of Sandro and his dancing knife, thought of what fun he would have. I thought of it all, and then I let the lesser angels of my nature have their way. Sure, why not, and didn't he deserve to be the quarry that got Gregor off my back? But if it was going to work, if a single name was going to send Gregor off to do his part on this brutal night, I needed him to trust me. How could I get Gregor to trust me with two cops banging down the door? How indeed?

"Twenty-five percent," I said.

"You're being greedy," said Gregor. "We had deal."

"That was before you sliced up my chest like a London broil."

"Fifteen."

"Twenty."

Another knock.

"Yes, fine," said Gregor. "Agreed. Who?"

"Clarence," I said as I jerked my head out of his grip and stood up, clutched my now-bloody shirt tight. "Clarence Swift."

"No. Can't be."

"Yes it can," I said. "That little eel has it stashed away, mark my word. Now, if you boys don't mind, I need to talk to my friends in the constabulary."

Sims and Hanratty, back again to where it all began.

"Are we interrupting something, Victor?" said Sims, looking through the crack of the door and past my shoulder to the two nefarious characters in my living room.

"Nothing worth talking about."

He eyed my shirt, still clutched, a rough circle of blood beginning to appear on the cloth, took in the burgeoning bruise on my face, my bleeding ear. Then he peered into my eyes as if to figure out what the hell was going on.

"You mind if we come in?" he said.

"Does it matter if I say yes?"

"No."

"Then by all means," I said as I opened the door wide, letting them through. Once in the apartment, the two cops stood side by side—Sims dark and furtive, Hanratty solid as granite with a Mount Rushmore jaw—and stared at the two other men in my apartment like a pair of fighting dogs sizing up the competition.

"Aren't you going to introduce us to your guests?" said Sims. "We so much would like to meet them, wouldn't we, Hanratty?"

Hanratty glowered and said nothing.

"Hanratty is always looking for new friends," said Sims, "since he tends to break the old ones."

"I'm sorry," I said. "How rude of me. Detective Sims, Detective Hanratty, this is Gregor Trocek and his boy toy Sandro."

Sandro hissed at me with his Andalusian lisp.

"Gregor Trocek," said Sims. "Gregor Trocek. Where have I heard that name before?"

"It is quite common," said Gregor. "Pleasure meeting you both, but we must be going. We have business meeting to attend."

"At this time of night?" said Sims. "It must be some business. Gregor Trocek. Gregor Trocek." He tapped his chin twice, and then his eyes lit up. "Of course. Gregor Trocek. What a coincidence. I was just this evening reading the Interpol file of a Gregor Trocek. A rather nasty villain."

"Must be different Gregor Trocek," said Gregor Trocek.

"Oh, I don't think so," said Sims. "The Gregor Trocek I was reading about was approximately your height, approximately your weight, had the same beady eyes and unkempt beard, the same air of perverse dissoluteness. He is wanted for questioning in Belgium about a notorious sex crime. A young girl violently assaulted. Shockingly young, actually. The community is still in an uproar. He is under investigation in Albania. Something about trafficking in young women. What was the term in the file? Oh, yes, the white slave trade. Quite evocative, no? And he is barred from entering Thailand and Cambodia. I can't imagine what bestiality one must commit to be banned from entering Thailand and Cambodia. Care to comment?"

"I am innocent of everything," said Gregor.

"Yes," said Sims, eyeing him up and down. "You look like an innocent. What should we do with this piece of trash, Hanratty?"

"Take him in," said Hanratty, "put him in the box, ship him FedEx to Brussels."

"You have no jurisdiction," said Gregor.

"Maybe not, but Immigration does. When I talked to them this evening, they seemed quite interested in your case. They were already looking for you. Apparently, you didn't inform them of any criminal problems on your visa application. They are making a recommendation to the FBI tomorrow."

"Let's hold him until then," said Hanratty.

"If only we could," said Sims. "If only we could."

"But I assume from your tone of regret that you can't," said Gregor. "So that is it, then. Off we go. It was an experience being introduced to you both. I will be in touch, Victor."

"Enjoy your meeting," I said.

"I intend to. Come, Sandro."

Gregor, with a hurry-up hitch in his stride, headed for the door, Sandro right behind.

"Oh, Mr. Trocek," said Sims. "One more thing."

Gregor stopped, turned around. His hands trembled, as if he were straining to keep them from wringing Sims's neck.

"If I see you again," said Sims, "I'll shoot you in the face."

Trocek stood there for a moment, staring back at Sims, before the slightest smile broke beneath the thatch of his beard. Something burst to life between them just then, some spark, containing in its charge a combustible mixture of greed and violence. I sensed that someday soon Sims and Trocek would meet again, and two of my problems might disappear all at once.

When Gregor left, Sims turned to me. "Quite a disreputable crowd you're hanging out with," he said.

"Not by choice," I said. "Very little that has happened to me as of late has been by choice. Take you two guys always popping in uninvited. Before we chat, do you mind if I go into my bedroom and get a new shirt? This one is a little worse for wear."

"Yes, we do mind," said Hanratty as he reached into his jacket pocket, took out a pair of blue rubber gloves, slipped them onto his huge hands.

"What are you doing? My prostate is fine."

Sims pulled a document from his overcoat and waved it once before putting it away. "We have a warrant. Hanratty's going to search your bedroom. Relax, Victor. This won't take long."

"That's what they say when they check your prostate."

While Hanratty disappeared into my bedroom, I sat down on the edge of the couch, leaning forward, one hand still clutching the shirt to my chest. Sims sat with a certain ease in my easy chair, leaning back comfortably, one leg crossed over the other.

"I'd ask about your shirt and the blood," said Sims, "but I try not to get into people's sexual practices unless absolutely necessary."

"This has nothing to do with—"

"Not yet, Victor. We'll talk, we'll have quite the conversation, but not just yet."

"What kind of—"

"Shhhh," said Sims. "Save it all for later. For now let Hanratty do his work."

From my bedroom came the sound of clothes rustling, of furniture being moved, of objects being tossed carelessly about. Something shattered against a wall. Sims didn't so much as flinch.

"Can I see the warrant at least?" I said.

"No."

"But the law says—"

"I know what the law says," said Sims. "Just be patient. Everything will come clear, one way or the other, soon enough."

And soon enough it did. From the doorway to my bedroom appeared Hanratty, a crooked smile on his stalwart face. And in one hand, still sheathed in blue rubber, he held out, like a magician displaying a startled rabbit pulled from his hat, a plastic bag.

And inside the plastic bag was a gun, big and shiny, and though I had never seen it before, I knew right away which gun, of all the guns in the world, was this gun and whom it had killed.

It's hard to parse the swirling swill of emotions I felt at that very moment. There was the inevitable shock, though how I could have been shocked was a mystery. And there was anger, a generalized anger at the bastards who had set up the frame and the two cops who were walking right through it. And there was fear, yes, fear that after all the crimes and misdemeanors in my life, I was being caught at something I hadn't done. The UPS guy always rings twice, I suppose. And let's not forget the sadness, too, yes, of course, I admit it, sadness at the past that was obliterated and the future altered by the sheen of the gun's silvery barrel.

But most of all, and this may be the truest revelation of this whole sordid tale, even as I felt the frame of guilt close in on me, what I felt surging through me at the sight of that gun, planted in my bedroom by my old lost love, was a great heaving sense of relief.

"What are you going to do now?" I said, my jaw tight with dread. Whatever relief I felt at the vision of Julia disappearing from my future was suddenly overwhelmed by visions of prison bars taking her place.

"We're going to book you for illegal possession of a firearm," said Sims as he calmly straightened out the fabric on his pant leg. "And when the tests show conclusively that your gun killed Dr. Denniston, we're going to book you and hold you without bail until a grand jury indicts you for murder."

"I didn't do it," I said.

"Save it," said Hanratty. "The judge might care, we don't."

"Hanratty," said Sims, "why don't you go down to the car and call in what we found. Maybe see if anything else has popped up that we should know about."

"I could call from here," said Hanratty.

"I know, but do it from the car. Leave me a few minutes alone with Victor."

Hanratty stared at the back of Sims's head for a moment, his stone features hardening, then put the gun in his pocket and stalked out the door. Sims and I sat there for a while in silence. Sims had something to say, but he wanted me to wait and stew a bit first. Except I had done enough stewing and waiting that night.

"The gun was planted," I said.

"Probably," said Sims.

"I know who killed him," I said. "I can prove it."

"You can prove it? Really? That's so encouraging for you."

"Don't you want to know who killed the doctor?"

"Not really. I have you here, now, and that's all I need. The young and pretty wife naked in your bed. You, as always, hoping for a big payday. The fingerprint. The letter you wrote as Miles Cave. The gun in your apartment. Open and shut, Victor. Open and shut. We'll check Dr. Denniston off the board and move on. When the grand jury rubber-stamps the indictment, we'll hold you for a year or two, depending on delays, until your trial. By then, with the help of a few cooperating witnesses from the prison, we'll have more than enough evidence to throw at a jury. And won't the prosecutor have fun waving the gun in his closing?"

I closed my eyes, imagined it all, felt the quease rise in me. "But I have a witness."

"Good for you. And you can present him at the trial, if he doesn't disappear before then. Like Mrs. Denniston's alibi witness disappeared."

I snapped my eyes open. "You chased him away on purpose."

"Now, why would I do something like that?"

"I don't know," I said. "But I suspect I'm about to find out."

"I wanted to help you from the first, Victor, remember? But you were all about attitude and nothing about gratitude. I felt only a smart-alecky disdain from you. Quite insulting. But the worm turns, doesn't it? And now all I see is your soft underbelly.

And so here we are. You with the murder weapon in your bed-room, me with a prime suspect. See how neatly it works? But I'm still willing to help."

"What do you want?"

"To see justice done," he said.

He stared at me briefly, and then he started laughing, and I couldn't help but laugh, too. His laughter was full of merriment and mirth, mine was full of bitterness and dread, but there we were, laughing together at the idea that justice had any place in the discussion we then were having. And in that laughter I caught my first glimpse of a route out of the cage of guilt that had been hammered into place around me.

"Let me tell you what I'm willing to do for you first," said Sims. "I can make this all go away. The gun was planted, of course it was. You are innocent, of course you are. You know who did it, of course you do. I'll follow your lead, I'll find the culprit, I'll make him pay. You tell me who. Clarence Swift? Fine. Someone else? Great. Your mother? My mother? My wife? Please. I'm flex-ible, really. It will all take some doing, and I'll suffer the heat from my superiors, but nothing I can't handle in the end. And for you, life goes on. Your fine legal practice, your new flat-screen television, your pleather couch. And finally, Victor, you can con-summate your renewed relationship with Mrs. Denniston. How sweet would that fruit taste? I grow weak myself, merely think-ing about it."

"I can tell by the slobber on your lip."

"I'm just so excited for you, Victor."

"And in exchange for all this happiness?"

"A little bit of truth. Do you think you can handle that? One honest word out of you. Do you think that can be arranged?"

"It depends."

"Yes, I know it will be hard. But try. Try as if your life de-pends on it, which it does."

"Go ahead."

"Okay, here it is. I need the answer to one simple question: Where is the money?"

"The money?"

"The one point seven million dollars that the murdered man stole from that bearded pervert Gregor Trocek. It's somewhere, I know that. The U.S. Trustee is looking for it. Gregor Trocek is looking for it. You, too, are looking for it, are you not? It is in play, and I want it."

"You've been after it from the first."

"Not from the first. At first I was looking for a killer. But then, after my meeting with Mr. Nettles at Inner Circle Investments and a careful look at the books, I had something loftier on my mind."

"That's why you chased Jamison away."

"I thought Mrs. Denniston could lead me to it. I needed to keep the pressure on her."

"And now you're putting the pressure on me."

"I didn't plant the gun, Victor, but I know opportunity when it bitch-slaps me in the face."

"And you think I know where the money is?"

"I'm sure of it."

"How?"

"Because you're clever and you're inside, and because Gregor Trocek wouldn't have sliced a ring in your chest if you didn't know."

"And if I tell you where it is, my problems disappear?"

"Absolutely. You'll still have to go down to the Roundhouse with Hanratty and be booked—there's no escaping that with the gun found in your bedroom. But as soon as the money is in my hands, I'll pull the strings to have you released immediately and the charges dropped. You'll be off scot-free."

"And you'll retire in style in Montana."

"Yes, exactly. Or Saint-Tropez. I hear it's quite nice."

"They don't fly-fish in Saint-Tropez."

"With the money, Victor, I can buy my fish at a restaurant, which I suspect is far preferable."

"What about Hanratty?"

"I'll take care of Hanratty."

"You'll pay him off?"

"Hanratty can't be paid off. But he can be led, like a dog can be led. It's just a matter of burying the bones shallow enough. Don't worry, Victor, I'll hold up my end."

And I was sure he would. I had been confused as to Sims's motives during the whole of this case. He seemed a complex character. Was he out for justice, out for political gain, out to screw me for the sheer pleasure of it, or was he simply too lazy to run an investigation on the ups? All valid motives, and each I could appreciate, but which was it? I hadn't known, but now I did, the son of a bitch. He only wanted what the rest of us wanted. It's always a little disappointing, isn't it?

So here I was, in a tough spot, with an easy way out. I was being framed for a murder. Framed by whom? By Clarence Swift and, sadly, by Julia. I had given her a chance to save us, she had taken the chance to bury me. How sweet, how so much like her. It's why I'd felt relief the moment I saw the gun she planted; my future would be free of her. But now, as a result of their framing, this piece-of-crap corrupt cop was suddenly in a position to blackmail me into telling him about the money. And the thing was, he was right, I did know where the money was. But there was more here than an opportunity to get Sims rich and me off the hook. There was an opportunity to achieve the thing that had set us both to laughing just a few moments before, an opportunity for justice.

Justice, justice shall you pursue. It's right there in the Good Book, sitting like a road map for me to follow. Justice for everyone, justice for all. An appropriate justice for Clarence Swift and Terrence Tipton, for Gregor Trocek and Detective Sims, that crooked son of a bitch, justice for Julia Denniston who had betrayed me once and again, and yes, justice of a sort for me, too. A laughable thing to find in this world, justice, but a beautiful thing as well, when meted out with just the right dose of bitter vengeance.

I sat across from him as I figured it out, all the while watching his face shine with an unwholesome eagerness. It would take a betrayal on my part, sure, but really now, what's a little betrayal among old lovers?

"You want to find the money, Detective," I said finally, after thinking it through, after seeing the parts all fit together.

"Yes, Victor," he said, with as much sincerity as he could muster. "I truly do."

"Then you just need to follow Mrs. Denniston. She'll take you right to it."

"And where would I find her at this time of night?"

"I don't know where she is now, but I know where she'll be."

And then I gave him a Kensington address.

There wasn't much time to change Hanratty's mind.

The trip from my apartment to the Roundhouse, even in the middle of the day, was not a long one, and in the middle of the night, if you caught the lights right, it could be positively swift. Once we hit the Roundhouse, I'd be sent straightaway to processing, and then to arraignment court, and then to jail until a bail was set that I could pay, which, considering the charge of murder and the state of my bank account, seemed unlikely. My future freedom would then depend on Sims, who, with the money scent now in his nostril, was as dependable as a rabid dog. So I had to somehow alter Hanratty's destination before we hit the Roundhouse. But it wasn't just to keep my butt out of jail.

Like a demented chess player, unmindful of the consequences, I had set the pieces in motion. At some point, probably on the road out of town, the paths of Sims and Trocek and Clarence Swift would intersect and the bullets would fly. Just the thought of it brought a little pitter-patter to my heart. But it wasn't long after I sent Gregor to chase Clarence, and Sims to meet up with them, that I realized that when the bullets flew, Julia would be caught in the middle, and her predicament would be my responsibility. I had to do something about it, and I had to do it fast.

But I was now in the backseat of a cop car, with my hands cuffed behind my back and without an easy way out. And it didn't help that the man in the driver's seat had an emotional temperament and a skull both of which could only be described as igneous. Still, I had one card to play that might crack even his stone demeanor.

"Your partner is a crook," I said to Detective Hanratty as he drove me east, toward police headquarters.

Sims had dashed off in his own car to chase after Julia, and so I was alone with Hanratty. He actually wasn't playing it as hard I thought he would. He had let me bandage my chest, clean the blood from my ear, put on a new shirt and tie just like the old shirt and tie, let me grab my suit jacket before we left. He had cuffed me, sure—rules are rules—but he didn't tell me to shut the hell up when I called his partner a crook, like I had expected. All he did was clench his jaw and set his features, just as he had when Sims had sent him from my apartment, which was a promising start.

"Sims isn't trying to solve Wren Denniston's murder," I continued. "Instead he's running after the one point seven million in cash that the good doctor embezzled from the Gregor Trocek who was in my apartment. That's why Sims stuck you with the task of taking me to the Roundhouse, so he could chase the money."

Hanratty gave me a quick and ugly glance in the rearview mirror as he kept driving. We were headed north now, toward Race Street, where we would turn east again. The Roundhouse was only a few minutes away.

"I know who killed the doctor. It was a drug-addicted Byron

wannabe by the name of Terry Tipton, who is an old boyfriend of Julia's. The story is sad and sordid and Shakespearean in the literal sense, but he admitted it to me and to someone else and on tape."

Hanratty cocked his granite face without saying anything.

"Ah, so you are listening. Good. No, I don't have the tape. Julia Denniston has the tape, and she'll do anything she can to protect this Tipton. But Sims doesn't care about the tape, or this Terry Tipton, or anything other than the money."

Hanratty's jaw clenched the way it seemed to clench whenever I mentioned his partner. But he still was headed to the Roundhouse and my appointment in arraignment court.

" 'What about the gun?' you might ask. It was planted in my apartment by Mrs. Denniston just before you showed up. She tried to convince me not to give you the tape. I tried to convince her to give up her old boyfriend. As always, neither of us convinced the other of anything. She took the tape and left the gun. Where'd you find it anyway?"

He glanced at me again.

"Let me guess," I said. "In the desk drawer."

His eyes blinked.

"That's her place. She likes to hide things there. And it's funny, isn't it, how you missed the gun the first time you searched my apartment? But your slimy partner isn't the only one chasing after the money. Gregor Trocek is after it, too. Nice guys, the two of them. It would be quite the show if ever they meet again. And it should happen soon, since I set the two of them on a collision course."

The car swerved. We were on Race Street now, racing through Chinatown and toward the Roundhouse, and the car swerved, hard left, before straightening again to the bray of horns.

"I sent Gregor Trocek after Clarence Swift, who was Wren's partner in the embezzlement. I sent Sims after Mrs. Denniston, who is the object of Clarence Swift's affection and who will, this very evening, I believe, meet with him on her way out of town. I expect it will end in extreme violence well away from here before it's over. Which, except for Mrs. Denniston's presence in the middle of it all, suits me just fine, because I think I know where the money is, and we can beat them both to it. And once the money is tucked safely away with the U.S. Trustee, we can deal with this whole situation like gentlemen."

"You want to take me to the money?" said Hanratty, shock in his voice.

"Yes, I do."

"You don't want to keep it for yourself?"

"If I thought I could get away with it, sure. But I can't. There are too many people looking for it, too many willing to perpetrate anything to get their hands on it. Gregor Trocek thinks I'm hoping he ends up with it, because I negotiated a piece of what he recovers, but I know he'd kill me before I got a cent. And Sims thinks I want him to find it, because he promised he'll keep me out of jail, but I trust him like I'd trust a ferret in my pants."

"And what about me?"

"Sims says you're a fool who's too honest to deal with. McDeiss says I can trust that you're after the right thing. Both pretty good recommendations in my book. So let's you and me, Detective, go get the money and then solve the murder and then save Mrs. Denniston while we bag a couple of crooks."

"Are you crapping in my hat?"

"Would I get away with it if I did?"

"No."

"There you go."

We were stopped at a red light at Eighth and Race. To our right, filthy with grime, was the ugly, circular skin of the Roundhouse. Straight ahead and to our left was the entrance to the Benjamin Franklin Bridge, the blue paint of the bridge gaily striped with light.

"You could take a right here, send me to arraignment court,

and let everything play out for better or for worse without you. Or you could get into the left-hand lane and follow the signs for the Ben Franklin."

"New Jersey."

"That's the place."

"I think you're full of it."

"But you're not sure," I said. "You don't like me much, do you?"

He glanced at me again in the rearview mirror. "Every time I see your face, I want to smash my fist into it, over and over, until the blood bubbles."

"I tend to have that effect on people."

Hanratty didn't respond, he just stared forward, letting his jaw work as if he were cracking walnuts between his teeth.

The light turned green.

The car stayed still for a moment and then started forward, eased left, slid into the lane of traffic headed over the Delaware River and into New Jersey, where a cat, gray and fluffy, waited for us.

The cat sat in the window well of a little Cape Cod in Haddonfield, New Jersey. The house was white and freshly painted, the lawn cared for, the perennials beneath the dogwood neatly weeded. As I rubbed my wrists while we made our way up the walk, from behind the brightly lighted window the cat hissed. It remembered me. Of course it did, it was a cat. And maybe it had the same reaction as Hanratty every time it saw my face.

Then the cat reached out a foreleg and gently tapped the window with the pads on the underside of its paw, leaving a streak of red.

Hanratty was on the phone to 911 even as he slammed his shoulder into the door, once, twice, and then thrice, shattering it to bits. He climbed over the splintered wood into the living room, one hand on the phone, the other gripping his drawn revolver.

"That's right," he barked. "Blood on the window." He looked around. "Blood on the floor. I'm inside now. Get an ambulance here and a bunch of black-and-whites. And tell your guys not to come in shooting. I'm going to find the victim, see if there's anything I can do."

Following behind the rampaging detective, surveying the scene for myself, I doubted there would be.

The tracks led through the undisturbed living room, into the dining area, and then into the kitchen, where they were most vivid on the white linoleum. Cat tracks, leading backward to the scene of the crime, as if gray and fluffy itself had done the vile deed.

"She'll be in the basement," I said.

"Where's the door?" said Hanratty.

"Through the kitchen."

With his gun leading the way, Hanratty stepped carefully around the cat tracks into the kitchen and then halted at an open door that led to a set of rough wooden stairs descending into darkness.

"Hello," he called down. "This is the police. Is anyone there?"

No answer.

He looked around, found the switch, flicked it. A dim light flowed up the stairs and out the doorway. Hanratty carefully stepped toward it, and then, moving sideways with the gun held in both hands and pointed forward, he slowly climbed down. I followed.

The basement was unfinished, old, about twenty by ten, with the ceiling beams bare, the concrete floor cracked, the uneven plaster on the walls flaking off. There was a concrete sink, there was an old washer and dryer, there was a small tool bench and a sump pump in the corner.

And there was the freezer.

It was a chest model, white, about five feet long, with its lock clasp broken and blood smeared about its sides. Tossed haphazardly around it were frozen steaks, still in their tight plastic wrapping. A dark red puddle, just to the right of the chest, was the apparent source of the cat's prints, with paw marks circling back and around in a sad record of feline agitation. Beside the puddle was a red plumber's wrench.

The freezer's lid was propped open, just a few inches, and, other than our breaths, the sound of its compressor was the only noise in the room, a hopeless churning, grinding.

And out of the top of the chest, like a thawing piece of mutton, stuck a leg, large and round and meaty, a human leg, with a sturdy pump still firmly on the well-pointed foot.

SATURDAY

By the time we got to Front Royal . . .

It sounds like a bad country-western song, doesn't it, chock-full of star-crossed lovers and dead bodies and too many miles of open road?

By the time we got to Front Royal, it was nigh on noon. But it's not so easy to slip out of Haddonfield, New Jersey, when there's a dead body in the freezer. The cops seem to have all these annoying questions, like who, when, where, and what the hell is going on. My tendency as a defense lawyer is always to button my lip and get out of there saying as little as possible, but Hanratty was made of different, perhaps more reliable, cloth. So, with the police lights spinning outside and the television crews filing their live reports, we sat in the kitchen with the New Jersey detectives and tried to make sense of what had happened in that house.

"There was hidden money?" said the lead Haddonfield detective, young and blond, scratching the stubble on his jaw.

"I think so," I said.

"How much?"

"Over a million in cash."

"From where?"

"It was illegal money brought here to be laundered by an international crook named Gregor Trocek, but that was stolen from him instead in a complex swindle. The trustee in Philadelphia, a fellow named Nettles, has all the details."

"And how did it get here?"

"Hidden here by a dead doctor in Philadelphia and a little weasel named Clarence Swift," I said.

"Hidden where?"

"Same place as the body."

It was the freezer that had sent me back to Haddonfield, this time with Detective Hanratty. The way Margaret bit her lip when first she mentioned it, as if a blunder had been made, and then got snippy when I brought it up again, was what got me to thinking. They had a sadly uneven relationship, did Margaret and Clarence Swift. She was in love with him, he was in love with her boss's wife. Whatever romance he had once felt for Margaret, if any, had been bled pale by time. Her plain living room made it clear that he was not one to smother her in tender little gifts. And yet he had bought her a freezer. To hold the meat. For their romantic dinners.

It was a strange gift, unless you figured it wasn't for storing the meat after all. And the timing seemed right, too. As soon as Gregor shows up with his briefcase full of cash for Youngblood Investments, LP, a freezer arrives at Margaret's place. It wasn't there to store the Omaha Steaks, it was there to stash cold cash. And the lock on the freezer seemed to prove the point, unless there'd been a rash of sirloin thefts in Haddonfield, New Jersey. But the lock was now broken and the money was now gone.

Someone had come for it. Margaret had objected. Her objection had been overruled with the plumber's wrench. Smack dead, as simple as that. The lock was snapped, the steaks on top were scattered, the money absconded with, the dead body stuffed in the freezer to keep the smell at bay.

"So who did it?" said the detective. "This Gregor Trocek character?"

"Maybe," I said, feeling the guilt that had been weighing me down as soon as I saw the bloody paw print now rise up to throttle me. I had cleverly sicced Gregor onto Clarence; if he had followed him here and then made his move, I was in large part responsible for the murder. I hadn't much cared what happened to Clarence, but the vision of Margaret in that freezer choked my throat. Except something didn't seem right.

"It was his money," I continued, "and he's looking hard for it. But he has a Cadizian henchman named Sandro who favors a knife over a wrench. The whole scene down there doesn't seem like Sandro's handiwork. And there were no trophies taken."

"Trophies?"

"Sandro collects body parts," I said. "Smokes them over mesquite."

"You're shitting me."

"I shit you not."

"Then who else could have done it?" said the detective.

Who else indeed?

When the grilling was over, but before we were permitted to leave the crime scene, both Hanratty and I got on our phones. There were six voice mails and fifteen missed calls on my cell, all from the same number. He had been pining for me.

"Where you been, bo?" said Derek. "I been trying to call you for like hours. You're killing me."

"You wouldn't be the first of the night."

"What? You sound tired for some reason. Get yourself some

Starbucks. What I been trying to tell you all this time is that your lady friend, she didn't go to the Roundhouse."

"I figured that out already. Did you stay with her?"

"You told me to, right. And at fifty dollars an hour, I been doing just what you said."

"I thought it was forty."

"This is above and beyond, bo. Overtime and on the road. Time and a half would be sixty, so I'm giving you a break."

"And it feels like it, too."

"And I got to charge you for the gas and the mileage I put on the car."

"Mileage?"

"Sure."

"But it's my car."

"Expenses, bo. I'm just following procedure."

"Who's killing whom now?"

"It's all business, baby."

"So what happened?"

"She didn't go to the Roundhouse. Went instead to some big mansion in Chestnut Hill."

"Her house."

"That's a smacking crib there. I see why you trying to hook up with her."

"She still there."

"Hell, no. She picked up a suitcase and a friend, an old withered lady with a hat."

"That would be Gwen. I'm surprised she's allowing herself to get mixed up in this, too."

"Picked her up and headed guess where."

"Kensington," I said.

"There you go. Went inside, found that skinny addict with the bum foot, brought him and his bag into the car, and then was off again, into the night."

"Where?"

"South."

"Where?"

"You ever hear," he said, "of a place called Front Royal?"

"Yeah, I heard of it. Virginia, right?"

"That's it. They all ended up at a low little joint called the Mountain Drive Motel."

"Did a weasel with a bow tie and a black Volvo show up, too?"

"Not that I saw. Maybe I missed him."

"Keep your eyes open," I said. "He'll be coming. Okay, stay with it, but don't get too close. Things are going to come to a head, and you don't want to get caught in the cross fire. We'll be down soon as we can."

"On the main road, there's a diner with a fox on the sign. It's got a view of the motel. I'll just be sitting there drinking coffee and peeing. Drinking coffee and peeing."

"You going to charge me for that, too?"

"By the pee."

"Not a surprise," I said. "Give us a couple of hours."

When I hung up, Hanratty was waiting on me.

"Sims check in?" I said.

"He called in sick," said Hanratty. "Said he'd be out a few days."

"Don't worry, he'll be fine. And I know just where we'll find him."

When finally the young detective released us from the crime scene, dawn was just breaking. Still, we had no choice but to walk hurriedly through the pack of photographers flashing their flashes at us and reporters shouting their questions.

"No comment," said Hanratty tersely as he barreled his way past.

I stopped to chat with a television lady, lovely blond hair cemented in place. She had nice teeth, and she patted my forearm suggestively as she positioned me in front of the camera for the interview, but before I could even make sure she had my name spelled correctly, Hanratty grabbed hold of my arm and yanked me the hell out of there.

"Hey," I said in a high-pitched whine as he dragged me to his car. "She was cute. And you know what they say about free publicity."

Funny how Hanratty didn't seem to care.

And just that fast we were on our way out of Haddonfield, over the Commodore Barry Bridge, onto I-95 south, and headed toward Front Royal, Virginia, gateway to the Skyline Drive, located in Julia Denniston and Terry Tipton's own home state. I suppose they were like the noble salmon, who, at the end of their run, have the instinctual urge to swim back to the very stream of their birth.

Where they are promptly eaten by a fat brown bear.

By the time we got to Front Royal, it was nigh on noon.

"When did the Volvo get in?" I said to Derek as we sat together in a small booth in the Fox Diner, a tiny stainless-steel and glass box with a turquoise counter and a view of the Mountain Drive Motel across the street. The motel was a two-story pile of brick and rust and chipped tile, shaped like a V with its point facing the road.

"About an hour after you called," he said. "A little fellow with a bow tie was driving. I tried to call back but was sent right to voice mail."

"The battery died on me."

"You don't carry a spare?"

"No, actually. Do you?"

"Sure I do. In this business you got to think ahead."

"In this business, huh? What business is that?"

"Don't be a fool. The detecting business, I mean."

"You been in it long?"

"Long enough to get fifty an hour. The secret's in the prepa-
ration. Like, even though I was in your jalopy, I filled up with gas
before we started so I wouldn't have to stop along the way. And
I brought an empty water jug."

"What was that for?"

"You know."

"Ah, yes."

"More coffee?" said the waitress with a pot in her hand.

"Thank you, Lois," he said. "And I think my friend will want
coffee, too. And the other guy who's in the head."

"I'll come back with menus," she said as she filled his cup.

"Thank you, sweetie pie," said Derek with a wide smile.

"Sweetie pie?" I said.

"That Lois is a doll. We got a thing going. She wants a little
Derek for herself."

"Sure she does, or why else would she be plying you with
coffee?"

The motel was at the mouth of the Skyline Drive, which runs
through the Shenandoah National Park. There was a McDonald's on its right flank, a gas station on its left. The motel's sign
showed a picture of a snowcapped rocky peak, which didn't
quite fit, and had the word POOL in big white letters. Weeds
sprouted tall through the cracks of the two desolate parking lots
in front. In one of the lots, there was a battered brown van, a big
black pickup, and a Corvair; in the other lot was Julia's large
blue BMW and Clarence Swift's Volvo, parked side by side. And
in the small circular drive at the motel's entrance, a big white
Buick sat, its engine running.

"What's with the car in front?" I said.

"Pulled in about fifteen minutes ago. There's an old man in
the driver's seat, just waiting there."

"Anyone get out of the car to check into the motel?"

"Nope."

"Any idea why it's sitting there?"

"Maybe he likes the view. What happened to your eye?"

"The two guys you saw coming into my apartment."

"I bet you just let them in."

"You win."

"I warned you, didn't I?"

"Yes, you warned me. Was anyone following the Volvo?"

"Not that I saw."

"How about Julia and her Beemer?"

"Not sure. Was a boxy brown car that passed by a couple times, but it hasn't come back lately."

I scoured the street looking for something brown parked somewhere. Not at the McDonald's, not at the gas station. Maybe it was just someone passing by. Sure, and maybe we all were there to see the splendiferous Shenandoah.

"You check the place out?"

"Not a high-class accommodation, I'll tell you that. It smells inside, like that Maurice from the neighborhood."

"Maurice?"

"You don't want to know. There's a door in front that goes past the desk, a door in the back that goes to the little pool in the rear. Two emergency exits on the side with signs what say they ring the alarm."

"Do they?"

"How the hell would I know?"

"You could try one."

"But the alarm would ring."

"That's the point. It's called scoping the scene."

"It's called setting off the alarm, is what it's called. Derek isn't a fool. Derek doesn't set off alarms on purpose. Get a grip, bo."

Just then Hanratty came back from the bathroom. He sat down across from us, grunted twice, squinted at the motel.

"What color car was Sims driving?" I said to Hanratty.

"He had an official car," said Hanratty. "Brown. Listen. I got a call from a detective in robbery. There was a break-in and a beating. An older lady in Center City. She's still in a coma. The detective, knowing about the details of the Denniston murder case, thought I might be interested. Her name is Swift, Edna Swift."

"Crap," I said, a ripple of relief sliding up my spine even as I imagined Edna on a respirator in the hospital. "When?"

"It happened about three hours ago."

"Then we don't have much time," I said.

"You think it was Trocek?"

"Of course it was Trocek. He's looking for the money, he thinks Clarence has it, he went after the mother to find him. If she knew anything, he's on his way here."

"So Trocek didn't kill that woman."

"Guess not."

"Then who did?"

"What was the guy with the bow tie carrying, Derek?"

"One of those huge black briefcase things lawyers are always bringing to the courthouse."

"Clarence has it."

"I guess that's it, then. I'll call in the local police and the FBI."

"But before you do that," I said, "I have to go over there."

"You'll do nothing of the kind," said Hanratty. "From here on in, this is a police matter, and you will stay the hell out of it."

"I can't do that."

"Coffee?" said Lois, bringing over the pot, two cups, and menus.

"Not for me," I said. "I have to be going."

"I'll cuff you to this table if I have to," said Hanratty.

"I'll yank it out of the wall and take it with me."

"I'll have the coffee," said Hanratty, staring at me all the while, "and a couple of eggs over, home fries, bacon, and some thick sausage links well grilled, rye toast."

"Sure thing, hon."

When Lois had gone, I leaned forward over the table. "Don't you see what's going to happen? She's in the middle of a bad scene that's going to turn worse because of me. I can't just leave her there."

He dumped in two creams and stirred his coffee, unconcerned. "You'll only muck it up."

"I've already done that. I'm going."

"You'll tip her off and send her running, and we'll be doing this two states over."

"She's not going anywhere. Same time I go over there, Derek is going to take my car and park it right behind the Beemer and the Volvo so they can't get out."

"I am?" said Derek.

"Yes, you are, and then you're hightailing it right back to this booth. No one's running anywhere. I just need to get her out of there."

"No."

"Think about it, think about who she's with. Terry Tipton is a murderer. Clarence Swift is probably a murderer. Your partner is after her, and he's a crooked bastard, too. And then there's Gregor Trocek and his pal Sandro, who are speeding toward her as we speak. When the police and FBI close in, it's going to explode."

"She's made her bed."

"I think the bed made her, Detective."

"What the hell does that mean?"

I thought about it for a moment. "I have no idea. But I loved her once, and that means something, at least to me. I want nothing more to do with her, but I loved her once, and I'm going to do what I can to get her out of there before it all starts to burning."

Hanratty looked at me for a long moment. I could see the

calculation going on in his stolid face. On one hand I was a creep, and every time he saw me, he wanted to smash my face. On the other hand, for the whole of that night I'd been nothing but truthful with him, and he was only there because of me. But then again I was a creep, and every time he saw me, he wanted to smash my face. It was almost fun watching him try to figure it out. Then he snorted.

"Get the hell out of here," he said, disgusted.

"Thank you," I said.

"I'm going to drink my coffee and finish my eggs before I make a call. That's all the time you have."

"You know, Detective, you're proving to be almost human. Let's go, Derek."

And then we were off, out of the diner, Derek to the car and me to face my old flame one time more.

I watched while Derek pulled my car behind the Beemer and the Volvo, blocking their exit. Just that quickly, the desperate run of Julia and Terrence was over.

As Derek hustled back to the diner, I walked briskly toward the front entrance, to get a line on the white Buick. It was sitting there, its engine running, waiting for something. I reached the driver's side, leaned over, peered into the front window. A tall, thin man, quite old, wearing a houndstooth jacket and a tie. He was squeezing the steering wheel with both hands, his back was straight, his lips were moving up and down, though he wasn't eating or talking.

I knocked gently on the window. The man ignored me. I knocked harder. He kept his eyes forward for an awkward few seconds more and then turned to face me.

I gestured for him to lower the window. After an uneasy interval, he complied.

"How are you doing, sir?" I said.

"Just fine," he said in a hoarse croak.

"Can I ask what you're doing parked here?"

"You already did, didn't you? I'm waiting for someone, though I'm not sure how it's any of your business."

"Waiting for whom, if I may ask?"

"Now you're being impertinent," said the old man. He pursed his lips, turned forward, and pressed the button to raise the window.

I knocked again and waited. After a long moment, the window came down.

"You still here?" he said.

"I just thought I should tell you, sir, that this might not be the safest place to wait. Things are about to happen of a violent sort, and you'd probably be better off out of it."

"You're not telling me anything I don't know," said the man. "Why do you think I'm waiting here to begin with?"

"I have no idea."

"That's the first thing you said that made any sense. Now, just go ahead and skedaddle on out of here and mind your own damn business."

"I'm only trying to help."

"You want to know something, young fellow? I've made it seventy-one years without your assistance. Do you know how I did that?"

"No, sir."

"Then I guess we're done here," he said, just as something caught his eye. He turned nervously toward it. I followed his gaze and saw her, coming out of the front of the motel, a small, carpet-sided suitcase in her hand.

Gwen.

She stopped short. "Mr. Carl," she said. "Thank God." And immediately she dropped the suitcase, rushed forward, and gave me a strong hug.

"I've come to get Julia," I said.

"Of course you have," she said. "Why else would you be here? And she needs you, Mr. Carl, she does. She's in more trouble than she knows."

"Where is she?"

"Out back. By the pool. With Mr. Swift and the other one."

"Terrence."

"That's him. She says they're on the run. Like it's some romantic adventure, like Bonnie and Clyde."

"Well, her run is ending here and now. It's only a matter of how."

"What do you mean?"

"The cops are coming, the FBI. Her car has been blocked off, and so has Clarence's, so there's no way out for her. But there's also a few people showing up who are looking for the money."

"The money?"

"The money Clarence brought with him. The money in the big black briefcase."

"What money?"

"He didn't tell you?"

"That sniveling runt, he doesn't tell me a thing. To him I'm just the help."

"Forget about it. Do you want to come with me and try to convince her to leave?"

"I've tried already. She won't listen to me, she won't listen to anyone but that Terrence. The only reason I let her drag me along was to try to change her mind, but it's not changing. Maybe you'll have better luck than I. Bonnie and Clyde indeed. I know the way that story ended, with that handsome Warren Beatty turned to Swiss cheese. I don't need to see it again. That's why I called Norman to get me out of here."

"So that's Norman."

"He's taking me home."

"Back to Philadelphia?"

"Why would I go back there? With the doctor gone and Mrs. Denniston in a state and the house about to be seized by the bank, there's nothing in Philadelphia for me now. Norman is taking me back home to Georgia. I've earned a rest."

"Yes, you have."

She stepped forward and kissed me gently on the cheek. "Take care of her," she said.

"I'll try."

I watched as she made her way around the car and picked up her suitcase. Norman leaned over and opened the passenger door.

"Good-bye, Victor."

"When you get down there," I said, "I expect you'll be picking some pecans."

"The fattest I can find."

"Then you'll be making some pies, I suppose."

"I have no choice. Norman's been after me ever since I gave his last pie to you."

"Lucky Norman."

"I'll send you one, I promise."

"I'd like that."

She smiled at me and then eased herself into the white Buick, shut the door. Without looking at me, Norman pulled the Buick out of the lot.

I watched the car head toward Skyline Drive and the scenic road south, and then I jogged to the north side of the Mountain Drive Motel. I skulked around the corner and across a scabrous piece of crabgrass. When I reached the black wire fence surrounding the pool, I peered over the top. What I saw stopped me cold.

On two chaise lounges, pressed close together at the edge of the pool, a man and a woman lay side by side in the sun, their heads leaning one against the other, their hands entwined such that their fingertips just barely touched. He was in jeans and a T-shirt, his swollen foot swathed in gauze. She was in dark pants and a loose white shirt, her feet bare. Their eyes were closed, their lips moved softly in hushed conversation. They were in a world of their own, a universe of two, blissful and exclusive, perfect and unyielding. It was a place where nothing could intrude, not another suitor, nor a foul drug addiction, nor a murder or two, nor a sordid chase for sordid wealth, nor a pack of police and a pair of gunmen all closing in. But it wasn't this vision of steadfast love that stopped me cold.

What stopped me cold was the expression on the face of the third figure in the tableau. He sat on the edge of another chaise just a few feet away from the loving couple, a figure in a tan suit and a bow tie, with his bulky black shoes flat on the ground, his elbows on his knees, his hands wringing one the other urgently, violently. The sun shone brightly on his face, and I could see his features clearly, twisted in unrequited ache as he stared forlornly at the blissful couple, alone together in a foreign land he would never be permitted to enter. And even though I knew him to be the enemy, and I had seen the grisly fruit of his foul crimes, I couldn't help but empathize with his pain.

Welcome to the club, you murderous son of a bitch.

"You're the worst kind of fool," I said to Clarence Swift.

Clarence jerked his head up at my words and then shot to his feet. "How did you . . . ?" he sputtered. "Where . . . ?"

"Did you really think," I said, "that they would ask you to join them in their fatal embrace?"

"I don't . . . Victor . . . What are you doing here?"

"I came for Julia," I said.

"What have you done?" His head swiveled back and forth. "The police might have followed you."

"They didn't follow me, I brought them. But you should be more concerned about the madman who's trailing Julia. Or the killers following you, who will be here"—I checked my watch—"in a matter of minutes."

"We have to go," he said. He reached forward and put his hand on Julia's shoulder, shaking her. "Everyone's onto us. Carl betrayed you like I told you he would. We have to run."

"Victor?" said Julia, pushing herself up off the lounge, her eyes half open. She was calm, languorous, she looked slow, wrong. So it wasn't just love anymore that was creating for them their own separate world.

"I need you to come with me, Julia," I said carefully. "I need to take you to safety."

"Both of us?" she said.

Clarence's head spun, like he had been slapped.

"I'll take Terry, too," I said. "I'll even take Clarence."

"What about Gwen?" said Julia.

"She's gone already. She left with her boyfriend."

"With Norman? She left without saying good-bye? Where to?"

"Home, to Georgia. But the rest of you I need to take across the street. Right now. To Detective Hanratty."

"He's across the street?" whined Clarence. He turned to Julia. "He's across the street. We have to get out of here. We need to go."

"You need to, all of you, turn yourselves in. Before the shooting starts."

Clarence swiveled his head back toward me. "Shooting?"

"You didn't think you'd get away with it, did you, Clarence? You didn't think Gregor Trocek would just shrug resignedly and go on back to Portugal, leaving you with your million point seven, free and clear, did you? Really?"

"With the information I've been feeding the government, it's only a matter of time before Immigration takes him out of the picture."

"Trust me when I tell you it won't be soon enough. Who else knows where you are?"

"No one."

"Your mother?"

His eyes widened. "What does it matter?"

"Trocek reached her to find you. Now she's in a coma and he's on his way."

"He's coming? Here? That can't be. Do you know all I've done to get that money?"

"Yes, actually."

"We have to stop him."

"We can't," I said. "He's a more vicious snipe than even you. So let's all get the hell out of here before he shows."

"Shut up, you miserable crumb," said Clarence. "You've been meddling from the start, but no more. You'll learn like the others, cross me and pay the piper. Julia, we're getting out of here. My car's parked in front. Go to the car, I'll get the money."

"What about Terry?" she said. "I don't know if he's ready."

"Then leave him. We have to go."

He started running, stiffed-backed and awkward, toward the gate leading to the motel.

"Clarence, stop," she said.

"Just get in the car," he called out before he disappeared into the motel.

I watched him go and then turned back to see Julia kissing Terry full on the lips for an obscene amount of time. Terry remained immobile, his eyes remained closed. It was as if she were kissing a corpse. As if she were kissing a killer's corpse good-bye. She said something, and he barely nodded before she rose from her chaise and walked slowly toward me.

"What have you done, Victor?" said Julia, now just across the fence from me. She was unsteady on her feet, her dark eyes were hooded, her hopelessly pretty mouth was smiling kindly, as if she were smiling at a puppy.

"I'm trying to save your life," I said.

"Why?"

"If you want a pep talk about every life being precious, you're not going to get it from me. What did you take?"

"Only a little. Just a taste." She turned to look at Terrence. "Sometimes I follow him to be close."

"You should have left him on the balcony," I said.

"He left me on the balcony. But I've remained true to myself. Love, if it matters, if it's real, is forever."

"Maybe, but relationships end. That's what they do. Some end quickly, some end badly, some end in death, but they all end. It's the nature of the beast. At some point after they end you have to move on."

"But then I'd be like everyone else." She reached out and gently touched the bruise beneath my eye. "Do you ever wonder how we would have been?"

"Incessantly."

"Do you think it would have worked?"

"Not with him around."

She laughed lightly. "We didn't need him to screw it up, Victor, we had each other. I thought I was ready to move on this time and leave him behind. I thought I was going to be free of it." She turned her head to stare at Terry. "But I was wrong."

"He's a leech."

"He's my leech," she said, and I noticed then there was something strange about her manner, something other than the drugs.

"Come with me," I said. "Now. Let's get away from here. Now. Give me your hand."

"I can't leave him."

"Don't let him drag you down anymore. Don't let him kill all your hope."

"Hope? You were always so sweet."

"There's nothing you can do for him anymore except turn him in."

She placed the back of her hand lightly against my cheek. "Thank you for trying, Victor. But when Clarence comes back, we're going to run, all of us, run as far as they let us and then face what comes together."

"There isn't going to be any running. There's only going to be bullets and blood," I said.

"That's what Gwen said, too. Maybe you're both right, and if so, I'm ready. I've begun to think that *Romeo and Juliet* was mislabeled as a tragedy. I don't think the ending is sad, I think it's just right."

"They die in the end."

"We all die in the end, but they do it on their own terms, with their love still untainted. I think dying with love's sweet poisoned kiss still on your lips is about as perfect as we can hope for."

It was then that I realized what was strange about her. She was happy. For the first time since I had known her, she was truly happy. Just as that realization dawned, Clarence stumbled out the rear door of the motel, clutching at his head as blood leaked down his scalp.

"He took it," shouted Clarence, collapsing on the ground, arms still around his bleeding head. He tried to rise and failed. "He took all of it. He took my money. Stop him."

Julia and I both stared at Clarence without moving to rush and help, as if we both were rendered paralyzed. There was something cold in the way we stood and stared at the bleeding, babbling man. She had been driven to indifference by the drugs; I had been driven to it by the sight of Margaret in the freezer.

"There's the blood," I said.

Two shots rang out from someplace distant, a scream, then one shot more.

"And there's the bullets. It's from the front of the motel."

"My money," wailed Clarence.

From over the fence, I grabbed hold of Julia's arm and began to pull her toward the gate that faced the rear entrance. "Let's go," I said. "Let's get out of here."

She didn't fight me, she was too high to fight me. But as I pulled her along, she looked back at Terry, who was now sitting up, dazedly, on his chaise.

"What's going on, love?" said Terry, his voice dreamy and weak.

"Nothing, baby," she said.

"What's he doing here?"

"He's just leaving."

"Give him some money, that will shut him up."

"Okay, baby."

"Do you think we should get on our way?"

"In a minute," she said.

As I listened to all this toddler talk, and tried to keep from puking, I held on to her arm and edged her toward the open gate. Just as I pulled her through, the motel's rear door swung open and a small, angry man rushed out, a huge black briefcase in one hand, a snub-nosed automatic in the other.

Sims.

There was blood leaking from a dark crease on his neck, his hair was mussed, his expression was slow and dazed, like he had just come out of a midday porn film and was blinking at the afternoon light.

He stopped when he saw us and pointed his gun at me.

"What a surprise," said Sims, putting down the bag and touching the neck wound with his hand. He moved with an exaggerated, even frightening, air of calm. He checked his hand, rubbed his thumb across the blood that was smeared thickly over his fingers. Still looking at the blood, his face betraying no evident concern, he said, "I thought you'd be rotting in jail by now."

I wanted to say something smart and witty, but I was too busy clenching my bowels.

"Chasing her, I suppose," he said, waving the gun now at Julia. She staggered just a bit to the left but otherwise didn't seem affected by the sight of the barrel pointing at her heart. "Didn't I warn you from the start? Didn't I give you my best, heartfelt advice? But a foolish romantic, I suppose, will never learn. If I had time, I'd have some fun with both of you, but you'll have to excuse me for a moment while I take care of a quick bit of business."

Suddenly he pointed the gun down at the still-kneeling Clarence Swift, pointed the gun right at his head.

"All right, you sniveling little piece of crap," shouted Sims with an uncharacteristic loss of control, spittle flying from his lips, his voice now a vitriolic shriek that sent birds into flight and insects burrowing. "Talk now or lose the top of your skull. Where the hell is it?"

Clarence acted as if he hadn't heard the psychotic shriek of a money-mad cop. Instead of quivering for his life like a sane person, he started scurrying on his knees toward the heavy black briefcase on the ground by Sims's feet.

The briefcase was one of those where the handle fits through a slot in the top. The bright brass lock of the case had been broken open, so only the handle was keeping the case closed. When Clarence reached the case he, wrapped his arms around it and grabbed it to his chest.

"Mine," he said.

Sims stared down at Clarence in seeming fascination, as if he were staring at a fish flopping helplessly on the ground, and then kicked him in the head. Clarence spun onto his back, the case still clutched to his chest.

"There's the money," I said, indicating the briefcase. "Just take it and go."

"That's the money case, all right," said Sims. "But not the money. Instead it's two phone books, a Bible, and a wet towel."

"No money?"

"Just a few bills scattered on top to make it look good."

I turned to Clarence, still on the ground, still clutching the case. "Where is it, Clarence?"

"Mine," was all he said.

"He showed it to me in the room," said Julia. "It was filled to the brim with cash. We were going to take it with us to Mexico."

"That was your brilliant plan?" I said. "Mexico?"

"And south from there."

"That's the best you could come up with? Driving through the wilds of Mexico and Guatemala? With a briefcase full of money?"

"There wasn't much time."

"A briefcase full of money," said Sims. "Don't leave home without it. This is getting tedious. I'm going to start shooting if I don't get an answer soon. Where is it, Clarence?" He cocked his revolver, still pointed at Clarence, and then swiveled his arm to point the barrel at Julia's head. "Tell me or I'll kill her."

"Why her?" I said.

"Because I don't think he cares if I kill you," said Sims.

"Now, is this nice?" came an accented voice from the south corner of the motel. We all turned our heads to see Gregor Trocek, a sawed-off shotgun pointed at us from his hip, heading our way. "You are having party but did not invite me."

Sims calmly moved the gun away from Julia so it pointed at Gregor. Gregor kept approaching, his shotgun steady on Sims.

"Remember what I said I'd do if I saw you again," said Sims.

"Yes, I remember," said Gregor. "Which is why I brought my friend Peter."

Sims's head swiveled. "Peter?"

Gregor shook the shotgun. "Peter."

This is what I had plotted and planned for, that these two would face off over a suitcase full of money and hopefully murder each other in the process. But as usual, despite all my best efforts, my plotting and planning had turned ruinous. When the lead flew, both Julia and I would be in the middle. I looked around, hoping to see Hanratty or some other cop rushing in to save us, but all I saw was the desolation of the pool at the Mountain Drive Motel.

"Hello, sweet Julia," said Gregor with the shotgun still at his hip. "I always thought if your husband was dead and you were twenty years younger, we might have had ourselves some fun. At least part has come true. And Victor, yes, always pleasure, though I am sorry to say our deal is off. All this running around and guns and such. Clarence, I have regards from your mother. And who is that sitting like a drunken log on the chair?"

I turned to look at the man on the chaise, staggering to his feet and then dragging his gangrenous foot to the fence.

"That's Terrence," I said.

"Ah, so he's the one," said Gregor. "Well, thank you, Terrence. You saved me much trouble. I would have had to kill Wren in any event, and I so much prefer someone else to perpetrate my violence. But, unfortunately, Detective Sims has inconvenienced me terribly by killing Sandro. So here I am, Peter in hand, ready to perpetrate violence on my own. Okay, hop-hop. We must work quickly. Julia dear, be so kind as to take briefcase from your lawyer and give to me."

Julia didn't move.

"Now," said Trocek with a jerk of the shotgun.

"Do it," I said.

Julie kneeled over Clarence and gently took hold of the briefcase's handle. Clarence wouldn't let go even as Julia pulled. Julia pulled harder. Clarence said, "Mine, mine," as if the word were invoking some sort of spell.

"Oh, for God's sake," I said as I stepped over, grabbed the handle, yanked the case away from Clarence and tossed it at Gregor.

As the big black case twisted in the air, the top flopped open, and out spun a smattering of bills along with the phone books, Bible, and towel. As the bills flitted toward the swimming pool, and Terrence reached for them as if they were bubbles floating by, the books and case dropped with a series of thuds just in front of Gregor.

"What is this?" said Gregor. "Joke?"

"No joke," said Sims. "The money is missing."

"It can't be, not again," said Gregor, the European languor cracking. "Where is it, Julia my love?"

"I don't know," she said. "It was in the case."

"And now it's not," said Sims.

"Still in room?"

"I searched it," said Sims. "Nothing."

"Then where? Where is it?" growled Gregor. He tipped the shotgun toward me. "Victor?"

"No idea," I said. "I just got here myself." The second statement was true, the first no longer was, but I wasn't going to let these two thugs know it.

"How about you?" said Gregor, waving the shotgun toward Terry. "What do you know?"

"Not much," said Terry slowly. "Except I don't have it. And Julia doesn't have it. And Clarence doesn't have it. And Victor is an idiot. And that leaves—"

"There was a woman," said Sims. "Old, feeble."

"She's no one," said Julia.

"The maid?" said Gregor. "Gwen?"

"I waited for her to leave before I went into the room," said Sims.

"Gwen," growled Gregor.

"A white car was waiting in front," said Sims.

"Yes, I saw it," said Gregor. "A white Buick. It went south just as we pulled in. Okay, now we are—"

Just then, in the distance, a siren sounded, and then another, both growing louder quite quickly. The heads of the two men turned in unison, like the heads of two birds on a wire. Terry started laughing.

"My car's in front," said Gregor.

"That's no good," said Sims. He pointed beyond the back of the motel. "My car's through there."

Gregor waved the shotgun. "Take me."

"Fifty-fifty."

"Don't be crazy. Take me or I kill you."

"Then we'll both die, and without the money."

"I give you quarter, maybe."

"Fifty-fifty."

The sirens grew louder. A set of tires squealed in the parking lot on the other side of the motel.

"You are a dishonorable and murderous thief," said Gregor. "I admire that."

"Is it a deal?"

"Deal," said Gregor.

"This way," said Sims, beginning to run, with Gregor behind him. When Sims reached Terry at the fence, he stopped suddenly and turned to me. "Is this the perp who killed the doctor?"

"What do you care?"

"Of course I care," said Sims. "I'm a cop."

He raised his gun and fired.

"Case closed," said Sims, as Terry staggered backward and fell with a quick splash of blood.

And then Sims was off, past the pool and through a patch of weedy trees, with Gregor Trocek, lumbering like a bearded sasquatch, still behind him.

Sirens and footsteps. Tires squealing. Shouts and hollers. Orders to get down, get down. And above it all the plaintive desperate keen of a woman in love.

AFTER

There was a moment after the cops arrived and made sense of the scene and gave chase to Trocek and Sims, a moment before the ambulance careened around the side of the building to pick up what was left of Terrence Tipton, there was a singular moment in which things came clear to me. Julia, my Julia, was kneeling over the prostrate body of her lover in a posture of perfect devotion as a uniformed officer performed whatever CPR he could think of to keep the bleeding piece of meat alive. And then Julia looked up, her face full of panic. She searched around frantically until her search found me and our eyes met.

Help me, please, her expression begged. And all I could think was, Who the hell was she? How had this strange woman, whom I barely now recognized, twisted me into knots?

Yet in reality I had done all the twisting, hadn't I? What she had done to Terrence, by concocting a fantasy room for him to live in, I had done to her, by concocting a fantasy past for the two of us, where our love had been honest and pure, when in reality it had been neither. She was just a woman doing her best to hold on to the one true thing in her life; my feverish emotions had turned her into a femme fatale. But isn't that always the way of it when old love comes a-knocking?

I've been trying to figure out what it is about old lovers that causes so much perturbation of the soul, and I've come up with a theory. We have, all of us, an image of what love looks like, an image that evolves and ages as we move through life. But for some, tragically, the evolution slows or even stops dead. And if that image stalls when a relationship dies, as it had for me, then you remain haunted by the lover who disappointed you and then disappeared. Whoever you are with, whoever you kiss or ravish, can be only a pale imitation of the image that lies like a ghost in your soul. But here's the thing. When the old lover shows up again in your life, she is just as pale an imitation as everyone else. She is no longer twenty-four, and neither are you.

"You took your time," I said to Hanratty as we stood side by side and stared at the twisted little pietà inside the pool fence.

"You told me you wanted to bring her out," he said. "I thought I'd give you a chance. I waited as long as I could, and then the gunfight in front of the motel broke out."

"Did you know it was Sims who was shooting from inside?"

"When the shooter outside was felled with one shot, I figured it out. Sims and Trocek didn't get away so long ago, but Sims knows all the tricks. He's probably on his third car by now. I'd be surprised if we see him again."

"Maybe he and Gregor will end up killing each other over the money."

"We can only hope. You have any idea where they're headed?"

"Georgia."

"Why Georgia?"

"For the pecans," I said. "I didn't do much good here, but I appreciate your letting me come over to try."

"She's still alive, isn't she?"

"But I don't think she's happy about it."

"That's not the point. And at least you tried. I almost admire that. I still want to punch you in the face, but I'd feel bad about it now."

"It's a start." I looked around. "Where's Derek?"

"He stayed in the diner, said a pack of cops showing up with guns drawn made him a little nervous. And he said he had something going on with the waitress."

"Yeah, that's Derek."

"What are you going to do about her?" he said, gesturing to Julia, still looking around desperately for the ambulance.

"I'm going to wait until this whole thing settles down," I said, "and then I'm going to wrap her in my arms and kiss her good-bye."

But I never got the chance.

When the ambulance careened around the side of the building and lurched to a stop at the edge of the pool, she stayed with Terry. Even as they loaded him onto the gurney and lifted him into the vehicle, she stayed with Terry, climbing into the back of the ambulance with the paramedic before the vehicle rushed off.

They pronounced Terrence Tipton dead at the Warren Memorial Hospital in Front Royal, Virginia, shortly after the ambulance arrived. It was inevitable, I suppose, that Julia and Terry's romance would end in blood and anguish. In Shakespeare's play the very instant Romeo unsheathes his sword, even if with the best intentions, he seals his fate, and Juliet's, too. Violence begets violence, and love pays the price.

I imagine that Julia was in the room as the doctors worked frantically over her lover's body. I imagine she had to be pulled away as they pressed the paddles to his chest. I imagine that after death was pronounced and the time duly noted, they left her alone with the corpse and she hugged it and kissed it and swore her everlasting devotion a final time.

Love at its truest, ever as faithful as it is delusional.

And then, after all the hugging and kissing and swearing and pain, after it all, she simply slipped away. The police came looking for her, but she had disappeared. There were charges of obstruction of justice and abetting a murderer to deal with, there were financial matters concerning her dead husband's estate to deal with, there was me to deal with, but all that was evidently too much for her to deal with, because she slipped away and disappeared. She vanished into the thin of the air, as if without her one true love to keep her grounded she rose into the ether and dissolved.

But I eventually received a clue that she might not have dissolved into nothingness after all. It arrived in the mail, a package from a place called Corsicana, Texas, about fifty miles northeast of Waco. A pecan pie. It was thick and rich, so sweet it curled your toes, and the nuts on top were fat as toads. About as perfect as a pecan pie could be, but not homemade, not Gwen's, with its little imperfections and heirloom taste. She had promised me a pie, and she had made good on her promise, even if what she sent was mail order.

"We got us a ways to go," read the note, "but we'll get where we're going."

Was I delusional to believe Julia was there, in that lovely word at the head of the sentence? Was I a fool to hope that Julia was with Gwen somewhere, healing? And all I knew about the somewhere was that it wasn't in Georgia, because Gwen hadn't made the pie herself from handpicked pecans, and it wasn't in Texas, because Gwen was too smart to order from on close. I could see the three of them, Norman driving the big white Buick while Gwen fussed on Julia in the backseat, a sweet little family making do on the road, with just one another to rely on, and one point seven million in cash.

One point seven million minus the thirty bucks they sprung on my pie.

I was glad that Gwen had gotten away with it, glad that she had slipped through the clutches of Trocek and Sims, glad but not surprised. When I look back on it, through the whole of that time after the murder of Wren Denniston, I can see Gwen's fingerprints on much of what happened. She had sent me searching for Miles Cave, she had given the anonymous tips that kept Gregor on my case and the suspicions about me swirling, she had stayed by Julia's side until Clarence brought the cash right to her. No matter how clever those of us on the trail of the money had been, there had always been one person one step ahead. That she would stay a step ahead only made sense.

And did I feel a bit deprived that I hadn't had that chance to see my Julia again, to hold her in solace and feel the painful emotions wrap like barbed wire around my heart one more time? Not as sad as you might expect. Because I suspected I'd have my chance eventually.

An old lover is like the lumbago; no matter how free of the pain you might feel today, in the small of your back you always know that someday she'll return.

It was Detective McDeiss who eventually clued me in on what happened to Sims. It came over the Interpol wire, a warrant issued by the government of Croatia for the arrest of two fugitives suspected of murder: Gregor Trocek and an American named Augustus Sims. I suppose, with Sandro dead and Gregor in need of a new enforcer, Sims just naturally slipped into the role. And he'd do a hell of job, too. Though having a Cadizian hit man might make quite the statement in America, it probably carried a lot less weight in Cádiz. But having a slick-suited Philadelphia hit man on your side, well, that would be enough to make any Iberian quaver in his boots.

Any Philadelphian, too.

So I was rid of Julia and Sims and Gregor Trocek, but I was

not yet rid of Derek. He showed up at my outer office a few days after the shooting, showed up with Antoine at his side and a nine-page invoice in his hand. I read the letterhead on the first page.

DEREK MOATS—INVESTIGATIONS
No Girl Too Tall
No Case Too Small

"Nice motto."

"I came up with that myself," said Derek.

"Why am I not surprised?" I said, looking over the invoice.

It was quite a document, so overinflated in its self-importance, so rich in useless detail, so full of bogus items and bloated numbers, so nauseating in its final tally that for a moment I thought it could only have been drafted by a lawyer.

"Like it?" said Derek.

"I'm flabbergasted. How the hell did you come up with all this crap?"

"A man in my position, just starting out in the detecting business and never having done an invoice before, needs to find help wherever he can."

"So who helped? Antoine?"

"Not exactly."

"Then who?"

"I asked around, talked to people"—pause—"and Ellie had some ideas."

I snapped my head to stare at my secretary, who had bent over to pretend to be looking for something quite important in a lower desk drawer. "My secretary?"

"I just needed a sense of what a proper bill looked like," said Derek. "She helped me work on it while you were out."

"My secretary?"

"He looked like a lost puppy," said Ellie in a soft voice.

"A puppy?" I said.

"You should be proud as a papa," said Derek. "She told me that everything she learned about invoices she learned from you."

"This," I said, waving the invoice in the air, "this is outrageous." I stopped waving the document for a moment and looked it over again. "Which means you are well on your way, my friend. Well on your way. Now, if we can just negotiate some sort of a reasonable reduction among friends . . ."

"Can't do it, bo. That would be unethical."

"Unethical? But lawyers do it all the time."

"Which just proves my point. I got to follow the guidelines. Giving you a break wouldn't be fair to my other clients."

"But you don't have any other clients."

"Don't matter. I will, and, like you been telling me, it's time I start thinking about my future. So you going to pay up, or do I got to put that bill into my collection department?"

"You have a collection department?"

Antoine doffed his porkpie hat.

"Ah, yes," I said. "Now I see. Nice touch. You learn quickly, Derek, I'll give you that. Okay, you don't have to put it into collections. I'll write you a check. No matter how outrageous your invoice, you did a fine job and deserve exactly what you get."

"Thank you, bo. And now that that's settled, I see you have some empty office space."

"Yes I do, at least until my partner returns from overseas."

"When's he going to do that?"

"It's a she, and I'm not holding my breath."

"Because just now, we're in the market for some office space ourselves."

"You and Antoine."

"That's right. Derek Moats Investigations. No girl too tall—"

"Yeah, yeah. And no case too small."

I thought about it for a moment. It would be nice to get some income out of that office. But then I'd have to see Derek's face every morning, which would really put me off my appetite. But then, truth be told, I could afford to lose some weight. And I had to admit, in the whole of that terrible week, whenever I had asked for Derek's help, he'd been there. He had the makings of the real thing. It's one thing to lecture your clients on straightening up and making something of their lives, it's something else to give them the opportunity. I thought it over and glanced once more at the invoice.

"I'll need something up front," I said finally.

"Now we're talking business," said Derek. "Let's have it."

"First month," I said, "last month, a deposit for utilities and phone, equipment rental, furniture rental, secretarial usage—"

"Bo."

"Don't worry, Derek. It's only the usual fees." I gave him a car salesman's smile. "I'll just have Ellie work up the bill."

And so it all was settled, the whole old-flame thing. It hadn't worked out so great for Wren Denniston and Margaret and Sandro, I had to admit, but everyone else seemed to have gained something out of that week. I had come through it with my ghost lover finally put to rest, Julia had been freed from her fatal obsession, Derek had found for himself a new profession, Gwen would be living in the lifestyle she had earned all these many years, Sims had found his true calling as a murderous thug, and Hanratty had solved the murder. Even Terrence had finally found the thing he'd been searching for so diligently since his brilliant portrayal of the young, doomed Romeo: his death. All seemed to have come out okay in the end.

All but one.

"What do you want?" said Clarence Swift.

"To see how you're doing," I said.

"Do you care?"

"No, you're right," I said. "I really don't."

He was wearing orange prison overalls, which gave his face a green tint. His lips were pinched, his skin taut, his philtrum deep. And yet, without his usual tortured verbal phrasings and ostentatious humility, I sensed some calm within him that hadn't existed before, as if here, in this place, finally, he could fully express his true inner nature. Prison seemed to agree with him, which was good, because he would be here awhile.

"How's your mother?" I said.

"Disappointed."

"I meant physically."

"She's recovered from the beating, if that's what you mean. She's a stringy old hen. But it's the disappointment that is going to kill her. I'm her only child, she had such hopes for me. I was going to finance her retirement, cleanse her bony limbs when she was too weak to bathe herself, wipe her buttocks when she lapsed into incontinence. Now she has nothing to fall back upon except the street."

"You don't sound sorry."

"Well, it's not all bad. She does enjoy visiting. What are you doing here, Victor?"

What indeed? Why had I made a pilgrimage to the Curran-Fromhold Correctional Facility on the dark edge of the city to talk with a murderer? What was I hoping to glimpse?

A truth about myself, maybe.

It was in that tableau at the poolside, the three figures frozen in their postures just a moment before the bullets and the blood, when it was simply Clarence and Julia and Terry, the latter two in their own little world and Clarence looking on, miserable and shut out. Something resonated in that image for me, something vibrated deep in my bone. When it comes to an old lover, aren't you always sitting off to the side wringing your hands as the object of your affection and her lover cavort, seemingly oblivious to your devotion? And it doesn't matter if the two in their own world are you and your old lover at an idyllic moment in your youths. You're still just as shut out, your hopes to crack that bond and capture that same love just as futile.

"I have a question," I said. "How did you think it would work? I mean, you're a smart guy, you knew what you were up against. How on earth did you ever think you'd end up with the money and the girl?"

"Love," said Clarence.

"Love?"

"The only thing that mattered was that I loved her."

"So love's the answer."

"The night of Wren's murder, love spoke to me. Finally.

When I arrived at the house with the cash to make a last payoff to that vampire and found Wren dead on the floor with the gun by his side, I heard love's true voice. Now's your chance, it whispered into my ear. Now. With Wren dead, love told me that Julia could be mine. With Wren dead, I had the money to woo her and win her. With the gun in my hand, I had the power to frame whomever I wanted for the murder."

"And that meant me," I said.

"I had seen you two together. I had told Wren about your trysts. And when I found out Julia was in your apartment the night of the murder, there was no other choice. And I would have gotten away with it, too, if the police had arrested you as I demanded. You should be sitting here wearing orange, and I should be on the beach in Rio with Julia."

"And the money."

"Why not the money? Didn't I deserve it, all of it, the love and the money? Was that too much to ask?"

"Evidently. What about Margaret? What did she deserve?"

"Margaret," he said, his voice spitting with derision. "She had a thick neck and no ankles. I could barely stand to look at her."

"She loved you."

"She believed she was the best I could do. Imagine what she must have truly thought of me."

"She didn't deserve what you did to her."

"You weren't engaged to her, you never felt the press of her muscled fingers in your flesh. The one time I let her dance with me, the bones in my back cracked. She tried to stop me from taking the money, but I opted for love."

"It almost sounds sweet. Except Julia loved Terrence, always had, always would."

"It wouldn't last. He was a nothing, less than a nothing, less than a man. Did you know that? Something went wrong in fetal development. He was totally dickless."

"It didn't matter, Clarence."

"Don't be a fool. Of course it mattered. What could matter more? In time she would have needed something real. In time she would have turned to the one man who had always been there for her."

"You."

"Why not me? Why is love only for pretty boys like Terrence Tipton, or wealthy fools like Wren, with his arrogance and his mistresses? He grew up with everything, a rich father, a big house, a private-school girlfriend. I can still see her, the way she hung on to him, long legs and blond hair, like the world was formed just so she could ignore boys like me. I see her every day, I close my eyes and see her sneer as she turns away from me and reaches her hand into the front pocket of his jeans. Why shouldn't I get the slim white hand in my pocket? And with Julia I had my chance. She was everything I had ever wanted, beautiful and thin and Wren's. And there was some lovely sweetness within her that made it all seem possible. That made it seem that her affections could be twisted my way."

"It wasn't sweetness," I said. "It was an emptiness."

"That I could fill. With my love. That I could pump full. With my love. Whether she wanted it or not, whether she needed it or not, I would give it to her. I. Me. My love, all of it, pure and rich, as clear as a kiss. Love. I killed for it. Who in this world deserves it more than me? Who? No answer to that, Victor?"

"No," I said, and it was the truth.

For once I was left speechless. But not for lack of understanding. Because I identified with him all too well. Watching Clarence Swift wax earnest on love was like watching myself in one of those funhouse mirrors. Here you're tall and thin, here you're short and fat, here you're a homicidal maniac.

Love is all you need, sure, if it doesn't drive you mad.

ACKNOWLEDGMENTS

This is my seventh Victor Carl novel, the latest in a span of stories in which Victor has moved from callow youth to something slightly less callow and slightly less youthful. Writing about Victor has been one of the great joys of my life, and I intend to keep doing it for as long as it's legal. And yet, in order to keep our relationship fresh, Victor and I have decided to take a short break from each other. It's nothing serious, it's just that he's been reading the paper in the morning instead of talking, and I occasionally have the urge to stick his head in a pasta pot. Before we get into a rut, we both thought it best to start hanging out with different people. For me, that means I'll be writing novels with different main characters for the next few years.

So this would be a grand time to pause and thank some of those who have been in my and Victor's corner over the years. Michael Morrison and Lisa Gallagher have been the most supportive publishers a writer could have and I am so grateful to them both. I also want to thank Jane Friedman for taking a personal interest in my work; it's been more encouraging than she realizes. The entire publicity staff at William Morrow, including Debbie Stier, Sharyn Rosenblum, and Danielle Bartlett, have been tireless campaigners and I thank them all. Thanks also to Wendy Lee and Jennifer Civiletto for keeping me on schedule, and to my mother for maintaining her lifelong passion for the cause of correcting my grammar. Wendy Sherman, my agent, has been an advocate and a friend and I am so appreciative to her for being both. My brilliant editor, Carolyn Marino, has done more than anyone to get Victor in and out of trouble with his spirit, if not his flesh, intact. Whatever strange ideas I come up with—mysterious tattoos, insane dentists, or that most dangerous of entities, old girlfriends—she accepts it without a bat of the eye and then works tirelessly to make sure it all comes together into a Victor Carl kind of novel.

Finally, I want to thank all those who have picked up a Victor Carl book over the years and given it a try. From the feedback you've passed on I know you've laughed and cried and thrown the books against the wall, all of which suits me just fine. Writing is a strangely communal enterprise in which the reader is complicit with the writer in creating the world of the novel. Without you there would be no Victor Carl, and I'd still be answering interrogatories. Believe me when I tell you, I could not be more obliged.